Was she plague ...
ing attraction he felt?

Or was he the only one whose equilibrium was being tested by forbidden urges? Somewhere along the line, Josh's protective feelings and aesthetic appreciation for Professor Rachel Livesay had gotten tangled up in a sexual tension that was at once irresistibly intriguing and damnably inconvenient.

His physical response to her had been tempered by the absolute awe of learning the elusive differences between her pregnant body and the body of any other woman he'd known. There was a vulnerability about a woman whose normal state of grace had been altered by the fragile miracle of life growing inside her belly. Everything about her seemed like femininity intensified.

He'd wanted to touch her belly, feel the life within her.

He'd wanted to kiss her.

Oh, boy. Talk about blowing his cover!

Dear Harlequin Intrigue Reader,

Happy Valentine's Day! We are so pleased you've come back to Harlequin Intrigue for another exciting month of breathtaking romantic suspense.

And our February lineup is sure to please, starting with another installment in Debra Webb's trilogy about the most covert agents around: THE SPECIALISTS. *Her Hidden Truth* is a truly innovative story about what could happen if an undercover agent had a little help from a memory device to ensure her cover. But what if said implant malfunctioned and past, present and future were all mixed up? Fortunately this lucky lady has a very sexy recovery Specialist to extract her from the clutches of a group of dangerous terrorists.

Next we have another title in our TOP SECRET BABIES promotion by Mallory Kane, called *Heir to Secret Memories.* Though a bachelor heir to a family fortune is stricken with amnesia, he can't forget one very beautiful woman. And when she comes to him in desperation to locate her child, he's doubly astonished to find out he is the missing girl's father.

Julie Miller returns to her ongoing series THE TAYLOR CLAN with *The Rookie.* If you go for those younger guys, well, hold on to your hats, because Josh Taylor is one dynamite lawman.

Finally, Amanda Stevens takes up the holiday baton with *Confessions of the Heart.* In this unique story, a woman receives a heart transplant and is inexorably drawn to the original owner's husband. Find out why in this exceptional story.

Enjoy all four!

Sincerely,

Denise O'Sullivan
Associate Senior Editor
Harlequin Intrigue

THE ROOKIE
JULIE MILLER

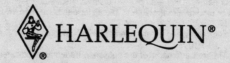

TORONTO • NEW YORK • LONDON
AMSTERDAM • PARIS • SYDNEY • HAMBURG
STOCKHOLM • ATHENS • TOKYO • MILAN • MADRID
PRAGUE • WARSAW • BUDAPEST • AUCKLAND

If you purchased this book without a cover you should be aware
that this book is stolen property. It was reported as "unsold and
destroyed" to the publisher, and neither the author nor the
publisher has received any payment for this "stripped book."

ISBN 0-373-22699-3

THE ROOKIE

Copyright © 2003 by Julie Miller

All rights reserved. Except for use in any review, the reproduction or
utilization of this work in whole or in part by any form by any electronic,
mechanical or other means, now known or hereafter invented, including
xerography, photocopying and recording, or in any information storage
or retrieval system, is forbidden without the written permission of the
publisher, Harlequin Enterprises Limited, 225 Duncan Mill Road,
Don Mills, Ontario, Canada M3B 3K9.

All characters in this book have no existence outside the imagination of
the author and have no relation whatsoever to anyone bearing the same
name or names. They are not even distantly inspired by any individual
known or unknown to the author, and all incidents are pure invention.

This edition published by arrangement with Harlequin Books S.A.

® and TM are trademarks of the publisher. Trademarks indicated with
® are registered in the United States Patent and Trademark Office, the
Canadian Trade Marks Office and in other countries.

Visit us at www.eHarlequin.com

Printed in U.S.A.

ABOUT THE AUTHOR

Julie Miller attributed her passion for writing romance to all those fairy tales she read growing up, and to shyness. Encouragement from her family to write down all those feelings she couldn't express became a love for the written word. She gets continued support from her fellow members of the Prairieland Romance Writers, where she serves as the resident "grammar goddess." This award-winning author and teacher has published several paranormal romances. Inspired by the likes of Agatha Christie and Encyclopedia Brown, Ms. Miller believes the only thing better than a good mystery is a good romance.

Born and raised in Missouri, she now lives in Nebraska with her husband, son and smiling guard dog, Maxie. Write to Julie at P.O. Box 5162, Grand Island, NE 68802-5162.

Books by Julie Miller

Don't miss any of our special offers. Write to us at the following address for information on our newest releases.

Harlequin Reader Service
U.S.: 3010 Walden Ave., P.O. Box 1325, Buffalo, NY 14269
Canadian: P.O. Box 609, Fort Erie, Ont. L2A 5X3

THE TAYLOR CLAN

Sid and Martha Taylor: butcher and homemaker
ages 64 and 63 respectively

Brett Taylor: contractor
age 39
the protector

Mac Taylor: forensic specialist
age 37
the professor

Gideon Taylor: firefighter/arson investigator
age 36
the crusader

Cole Taylor: the mysterious brother
age 31
the lost soul

Jessica Taylor: the lone daughter
antiques dealer/buyer/restorer
age 29
the survivor

Josh Taylor: police officer
age 28
at 6'3", he's still the baby
of the family
the charmer

Mitch Taylor: Sid's nephew—raised like
a son
police captain
age 40
the chief

CAST OF CHARACTERS

Josh Taylor—His youthful smile and irresistible charm make him a natural for infiltrating a meth ring on campus. Will his assignment put his pretty professor in even more danger?

Dr. Rachel Livesay—Eight months pregnant and on her own—just the way she's planned it. Until someone threatens to take away her baby. She turns to a younger man for protection. But can she risk turning over her heart, as well?

Dr. Simon Livesay—Rachel's ex-husband and former business partner. Once he cheated on her. Now he wants to replace her.

David Brown—He didn't take kindly to being kicked out of the good doctor's class.

Dr. Curt Norwood—He and Rachel were old friends from college.

Dr. Andrew Washburn—His sperm bank offered only the finest in father candidates and promised the utmost discretion.

Kevin Washburn—What secret was the lonely young man hiding?

Lucy Holcomb—Rachel's troubled client knew what it was like to lose a baby.

AJ Rodriguez—The wounded cop owed Josh a favor.

#93579—The not-so-anonymous father of Rachel's baby.

For Marilee Mathine.

A good friend and co-worker for many years,
and the unofficial goodwill ambassador
for St. Paul Public Schools.

Thank you for all your support
in both teaching and writing. Thanks for
fielding those phone calls. Thanks for easing my stress
and sharing my excitement.

May good fortune and good health
be your lifelong friend.

With thanks to the Kiss of Death ladies
(the Mystery/Romantic Suspense Chapter of RWA)
for answering my research questions
with expertise and enthusiasm.

Prologue

Joshua Taylor hunkered down behind the stack of crates in the old warehouse, alternately scanning the shadows for signs of movement, and eavesdropping on the soft yet tense conversation playing into the receiver wedged inside his ear.

His black slacks and fur-collared uniform blended into the night. The only signs that might give away his presence were the shiny brass badge pinned above his heart, and the sleek bulk of the steel pistol he gripped between his leather-gloved hands.

"You told me you could deliver." That was A. J. Rodriguez, at one time the partner of Josh's older brother, Cole. He'd been masquerading for the past three weeks as a drug dealer trying to move his business into Fourth Precinct territory. "And now you want to short me twenty bags when I come with my arms—and my briefcase—wide open?"

"It's risky, putting my faith in new neighbors." That cranky, drug-damaged voice belonged to Randall Pittmon. He'd been in and out of jail more times than Josh had taken a date to the local amusement park—and that was saying something. That ageless scumbag was going down for the count this time, though. No misdemeanor charges. No plea bargains. This was a major bust.

As soon as Randall put his cards on the table. Cards filled with street-ready methamphetamine. Vacuum-packed crystals ready to smoke or melt down to inject. The same kind of home-brewed high that had taken one of the kids he coached at the local gym last month.

Josh swallowed his impatient huff and shifted his position. The concrete floor was chilling his butt, and this guy wanted to philosophize! Josh turned his chin toward the microphone clipped to his shoulder strap and whispered, "Does anybody else think this guy's stalling?"

"Maintain silence, Taylor." That would be Lieutenant Cutler.

Josh nodded in lieu of a *yes, sir,* and peered into the darkness, trying to pinpoint the location of the other uniformed officers who'd been assigned as backup for A.J. and Cutler's men. No one. Nothing. He was stuck like a frog at the bottom of a mud-hole, blindly waiting for the predator to strike. Able only to listen and wait for Cutler's command.

One day soon he'd make detective, and he could take the lead on cases like this one. At age twenty-eight, he was ready for it. He'd passed the test. He had the college degree. He had the experience under his belt.

What he needed was a different last name.

Being the baby of a large brood of law enforcement brothers, he had an almost legendary reputation to live up to. Proud as he was of his family's accomplishments, he found it hard to measure up. He couldn't just be a competent patrolman with a decent arrest record. He couldn't just have good instincts on the street. He had to be better than anybody else up for the new detective slots in the Fourth Precinct.

He had to walk a fine line between taking orders and taking risks, and prove that he was the best.

A.J. tried to urge Randall into a decision. "My offer's not going to be on the table much longer. If you have the goods, deal. If not, I'll take my business elsewhere."

Definitely stalling. Josh rolled over onto the balls of his feet and crouched low, maintaining his cover behind the crates. He ventured a whisper, almost touching his lips to his mike. "Lieutenant."

Josh ignored the lieutenant's succinct curse and reported what his ears and his gut told him, even if his eyes couldn't see it. "Pittmon's waiting for a third party. Does A.J. know that?"

Detective Rodriguez had been thoroughly searched by Pittmon. So there were no wires on him. And no weapon. At least, none that Pittmon knew of. A.J. might be a sitting duck.

Josh's earpiece crackled as another officer came on the line. "I've got a blue pickup coming in the back. Local plates. I'm running 'em now."

Cutler swore for all of them. "Anybody got a clear view of what's going on? Pittmon just stepped out of the camera shot."

Josh tuned out the roll call of reports. He slipped to the end of the stack of crates and pressed his belly flat to the floor. Turning the bill of his KCPD cap to the back of his short, dark-blond hair, he made himself point man to A.J.'s backup. Keeping himself aligned with the shadows, he inched forward just enough to get a bug's-eye view of unfolding events.

"Pittmon's headed toward the garage door," Josh reported, his deep voice barely a whisper. "A.J.'s at the desk. The only package is the briefcase with the money. Wait. Somebody's coming in."

The buzz of voices in his ear fell silent. Randall laughed and swatted the third man on the arm as he walked in. The new man was smaller in stature. He wore jeans and sneakers.

And a letter jacket.

"Crap. It's just a kid." A slew of other, choicer, more damning curses filled his brain. Josh pushed them out of his mind, along with the image of Billy Matthews's strong young body lying still on the gym's hardwood floor. No spasms. No sweats. Nothing. He just dropped like a stone. Josh could suddenly hear his own rapid breathing, his heart pounding as it had that day. "The kid's about eighteen. I can't make out what they're saying."

Neither could A.J., it seemed. Calm as always, the compact, muscular detective rose to his feet. "Is there a problem?"

"Bingo on the plates." An officer from the command-post van chimed in. "Tyrone Justiss. He's on probation from juvie hall."

Not for long, thought Josh.

"Do you have it or not?" A trace of impatience filtered into A.J.'s voice.

"Yes, sir." Tyrone received a nod from Randall and carried the nylon sports bag to the table. "Right here." The teenager unzipped the bag and pulled it open, displaying the shrink-wrapped blocks of pure meth with all the pizzazz of a game-show model.

Oh boy.

Josh chomped down on his anger and started counting off the seconds in his head until A.J. was clear and they could apprehend Pittmon. And the kid.

Didn't the teen know what he'd gotten himself into?

"Looks good to me." A.J. had inspected the goods and

closed the bag. He slung it over his shoulder. "Next time, don't keep me waiting."

"Next time, don't be so quick to make yourself at home in my backyard."

When Pittmon reached inside the front of his jacket, Josh's senses went on full alert. "Gun!"

The next few seconds unfolded with the heart-stopping clarity of a slowed motion picture snapping by, frame by frame.

Randall squeezed the trigger. A.J. twisted his shoulders, grunted with the impact of a bullet and sailed back into a stack of shipping crates. A spray of police bullets cut the old desk in two and chipped up concrete at Randall's feet.

As Josh charged, the kid pulled a Saturday-night special from his pocket. He pointed the revolver at A.J., then at Josh. Sweat popped out on the kid's forehead as panic swept across his face.

"Drop it." Josh approached the youth, their guns facing off like an old-fashioned showdown.

"Drop your weapons!" Lieutenant Cutler joined the swarm of officers surrounding Pittmon.

Seeing the wisdom of surrendering when he was outnumbered, Randall set his gun on the floor and raised his hands. In a matter of seconds, he was facedown on the concrete, wearing a set of handcuffs.

But the kid started to backpedal. "I ain't goin' back!"

"Drop the gun before somebody shoots you," warned Josh.

"*You* gonna shoot me?" he challenged, his eyes darting like a cornered animal's, his gun trained on Josh's chest. "I'll shoot you first."

A TAC team officer, dressed in black from his cap to his bullet-proof vest to his boots, circled behind the kid.

Josh took his right hand off his gun and tried to placate

the teenager. Using only his eyes, he urged the officer to move aside. The kid was already on the edge. Any sudden move, and he might just make good on his threat to pull the trigger.

Then the rest of hell would break loose and the kid would end up dead instead of in jail.

"Give me the gun," Josh urged in a quiet, firm voice. "Hand it over and you won't get hurt."

Something alerted the kid to the other officer's presence. "Hey!" He whirled around.

Josh lunged, catching the youth by the wrist and twisting his arm upward. The shot pinged off the exposed steel beams of the warehouse ceiling and landed with a *thunk* in a crate somewhere.

In a matter of heartbeats, Josh had the kid pinned to the floor. His gun was safely tucked in the back of Josh's belt. The TAC officer plus two more men had their rifles trained at the boy's prone figure.

"Back off," Josh ordered, as if he had the right to give an order to three superior officers.

"Taylor!" Lieutenant Cutler. Josh snapped his cuffs around the boy's wrists and exhaled a weary breath. He knew what was coming.

"Don't argue with these men," Josh whispered in the youth's ear. "I just saved your life."

"Don't do me no favors."

So much for gratitude. While the TAC team officers carted off the kid, Josh climbed to his feet, holstered his gun and straightened his cap before facing Cutler.

"I told you my men had point on this. Your job was to back up and secure the perimeter."

"I was protecting the kid."

The older man planted his hands on his hips and glared

up at Josh. "He's just as guilty as Pittmon. His gun is just as deadly."

Josh stood a head taller than Cutler. He shook the tension from shoulders that were twice as broad. He felt annoyingly chastised, but the man was right. He had acted on the instinct to protect, rather than the task assigned to him. "Yes, sir."

"Go easy on him, Lieutenant." Antonio Josef Rodriguez eased his way into the conversation. He pressed a bloody compress to the wound at his left shoulder. With a nonchalance that betrayed neither pain nor gratitude, he nodded toward Josh. "Taylor here probably saved my life."

Cutler's nostrils flared as he considered A.J.'s remark. "I suppose that's another debt of gratitude we owe the Taylors."

Josh let his gaze travel from the unemotional support in A.J.'s golden gaze to the flash of sarcasm in Cutler's baby blues. "Just doing my job, sir."

It was all he'd ever wanted to do.

Now if the old guard at KCPD, like Lieutenant Cutler, would just back off and let him do it.

Chapter One

Dr. Livesay,
I'm watching.
I want what's mine.
The baby you're carrying belongs to me.
Take good care of it.
Daddy

Dr. Rachel Livesay stared at the snow-speckled piece of paper in her hand. Images of each boyfriend she'd dated through high school and college flashed through her brain. Of course, none of them could be the father. She'd married when she was twenty-five, and, unlike her philandering husband, she hadn't felt the need to betray her vows with a lover. And since the divorce over two years ago, she hadn't felt the desire to get that close to any man again.

Or maybe it was just her judgment in men she didn't trust anymore.

At any rate, *Daddy's* message was just a cruel joke. There was no father to speak of, no man who could lay claim to the miracle growing inside her.

''Jerk.'' Rachel wadded up the typewritten note she'd found stuck under her windshield wiper and stuffed it into her coat pocket. This was probably just a stupid, tasteless prank. Still, she couldn't help but survey the dull gray grounds and concrete buildings around her to see if anyone actually *was* watching.

Though the snow had stopped for the time being, the February morning still held the damp chill of a Missouri winter. The students, staff and faculty members hurrying to their ten o'clock classes from the parking lot and public transports huddled with their chins tucked inside their collars, or were bundled up beyond recognition beneath scarves and hats.

No Peeping Tom's. No unwanted daddies in disguise.

Rachel shook her head at her own foolishness. Someone was just trying to get a rise out of her. A disgruntled student, no doubt. The set of papers she'd returned at her last Community Psychology class had been less than stellar. True, she'd found a few gems, but she'd also given out *D*s and *F*s. Including one plagiarized paper titled "Psychoses of Inner-City Youth."

That's what this was about. Attack the pregnant professor where it hurts the most. Get your jollies at her expense. "That'll teach me to challenge them to think beyond my lectures." She inserted her car key into the lock, exhaling a sigh of relief. "What was I thinking? Expecting them to take notes *and* read the text." She raised her eyebrows in mock shock and opened the door, addressing the imaginary student. "Ooh, you got me this time."

With as much grace as a belly-heavy woman could manage, she bent across the seat and retrieved the stack of lecture notes she'd left inside her Buick. She shifted her balance back over her hips and straightened, relocking the car behind her.

She braced her gloved hand on the roof of the car.

I'm watching.

So much for not letting the note get to her.

A sudden shiver that had nothing to do with the temperature cascaded down her spine. She huddled inside her long, cocoa-brown wool maternity coat and turned to look beyond the Holmes Street parking lot toward the heart of downtown Kansas City.

Someone *was* watching her.

The creepy sensation sparked along her nerve endings and made her spin around an embarrassing 360 degrees.

The bustling energy of a city campus kept everyone moving quickly along the sidewalks and makeshift shortcuts. Sometimes alone. More often in chatty pairs or small groups whose animated conversations created a cloud cover of sorts in the cold air, preventing her from really making eye contact with anyone.

"Get a grip, Rache," she scolded herself.

She rubbed her distended belly, cradling her hand against the tender muscles where her miracle baby loved to stretch and kick. "Imagine." Her voice slipped into that breathy pitch reserved for mothers speaking to their unborn child. "Calling you an 'it.' That's probably why *Daddy* isn't doing very well in my class."

Right on cue, the baby kicked against her hand. Rachel smiled, imagining a shared high-five between mother and infant. Her tension eased on a cleansing breath.

There was no daddy in their lives, she reminded herself, slinging her leather tote over her shoulder and heading toward class.

As far as she was concerned, the father of her baby was 93579. A brown-haired Caucasian with an excellent health record, a high I.Q. and interests in classical music and Jayhawk basketball.

The dark hair and intellectual pursuits were to match

her own. The clean bill of health was to prevent any future need to contact the donor of the sperm she'd selected from the Washburn Fertility Clinic.

She'd paid good money to ensure anonymity. That stupid note meant nothing. This was her baby. No one else's.

It wasn't the way she'd planned to have a family.

But it was the way it had to be.

JOSH TANNER SAT in the second row of his Community Psychology class and watched his professor, Dr. Rachel Livesay, rub the small of her back. It was a subtle movement done with her left hand, hardly noticeable considering the way her right hand flitted through the air with the grace of an exotic dancer, emphasizing each point she made as she lectured.

He liked watching her mouth, too. Her lips were tinted with a frosty neutral shade of lipstick. They were full and sensual, and moved with the same fascinating grace as her hand, in spite of all the technical jargon and graphic examples that flowed between them. Her eyes were green and almond-shaped, a perfect foil for her dark-brown hair. As rich as a sable pelt, it fell thick and straight to her shoulders in a boxy cut that swung back and forth each time she lifted her face to look at the students sitting behind him, near the top of the banked, theater-style lecture hall.

But the best thing about her was her breasts. Ripe. Full. Sensuous treasures that could fill a man's hands and spill over into his fantasies.

With the cold of winter, she wore smooth-knit tunic sweaters that emphasized the shape and size and beauty of her breasts.

Josh breathed in deeply, slowly, silently. Savoring the

gentle course of heat that raised his body temperature by several scintillating degrees.

His psych professor was a hottie.

A very pregnant, and very off-limits, hottie. Despite the fact she wasn't wearing a ring on her left hand. He wondered about that last observation. He'd heard that pregnancy drew couples closer together. But Rachel Livesay seemed to be conspicuously alone.

His own sister-in-law had given birth just a few months ago, and Mitch Taylor, his cousin and boss—whom Josh considered his eldest brother—had mellowed considerably. Sure, falling in love in the first place had changed Mitch from a hard-ass workaholic into a much more grounded—though no less tough—precinct commander.

But with the baby... Hell, Mitch and his wife, Casey, had been downright frisky at the family's Christmas get-together. Always touching. Holding hands. Sneaking kisses. Cooing over their newborn and each other.

Where was Dr. Livesay's attentive mate? Was her pregnancy the accident of a misguided affair? The leftover burden of a messy divorce? The last memory of a deceased husband?

Why was a woman that beautiful and that smart walking around unattached? He couldn't imagine any sane man not staking a possessive claim on the mother of his child.

Or those luscious breasts. Those eloquent hands. Those beautiful green eyes. Those come-kiss-me lips.

Stupid bastard.

"Mr. Tanner."

Josh's heart skipped a beat at the sound of his alias, as if he'd been caught condemning the unknown father out loud. But no, the professor wasn't telepathic. And he hadn't been broadcasting his appreciation with an admiring glance.

Had he?

It still took him a split second to assume the Josh Tanner persona and make himself think like a coed, even after a month and a half of campus life. But without allowing more than a smile of acknowledgment to crease his face, he pulled himself from the politically incorrect yet inevitable trail of his thoughts to listen to Dr. Livesay's question.

"What do you think?"

Though he'd just turned twenty-eight, he knew a moment of juvenile panic. He broadened his smile until it dimpled on either side, buying himself some time to think. Technically, he'd been paying attention. He just hadn't been listening to what she was saying. But he was getting better at covering his mistakes. He rolled the dice and gambled that he could fake his way through this.

"I agree with you."

His answer earned a few snickers from his classmates. Dr. Livesay shushed them with an upraised hand. Oh, great. What had he just agreed to?

She stepped closer, moving her hand from the small of her back to the curve of her belly. "You think training in classical music and the arts is a way to help young, displaced teens stay away from gangs?"

Josh shifted in his chair, straightening from his slouch. Lady Luck was with him today. He could do more than catch up with the discussion. He took the topic and ran with it.

"Sure. If the arts is something that interests him or her, that's the way to go. For others it's sports." Like the group of teens he volunteered with at his neighborhood youth center. "Some do well helping out younger kids as a mentor or tutor. They like that sense of responsibility." He braced his elbows on the tiny piece of Formica that passed for a desk and leaned forward. She'd touched on an issue near and dear to his heart. One that had put him in this seat in her classroom in the first place. "There's no one way to reach every kid. But something clicks with each of them. It's a matter of finding the time and the patience and the funding to discover and supply that thing that clicks."

He began to move his hands in the same fluid way she had. "If they have nothing to live for or work toward, then the gangs and the drugs are there waiting for them. They all want to connect with something positive. Unfortunately, the trouble is usually easier to find."

Too easy, he thought, remembering his other life. The life before this one. The one in which one teenage boy could lie lifeless in his arms and another could damn him for saving his sorry hide. Such a waste. He clenched his gesturing hand into a fist and silently consumed his anger. The grim memories threatened to steal his ability to even fake a smile.

Such a waste.

A smattering of applause and a couple of appreciative whistles gave Josh the opportunity to look around the room. He nodded at the blond girl sitting two desks over. Kelly, he thought she'd said. Nine years younger than he, though she seemed to think he was eligible material— judging by the hooded sweep of her bright-blue eyes. Josh grinned and she giggled.

He looked beyond her, at the end of the aisle, two rows back. Joey King. A long-haired loner who wore his thick nylon parka to class every day.

To Josh's left, he glanced at David Brown, king of the class, surrounded by two thick-necked jocks, a nerdy-looking accounting major and a changing variety of pretty

girls. Today there was a redhead. On Friday, his conquest
had been a brunette.

Behind him, probably dozing in the top row, he'd find
Larry, Moe and Curly. Okay, so he knew they were really
Nathan, Rod and Isaac. But the nicknames fit them only
too well.

He was watching them all. Slowly but surely getting to
know each student. There were others in the class. He
recognized every face. Knew them each by name. But
those were the ones he wanted to know better.

One of them he wanted to get to know better than he
knew himself.

Because one of them could lead him to a killer.

But not today.

Today he'd do well to keep his cover intact.

"I don't think I can top that speech." Dr. Livesay
clapped her hands together and commanded their attention. "Don't forget that Wednesday you have your next
quiz. Be sure you've read all the chapters and reviewed
your notes."

An answering medley of moans and groans made Josh
smile again. He added his own complaint to the chorus
for good measure and reached for his backpack to load
up his books and pen.

"David?" As the students filed toward the exit, Dr.
Livesay singled out the self-proclaimed leader of the class
and motioned him down the stairs. "Could I speak with
you for a moment?" Judging by the tight expression
around her mouth, Josh figured David wasn't going to like
what she had to say. She thumbed over her shoulder toward the door behind the speaker's platform that led into
a wing of smaller, private rooms. "In my office?"

David Brown was a wiry young man in his early twenties with dark-brown hair and eyes. He stood a head

shorter than either of his pseudo-bodyguard buddies, though Josh suspected he possessed the explosive strength of a bantamweight boxer. His face was nothing remarkable to look at, but today's redhead sure seemed clingy. Josh supposed David was heartthrob material in a future-C.E.O. kind of way.

Josh noted the lack of visible tension in the young man's body. His laid-back nonchalance bordered on rudeness.

While Josh zipped his bag shut and reached for his padded leather coat, David Brown nudged his girlfriend *du jour* up the stairs and nodded to his linebacker friends.

After Dr. Livesay had gathered her things at the podium and exited through the rear door, the three young men traipsed down the stairs. Before the door closed behind them, Josh noted David's hand signals to his buddies.

Strange. What kind of college student needed the protection of two oversize jocks stationing themselves like guards at the end of the hallway?

Josh zipped his jacket and lingered a moment, digging into his pockets for the matching black leather gloves. The commonsense warnings of Lieutenant Cutler told him this was none of his business. Curiosity told him otherwise.

Trusting his instincts over his training, Josh grabbed his backpack and hurried after them.

He pushed the locking bar on the door and entered the oldest part of the building, onto which the lecture hall had been added. Sure enough, Jock One and Jock Two were pacing like sentries at the water fountain across from Dr. Livesay's office.

Boldy testing his theory, Josh walked right up between them and took a drink. They stood their ground as if ordered to do so, instead of scattering to a polite distance.

Josh was definitely sticking around to figure this one

out. Stepping back, he pulled his research paper from his backpack and crossed the marble floor to Rachel Livesay's office.

He had the doorknob turned before Jock One tapped him on the shoulder. "You can't go in there."

Jock Two framed him on the opposite side. "Yeah. The professor's got somebody with her right now."

Josh grinned his best good-ole-boy smile, pretending he hadn't heard the threat in their helpful comments. "No sweat. I can wait."

He sat on a bench beside the office door and evaluated the would-be guards. Intimidating in size, perhaps, but not terribly observant. He'd left the door nudged open a crack to hear what was being said inside. If the twin jocks had the brains to go along with that brawn, Josh would have his hands full justifying his presence. As it was, they dismissed his unassuming slouch and he faded into the woodwork.

"You can't kick me out of class for that." David Brown's too-cool voice shrilled with an unexpected whine from Rachel Livesay's inner office.

Josh snuck a peek at David's protective cohorts. They'd heard the same protest. They traded confused glances. Maybe no one had ever challenged their fearless leader's autonomy before. He gave a mental thumbs-up to Rachel Livesay and whatever law she was laying down.

"Yes, I can." She raised her volume a notch to command David's attention. "That's school policy. Read your handbook."

"But I need this credit for my major."

David's protest was followed by the screech of wood against wood, a chair sliding across a floor. Josh tensed at the sudden, forceful sound. Was it a burst of temper or a defensive maneuver? Was David making a threat? Or was the doc standing her ground?

Either way, he wasn't supposed to notice. He couldn't maintain the laid-back demeanor of his cover *and* show a reaction. He silently counted to ten, waiting for some sign to lessen the impulse to barge in, to Dr. Livesay's defense, to see if she was all right.

A door swung open inside, making her next words crystal clear. "You don't understand, David. Plagiarism is a probationary offense that can lead to expulsion from the university. I'm turning you in to the Dean's Office. You'll be required to appear before a review board. If you're lucky, they'll let you stay in school."

"We'll see about that. I'm talking to my advisor. He'll listen to my side of the story."

"Do that," she challenged.

David's temper seemed to dissipate as quickly as it had flared. "Is that all, ma'am? I need to get to my next class. I assume I should continue my regular schedule until I hear otherwise?"

The outer door to the hallway opened wide, and Josh sat up straight, more suspicious of this sudden mood change than of David's initial burst of anger. One of the bruisers standing guard at the fountain took a step closer. Josh stood, surreptitiously blocking the young man's path to the doorway.

"Of course," Dr. Livesay answered after a slight pause, as if she, too, had noticed the reinforcements heading her way. "Someone from the Dean's Office will be contacting you."

"Got it."

David brushed past Josh and sauntered down the hallway toward the outside exit. He disappeared through the double glass doors. His goons followed close on his heels.

In the sudden emptiness of the marbled hall, Josh heard a small catch of breath.

He turned and looked down at the pale color of Dr. Livesay's cheeks. Without thinking, he let his gaze slide up to meet hers. Her eyes had blanched to the dull gray-green color of a lake on a sunless winter's day. The vibrant energy that had animated her during her lecture was absent in the current sag of her posture.

Josh felt his body turning, shifting toward her. She seemed tired, spent, emotionally drained. She looked like she needed a shoulder to lean on right about now. He had two, size extra-large. And he was willing to accommodate her.

But then she broke their mutual gaze and retreated toward her office.

Josh debated a moment, hovering in the open doorway, wondering if he should say something. Worrying that he should stay to make sure she'd be okay after that unpleasant encounter with David Brown.

She stopped and turned. "Did you need something, Mr. Tanner?"

"Uh, no, ma'am. It can wait."

"Catch the door on your way out, okay?"

"Sure."

She closed the door to her inner office, dismissing him the way she did the other young teens and twenty-somethings.

And why not? Josh chided himself. If she saw him as a student, and not a fellow adult, that meant he'd created a convincing cover. Besides, she probably had a friend her own age whom she was calling right now. Someone whose sympathetic ear would mean something to her.

Adjusting his bag on his shoulder, Josh turned his back on Rachel Livesay and headed down the hallway.

It felt wrong to turn his back on anyone in trouble. But he had a different job to do right now.

And this time he'd play by Cutler's rules and get it done right.

A detective's shield and a lot of innocent young lives were depending on it.

RACHEL LOCKED HER DOOR and sank into her office chair. She stood up again, just as quickly, as the baby protested the change in position.

"Give me a break, little one." She rubbed at the tender skin on her left side, where the baby liked to wedge her foot up under one of Rachel's ribs. "Sorry about Mommy's blood pressure. You know how it flies when she loses her temper or gets upset."

And that confrontation with David Brown had really upset her. Of course, with her hormones so out of whack, she never knew what was going to set her off. And then there was that damn note.

Rachel blinked and pinched her nose shut, fighting off the salty rush of tears that stung her eyes. She would not let that stupid prank get to her. But she could barely remember what she'd discussed in class today. She'd spent half her time sizing up each student and wondering which one could be crass enough or desperate enough to threaten her precious baby.

The three deadbeats in the back row didn't seem to have enough brainpower between them to come up with something so devious. No, when she thought of devious, she thought of David Brown. Acting as if she was lucky he'd given her a moment of his time. He knew darn well what the consequences of his illegal actions were, and he had the arrogance to accuse her of persecuting him! And then to walk off as if stealing someone else's work and claiming it as his own was no big deal. He definitely had the brains and the audacity to threaten someone.

But she'd received that note *before* he'd learned of his certain probation and possible expulsion. Rachel released her nose and blew out a weary sigh. So much for motive.

She pulled her planner from her bag and read through the names on the class roster. Joey King? He certainly was quiet and mysterious enough, sitting there class after class in his dark coat and never saying a word. He was pulling a *C*. But at least he was doing his own work. Amber? Kelly? She shook her head. They were more interested in the young men in class than in anything she had to say. In fact, Amber had latched on to David's arm today. Not the wisest move, in Rachel's opinion. But a poor choice in men certainly wasn't a criminal offense.

Rachel laughed out loud and shared the joke with her baby. "If it was, I'd be in jail right now."

She had fallen for Simon Livesay's dark good looks that first day of residency at the private psychiatric center in Topeka. After working side-by-side for a year, sharing research and steamy nights of passion, they'd eloped to Las Vegas.

She'd loved his intellect, his sense of humor and his worldly ways.

She hadn't loved the string of affairs that started before their first anniversary.

With backgrounds as therapists, they couldn't help but attempt a reconciliation. But ultimately, their marriage had been doomed to failure. She wanted children. Simon only wanted the fun that came in making them.

They'd parted amicably enough, splitting their successful practice and their lives fifty-fifty.

Rachel closed her planner and dropped it onto the desk. She looked around at the spotless organization of her office and drifted to the window. Pressing her hand against the cool metal frame, she looked outside at the bustle. Students hurrying to class. A pair of professors talking intently. There was even a group of young men dodging and diving in the wintertime ritual of a snowball fight.

She turned and faced the empty silence of her office again.

Fifty-fifty. Half a life. That's how she'd felt for so long.

She cradled the precious being growing within her. She was honest enough to admit that fear of a life half-lived, as much as the loud ticking of her biological clock, prompted her to visit the fertility clinic. Since she couldn't trust a man to make her happy, she'd turned to her work, and she'd turn to her baby. They'd have a life together. A safe life. A life full of love, where an adult made a commitment and saw the relationship through, no matter what.

Satisfied with the choices she had made, Rachel ignored the baby's protests and sat down to review her notes for an upcoming counseling session. Gradually, the chill from outside worked its way into the room. Rachel pulled her coat from the back of her chair and shrugged it around her shoulders.

The comforting rush of warmth reminded her of a similar feeling she'd experienced earlier in the hallway. The idea of a warm hug made her think of Josh Tanner.

The big, brassy-haired student who distracted more than one set of female eyes during her lectures had hovered outside her office. She'd been relieved to find him standing there, strategically positioned between her and David's buddies, Lance and Shelton. Had she imagined something more than idle curiosity had prompted him to stay and witness the exchange with David Brown? As improper as the thought might be, she'd been grateful that he'd hung around.

David hadn't actually threatened her. But she'd still *felt* threatened.

If Josh Tanner hadn't been there, she would have been alone with David and his friends. That prospect was more unsettling than her fears of simply being alone.

Once David had left the office, she'd felt Josh's gaze on her. Like that warm hug. In a moment of weak relief, she'd ensnared herself in the bright-blue sky of his eyes. Those eyes had seemed older than they had in class when he'd pulled that B.S. answer out of his hat. They'd seemed kind. Concerned. For her. He'd been concerned for her.

Rachel shook aside the notion before that soft, tended feeling overtook her again. Josh Tanner had been raised right, that was all. The young man had compassion. No doubt she'd projected some damsel-in-distress pheromone that had prompted him to hang around.

Whatever his reason, she was glad he'd been there. For those few brief minutes in time, she hadn't felt quite so alone. She'd felt safe. She'd almost thanked him. No. She'd almost run into his arms and asked him to hold her. But rational thought had kicked in. Josh was a student. She was his professor, a good fifteen years his senior. It would hardly be ethical for her to turn to him for any personal sort of comfort.

She'd handle this threat—if there really was anything to it—alone. If she could raise a baby by herself, she could handle a disgruntled student. She could tackle a piece of paper stuck on her windshield.

Shoving aside any lingering fears or fantasies, she reached for her planner again and thumbed to the page of

phone listings. By the time she'd punched in the number
for the Washburn Fertility Clinic, her usual confidence
had returned.

It was high time she found out who *Daddy* was.

Chapter Two

"Dr. Livesay, all due respect, but you don't know what it's like to lose a baby."

Lucy Holcomb sat in the chair across from Rachel, wringing her hands. The twenty-year-old was even more nervous than usual today. Was she still taking her prescribed antidepressant medication? Or was there some new crisis turning the young woman's life upside down?

Rachel resisted the urge to stand and pace, keeping her eight months of pregnant belly out of Lucy's direct line of sight. "It's true I haven't personally experienced what you're going through, and I can't fix it for you. But I can help by listening. Look at all the progress you've made so far."

Lucy tossed her curly chestnut hair over one shoulder and stood to circle the room. Twice. "Ever since the miscarriage, it's like Kevin and I are fighting all the time. I blame him because he wasn't around when the contractions started, and he blames me because I didn't take care of the baby."

"You know it's no one's fault," Rachel reminded her. "Your O.B. doctor told you as much. There was something wrong with the development of the fetus, and your body handled the situation with a spontaneous abortion.

You were progressing with your pregnancy just as the doctor had ordered. Sometimes tragedies like that happen, and, unfortunately, there's nothing you can do about it.''

"But the guilt..." Tears welled up in Lucy's eyes and overflowed. "It's not just grief. I feel so guilty."

Rachel finally stood and took Lucy a tissue. She leaned her hip against the desk in a casual pose. "That's normal. You can't beat yourself up over that. We all deal with loss in different ways. Feel different emotions. This is the way that's right for you."

Lucy's mascara blotched in circles around her big, brown eyes. She blew her nose into the tissue. "But Kevin is so angry with me. Sometimes he's sad and we cry about it and we talk. Then, next thing I know, he's on my case over every little thing."

Her outburst of tears ended on a tiny hiccup. "He says we should have another baby."

Rachel kept her face a placid mask. Oh lord, two kids barely out of their teens, dealing with the loss of one child, anxious to dive into pregnancy again.

"Do you want another baby?"

"I don't know. Maybe—if it's what Kevin wants."

"What about what you want? I think you and Kevin should talk some more."

"But that's the problem. He won't just sit and talk to me like he used to." Lucy's gaze lit on Rachel's protruding stomach. "Maybe a new baby would make him pay attention to me again."

"Lucy, you and Kevin have issues you need to resolve before you engage in unprotected sex again." Creating a new life wouldn't solve the problems of the existing one. "Would he come in and talk with me?"

"I don't know." Lucy shrugged helplessly. "I could ask him."

"If not me, I can give you some names of several reputable counselors."

"Okay."

Her phone buzzed and Rachel leaned back over her desk to read the number of the incoming call. It was a message she'd been expecting. Rachel stood and smiled at Lucy. They'd run a few minutes over their scheduled time already. "I need to take this. Will you be okay?"

Lucy sniffed. "Sure."

Rachel urged Lucy to check out the bathroom and freshen her makeup before venturing out to catch her bus. "I'll see you next week, won't I? Even if Kevin doesn't come with you?"

The young woman dredged up half a smile that revealed the beauty in her face and made her seem terribly young to be dealing with such heavy emotions. "I'll be here."

"Good. I'll see you then. Call if you need to."

"Bye, Dr. Livesay."

When the door shut behind her patient, Rachel picked up the phone, blaming her tardiness on her laborious walk.

"Andrew Washburn here. You said you had a concern about the confidentiality of your pregnancy?" In person, he was a gruff, blustery man whose snowy-white hair and mustache reminded her of Colonel Mustard from her childhood game of Clue. But on the phone, he betrayed a blend of shock and concern that made him sound more like a doting old father figure. Which was an odd image to spring to mind for a man whose clinic had fathered hundreds of babies.

"Nothing like getting right to the point." Rachel pulled the wadded-up note from her coat pocket and spread it flat against the desktop. "I received a message this morning from someone calling himself 'Daddy.' Basically, he claims that my baby is his, and that he plans to take her from me."

Dr. Washburn's response was half laugh, half snort. "What? That's preposterous. Our donors and clients are completely anonymous, and are never informed as to when or even if their sperm have been used. Their relationship with us ends after their donation has been made."

Rachel sighed, schooling her patience. "Someone thinks he knows. He says he wants what's his."

"I assure you, the clinic is not to blame here." She heard a sound in the background, like the shuffling of papers or the tapping of buttons on a keyboard. "No one but myself and a few bonded staff members have access to the sperm donors' names. There is no way a donor could find out if he was the father of your child."

Rachel twirled her finger into the curling phone cord, wanting to believe him. "Are you sure?"

"The donor's name isn't even listed in your file. Here it is. Only the number is recorded. 93579."

"Can you tell me who 93579 is?" she asked.

Washburn's laugh this time seemed more genuine. "Now that would be betraying *his* confidence."

Rachel couldn't see the humor in anything that might pose a threat to her baby.

"Tell you what. I'll cross-reference the donor's file and see if there's anything there that would make me suspicious of his having the opportunity to contact you."

"What would make you suspicious?" Rachel pulled her shoulders back and stood up straighter. Was there a possibility the father knew her? "I thought you screened all your donor candidates."

"We do. We do. But his social circle might cross yours somewhere that we missed before. Perhaps you let the number slip and he recognized it."

Social circles, huh? That would require a social life. Of which she had none. Her life revolved around school and her baby. Other than a few solitary errands and her twice-weekly trip to the Y for a water-aerobics class, she spent her time either on campus or at home. "I don't think so, Dr. Washburn. The donor's number is nothing I've ever discussed with anyone but you. But I'd appreciate any information you could give me."

"I'll read through the file and call you tomorrow." She overlooked the patronizing gratitude in his voice. The man was probably relieved she hadn't pushed the issue any further.

"Thank you."

By the time she hung up the phone she felt exhausted. The baby had snuggled into a comfortable position and fallen asleep. But Rachel couldn't afford to surrender to her own fatigue—be it physical or emotional.

Maybe that note *was* just a stupid prank perpetrated by one of her students. But she couldn't afford to just let it slide without checking out every possibility.

Her baby's future depended on it.

JOSH STIRRED THE SPOON around in his mug of coffee. He hadn't added any sugar, but it gave him something to do while he waited for his contact to join him at the secluded table of the Bookstore Coffee House, a few blocks west of the UMKC campus.

Almost as if the thought had summoned him, a trim, well-built man with glossy black hair and golden-brown eyes slid into the seat across from him. "So, how's college life treating you? You flunking any of your classes yet?"

Josh looked up and grinned at A. J. Rodriguez. He was learning to appreciate the undercover detective's dry sense of humor. He responded in kind. "I'm doing well enough to maintain my self-respect, but not so well that I can't fit in with the party crowd."

A.J. sipped on the frothy cappuccino he'd brought with him. "Gotten any invitations yet?"

"Yeah. I'm heading to a party tonight. I've been told that if I can find my way into the back room, I can get my hands on more than a free beer."

His companion nodded. "Good. Remember, don't push too hard at first. Find out who your friends are. If you do spot some meth, just note who has it and if it's all for private use or split up for resale."

Josh shrugged. "I know the drill. I overlook the underage drinking because this is reconnaissance, not arrest time. I'll do my job. I know Lieutenant Cutler is waiting for me to screw up so he can deny my promotion. Besides the fact I've earned that detective shield, I don't intend to give him the satisfaction."

A.J. raised his hands in mock surrender. "Cutler rides everybody hard. 'By the book' is not always a bad way to go."

"You follow your own rules and *you* made detective."

A.J.'s smile flashed bright white against his olive skin. "That's because I'm a charming Hispanic and the precinct had to meet its quota for ranking minority officers."

Josh seriously doubted A.J. had ever achieved his successes on anything less than his own merit. But he played along with the joke. "So you're saying if you had blond hair, blue eyes and your cousin was captain of the precinct, you'd still be walking a beat?"

"If I had blond hair and blue eyes in the neighborhood where I walked a beat, I'd be toast." A.J. swirled the coffee around in his cup, then changed the joking mood before taking another sip. "I didn't agree to be your contact with the department just because Cutler assigned me. I've got your big brother to answer to.''

"Cole's not a cop anymore.''

A.J.'s gaze followed a pair of girls who walked past, his eyes convincingly glued to their curvy backsides. "You don't know that.''

"Cole walked away from the force two years ago. He does private security work now.''

"If you say so.'' A.J. dragged his gaze back to Josh. The detective had to be in his mid-thirties, but he blended into the scenery with these trendy young students as if he wasn't a day over twenty-two. Josh hoped his cover was half as convincing.

"Is there something you want to tell me?'' Josh asked.

The rest of the cappuccino disappeared in one last gulp. A.J. scrubbed the remaining foam from his lips with a paper napkin. "What Cole does now is his own business. But the man was my partner for eight years. Since you're looking to take his place in the drug enforcement division, it seems a natural step to start watching *your* back.''

Josh bristled at A.J.'s words. "I'm not taking anybody's place. I'm making my own.''

A.J. nodded, showing no reaction to Josh's declaration. "Poor choice of words. I apologize. Cutler can be a controlling SOB, but he's fair. You clean the meth off this campus, and he'll give you that promotion.''

"Can I get that in writing?'' Josh accepted the apology and support with a teasing smile.

"There are no guarantees in this business.'' A.J. slipped his hand inside his jacket and pulled out a piece of paper. "Here's a number where you can reach me at any hour. The line's secure.'' After he pushed the note across the tabletop, A.J. leaned back and rolled his shoulder. His mouth tightened with a wince of pain.

"Still stiff?" Josh knew A.J.'s wound from the Pittmon bust two months ago had done some muscle damage that would be slow to heal. The fact one of the precinct's best undercover men was out of commission was probably one reason Josh had gotten this assignment. That, and his youthful, wrinkle-free smile.

"A little. When the weather's about to change, it gets worse." He shrugged his good shoulder. "I'm not used to sitting on the sidelines."

"Don't worry. I'll call you if I need some backup."

"You better. I don't want to have to explain you getting hurt to anyone in your family." A.J. pulled a stocking cap over his head and stood. "Got any personal messages you want to send out?"

Josh considered the request. "Tell Ma hi and that I'm okay. She worries."

A.J. nodded. "Where does she think you've been these past few weeks? Lying on the beach with some sweet young thing?"

An unexpected image of Rachel Livesay popped into his head. With those kissable lips and expressive green eyes, his psych professor was sweeter than any young thing he'd seen waltz by this table or anyplace on campus. He'd dated a lot of women in his time. But never anyone more than a couple of years older than him, and never anyone who was pregnant.

He wasn't quite sure how to explain his fascination with the older woman. Maybe it was the fact that she'd been distressed over her run-in with David Brown—and for an instant afterward, they'd connected. He'd waited in that hallway to scope out David. But he'd stayed because Rachel had needed him. She'd needed somebody. At least, he'd thought she needed a friend. And he'd been more than ready to volunteer his services.

"Josh?"

A.J. snapped him out of his illicit imaginings and back to the present. "Nah. I told Ma I was at a training seminar in Jefferson City."

"With some sweet young thing."

"Right."

The two men shared the hearty laughter of acquaintances becoming friends.

But A. J. Rodriguez wasn't the best in the business for nothing. For a moment, the seasoned undercover operative with all those years of experience crept into his expression. "Be careful, Josh. This isn't the kind of work where you can afford to lose your focus. Wherever your head was a few moments ago, don't go there again. That's the kind of distraction that can blow your cover and get you killed."

An instant later, the street-savvy college kid was back in place. A.J. grinned. "Take care, man." They touched fists in what passed for a handshake. "Call me at that number to set up a meeting tomorrow. Let me know what you find out tonight."

"Will do."

After A.J. left, Josh stirred his coffee again, trying not to compare its color to the rich sheen of Rachel Livesay's hair. Avoid the distraction of the good doctor? Right. That should be easy enough to do.

All he had to do was imagine the unknown father of her child. The man who had the right to take her in his arms and comfort her.

RACHEL PULLED her bright red, rolled-brim hat down over her ears and stepped out into the cold. Though her body temperature had increased in the past few weeks of her pregnancy, she and her wool coat were still no match for the cold, whipping wind that stirred up the snow from the ground and pitched the tiny, icy flakes into her face.

After her water-aerobics workout and a dinner of salad and breadsticks from a local Italian restaurant, she headed for her brownstone condo just off the Plaza in southwest Kansas City.

But instead of turning in for a night of reading in front of the TV, she'd backed out of her doorway and retraced her steps to her car. She just couldn't shake the feeling of being watched. The sensation of unseen eyes learning which condo belonged to her. The unsettling quiet that, instead of offering respite and reassurance, taunted her with the realization that she'd be alone for the night. Completely and utterly alone.

Despite the protests of her weary body, she'd locked the door and drove back to campus. At least there she'd find plenty of people around—studying at the library, attending night classes and departmental meetings, going to play rehearsals and music practices.

But when the night janitor had checked her office to see why the light was still on, she'd joked about losing track of the time. She'd spent the evening grading makeup papers and editing her mid-term exam. But eventually, her baby's needs spoke louder than her own misgivings. She needed to get home. Maybe splurge on cookies with her nightly glass of milk. She needed to sleep.

As busy as the campus had been at seven o'clock, by midnight the place was nearly deserted. The bitter weather had chased all but the heartiest of souls inside.

Rachel's teeth chattered and she hugged her arms across the top of her belly, trying to retain her body heat. Snow and cold and damp air were nothing new to a Kansas City winter. They were nothing new to her. But by the time she reached the stand of streetlights bordering the faculty parking lot, she was puffing out quick, tiny clouds of air that warned her that the baby's round head was pushing against her diaphragm and impeding her ability to breathe deeply.

The baby was also sitting on her bladder. She'd used the facilities before leaving her office, but now she felt like she had to go again! Feeling cold, feeling damp, feeling miserable, Rachel hurried her pace and cut straight across the empty parking lot toward her car.

But she pulled up short and stuttered to a stop when she saw her left rear tire. The blowing snow had drifted around the wheels, but there was no mistaking the distinct lean from the hood to the trunk.

She had a flat tire.

Rachel cradled her belly and jogged the last twenty feet. The tire was flat. Definitely flat.

At midnight. In winter. When she was bone-tired and had to pee.

"Damn." She tipped her head to the curtain of snow swirling in the circle of light from the streetlamp overhead. "Double damn."

Then she looked down and rubbed her tummy, apologizing for the frustrated outburst. "You didn't hear that."

She looked around for options, pushed back her glove and checked the time, breathed in and checked the temperature. She could phone a tow truck and pay the extra charges for a nighttime call. She'd have to walk back to the building and wait or else she'd freeze. She could call campus security to wait with her until she could leave.

Or she could handle the situation herself.

Strengthening herself with a mental resolve, she unlocked the car and tossed her bag inside. "We're going to be on our own for a long time, sweetie," she explained to her unborn daughter. "We might as well practice fending for ourselves now."

But by the time she'd dug out the jack and the spare, she was breathing hard. Quick, shallow breaths in and out through her mouth. The baby kicked to protest the strenuous exercise, catching Rachel beneath a rib, forcing her to stop and clutch her side until the pain subsided.

But then she resumed her work, jacking up the car as quickly and efficiently as the numbing tips of her fingers through her gloves would allow.

She'd unloaded the jack and had the hubcap off and a couple of lug nuts loosened, before she realized she had company. Three figures, watching her from the shadows like snow wraiths. And then she understood what was really going on. An icy chill shimmied down her spine.

This wasn't about bad luck. This was about payback.

She locked the tire iron in her fist before pushing herself to her feet and turning to face David Brown and his two thick-necked jock friends.

"Dr. Livesay." David's smile was anything but genuine. "Having some trouble with your car?"

Rachel was oddly strengthened by the knowledge that David felt compelled to have backup when trying to intimidate her.

"I suppose if I check the stem, I'll find a tiny pebble wedged beneath the cap." She'd heard of the trick to slowly release air from a tire.

"I wouldn' know about that." David's cheeks were flushed pink, as if he'd just come from inside some nice warm vehicle or building. Or worse. She picked up on the slight slur in his voice. He'd been drinking.

Intoxicated meant unpredictable. Rachel was already at a disadvantage. She needed to keep her head and think more clearly than any of these boys could.

"Then, you stopped to help me change the tire?"

"Looks like you're doin' jus' fine on your own."

Rachel noticed one of the bigger youths moving toward the rear of her car. She jabbed the air with her tire iron. "Stay put. I want all three of you where I can see you."

David gestured to his friends and himself. His lips pouted and he took on a wounded expression. "We're not in your class anymore, Doctor. You can't give us orders."

She nodded to the two muscle men, Lance Arnold and Shelton Parrish. "I didn't kick them out of class. You're the one who stole that paper. I found an exact duplicate on the Internet."

David's chatty drunkenness vanished. In its place she caught a glimpse of temper flashing in his eyes, followed by cold, heartless rationality. He pointed his finger at her and advanced. "Maybe you shouldn't be such a tough bitch." Rachel backed up against the car, succumbing to a moment of self-preserving panic. "It's no wonder the guy who knocked you up didn't stick around."

"Get away from me!" When David was within arm's reach, Rachel jammed the tire iron in the middle of his solar plexus.

David clutched his arms across his stomach, doubled over and coughed. Rachel poked him in the chest, nudging him farther away.

"You stay away from me," she threatened in as succinct and even a voice as she could manage. "I'm calling the police right now."

"With what?" David's cough turned into a laugh as he straightened.

Rachel traced his line of sight and glanced over her shoulder, beyond the roof of her car. Distracted by the vile menace of David's advance, she hadn't noticed Lance circle around the front of her car. Her book bag—and the cell phone she kept inside—dangled from one big, meaty fist.

Fear—more chilling than the night around her—attacked her from within, robbing Rachel of her false sense of confidence.

The diversion was the opportunity David needed. He snatched the tire iron from her grasp.

Instinctively, Rachel circled her arms around her belly, shielding the most vital part of her from any harm.

David pointed the tire iron right beneath her chin, using it as a lethal extension of his accusatory finger. "I don't want back in your lousy class," he said, laying down *his* version of the law in unmistakable terms. "I just need you to clear my record so I can stay in school."

"That's out of my hands, David."

"Do it." Cold, cold iron tapped the end of her chin and she jerked away from its frozen touch. "Do it, or you might have to face worse than a flat tire."

A frisson of anger worked its way through the chill that rooted her in place. "How dare you threaten me. *You're* the one who broke the rules. *You're* the one who has to pay the consequences."

"It's one…stupid…paper!"

His voice flashed with anger augmented by the liquor that still coursed within him.

Oh God. Rachel shivered against the raised fender of the car, shrinking into herself. What had she done? Why had she argued? Why hadn't she stayed home?

This morning's cyptic note burned an incriminating hole in her pocket. Because of her stupid paranoia, she hadn't seen the real danger headed her way. Now she'd put not just herself but her baby in danger.

"David. Please…" For her baby's sake, she wasn't above pleading. "Lance? Shelton…?"

"Is there a problem, Doc?"

Rachel's heart jumped to her throat and collided with her fear. The dark, low-pitched voice had startled David, as well. It was a voice that brooked no argument, a voice that showed no fear.

It was a voice she would never forget or be able to repay.

Her knight in shining armor stepped from the shadows into the illumination from the streetlamp. Josh Tanner. With his black jacket and jeans, he'd been invisible in the shadows. She knew he was six-three or -four, and his broad shoulders required the extra space of an empty seat on either side of him in her lecture hall. But as he stepped into the light, with his feet braced for a fight, his hands hanging in loose fists at his sides, and his blue eyes dark with some unnamed emotion, he looked bigger and tougher than she'd ever seen him in class.

She hugged her stomach, keeping her baby close in her arms, half afraid to trust in the rescue he promised.

"Lose the tire iron, David," Josh warned.

David's gaze darted from Lance to Shelton to Josh. The look he spared Rachel was a mix of hatred and smug triumph. "There's three of us, Tanner." David's challenge dangled in the cold, damp air. "And this isn't any of your damn business."

"I've made it my business," Josh answered, unmoved by David's bravado. "Now, are you going to leave with your face intact, or with a bloody nose? The choice is yours."

Chapter Three

"Well, David, what's it gonna be?"

Josh patted his jacket, wishing his gun were strapped to his shoulder instead of locked with his badge in the glove compartment of his truck. He forced his hand back to his side, clenching and relaxing his grip, testing his readiness for an old-fashioned fist-fight.

"Are you as tough as you talk?" David challenged.

If Josh hadn't made a lonely trek across campus through the frigid midnight air to clear his head and temper after that frustratingly unrevealing party he'd attended, he never would have happened onto the tense situation unraveling before him in the faculty parking lot.

No one would have.

Three taunting drunks cornering a defenseless woman.

Josh breathed in a long, silent, steadying breath. He was about to even up the odds.

"I'm tough enough."

And smarter, too. He hoped.

He balanced himself over the balls of his feet, making a quick peripheral sweep of the scene, noting the slippery layer of new snow on the asphalt, measuring the distance between him and each of his opponents. The flushed skin and bleary eyes of the linebacker duo and their self-proclaimed leader indicated a dangerous level of alcohol in their bloodstreams, making them slow-witted yet unpredictable threats.

The back room of the off-campus party had been a seller's market for pot, not meth. Though the marijuana was as illegal as the underage drinkers holding their beers in the main room, he couldn't do a damn thing about it. His hands were tied with the burden of maintaining his cover. So he'd flirted with a few pretty girls and sipped his own beer.

Unlike Josh, though, Brown and his buddies had been nursing something considerably more potent.

He took special note of the only visible weapon—the tire iron—and how David kept it pointed directly at Rachel Livesay's pale face.

Despite the liquor, David managed to articulate his underlining meaning with crystal clarity. "We were just having a little chat about a flat tire. Weren't we, Dr. Livesay?"

The tire iron tapped Rachel's chin. Her breath stuttered through her teeth.

Screw his good-ole-boy persona.

Nobody, but nobody, threatened a woman on his beat. A pregnant woman, no less. Not on his watch. Undercover or not, it just straight wasn't going to happen.

Though Rachel's eyes had swelled with panic, she was smart enough to keep her focus pinned on her immediate threat. "Don't do this, David," she pleaded in an urgent yet even voice.

Debating the reason in her words, David's gaze slipped over to Josh, then to his two muscle-bound sidekicks. Lance and Shelton were more panicked than David by Josh's unexpected appearance. They were looking to their leader for guidance. Retreat? Attack?

Lance dropped Rachel's bag onto the hood of the car, prepping himself to either charge or run away. Josh seized on the young men's hesitation. "Leave now, while you still can."

Shelton, too, seemed indecisive. "David?"

The tire iron was still too damn close to Rachel for Josh's peace of mind and pounding pulse. And Brown was no idiot. He could read Josh's distraction. He probably sensed that Josh's first priority would be keeping Rachel safe rather than defending himself.

Josh knew the moment David made his decision. The cocky young man's lips curled into a smug smile. He pointed the tire iron at Josh.

"Show him who's in charge here."

"No!" Rachel lunged at David's arm, but he whipped the tire iron up in front of him like a defensive shield and backed her against the car. Her protest was drowned out by his shrill laughter.

"Get away from her." It was Josh's final warning.

"Now, gentlemen," David commanded.

Like a skewed version of a Dr. Seuss book, Jock One and Jock Two—Lance and Shelton—obeyed their master and attacked like two well-trained guard dogs. Josh had to get his licks in first. Dazed and drunk or not, these two were almost as tall as he was, and at least as stocky. He had to scare them off while he could, before he lost the advantage of clearheaded sobriety to the fatigue that would weaken him in a drag-'em-out fight.

But Lance and Shelton were thinking *power* instead of *endurance*. Josh took a step toward Lance, who struck first. Deflecting one meaty fist with his forearm, Josh bent at the waist. With his shoulder he caught the younger man square in the gut and rammed him hard against the front fender of the car.

Shelton was on him next, throwing his considerable weight onto Josh's shoulders. The propelling force of two men on top of him bent Lance over backward. Jock One conked his head on the windshield and swore. Dazed, he blinked and shook his head, out of the game until the world came back into focus.

Jock Two still had fight in him, though. With the wrenching force of a clothesline tackle, Shelton flung his arm around Josh's throat.

Josh had quick enough reflexes to duck his chin to his chest and protect his Adam's apple from a crippling blow. But Shelton's extra weight pulled him off balance. He stumbled back a couple of steps, heading for the ground and certain vulnerability if the two attackers could get on top of him.

"Stay out of this!" David's warning drew Josh's attention as he landed hard on top of Shelton. Rachel had picked up the loose hubcap to use as a weapon. But with the reverberation of two cymbals clashing, David smacked it out of her hands. The dented metal disk hit the snowy pavement and skidded out of sight.

The brief diversion gave Shelton the opportunity to land a solid punch against Josh's kidneys. Swearing at the bruising pain, Josh refocused his attention and retaliated.

With his hand squeezed into a rock-hard fist that turned his muscular forearm into a battering ram, he jabbed back with his elbow. The first blow hit Shelton's diaphragm, pushing out his breath on a stifled grunt. The second loosened his grip on Josh's throat. The third connected with a rib. Shelton released him and tried to scoot away across the slippery asphalt. In milliseconds, Josh was on his knees above him. He spun around and planted his fist in Shelton's jaw, putting the big kid out of commission.

Josh spared a glance for Rachel as he climbed to his

feet. David squared off against him, shoving the professor aside. But her green eyes widened and darted to the right, warning Josh of the threat advancing behind him.

He spun, ducked a swinging fist and kicked out, nailing Lance right in the groin. Jock One's bloodshot eyes narrowed into slits. His knees buckled and he hit the ground, clutching himself and moaning in pain.

Josh's breath steamed out on heated clouds in the cold air. Enough of this crap. "Doc—?"

"Josh!"

At Rachel's shout, he saw the glint of shiny black metal hurtling toward him. He dodged to the side, trading a potentially fatal strike to the head for the stinging smack of iron against the flank of his rib cage. The force of Brown's glancing blow was enough to knock Josh back a step. His feet tangled with Shelton's and he tripped in the snow, hitting the parking lot flat on his back.

Josh swore as the initial paralyzing shock gave way to a fiery web of pain that mushroomed through his left side.

"Oh God." That was Rachel.

"You son of a bitch." David raised the tire iron to strike again. "Mind your own business!"

A snowball smacked the side of David's face. His dark eyes widened above his reddened cheek at the unexpected attack, providing enough of a diversion to throw off his aim.

Josh seized the advantage and rolled as the metal club crashed down. The tire iron clanged against the pavement. The unyielding forces of cold iron meeting colder asphalt vibrated through the iron into David's hands.

David swore. His grip popped open. Josh kicked the weapon aside, sending it clanging beneath Rachel's car.

"Let's go." David wiped his dripping cheek and straightened as he gave the order. His brown eyes promised retribution as he glared down at Josh and back at Rachel, who stood poised with a second wad of snow clutched in her gloved hand. Shelton crawled to his feet and helped Lance, whose stooped posture revealed the pain he was in. "Let's go, let's go, let's *go!*"

David urged his thugs back into the shadows of the snowy night, while Josh stood and positioned himself closer to Rachel. "I never expected a sweet-talker like you to be so good in a fight, Tanner," he said. "I'll have to remember that next time." Then he dredged up a false smile for Rachel. "We'll be talking again soon, Professor. *Before* my hearing."

Over the sounds of his own labored breathing, Josh heard the crunch of snow beneath hurried footsteps fading as David and his cohorts disappeared. He didn't plan to wait for them to regroup or gather reinforcements.

He allowed himself only a moment to press his hand against his rib cage to ascertain the extent of his injury. "Ow." He muttered something cruder beneath his breath at the pain that resonated through swollen tissue. Tender. But nothing sharp stabbed him internally. He was bruised, but not broken.

"Are you all right?"

"Are you all right?"

If his side didn't ache so much and her fingers didn't have such a firm, questing grip on his forearm, Josh might have laughed at their simultaneous show of concern for each other. Under the circumstances, though, sparing time for laughter didn't seem the wisest choice.

He covered her gloved hand with his own, offering a silent reassurance as he made another visual sweep of the darkness beyond the circle of illumination the streetlight provided. Convinced the threat had departed—for the time being, at least—he finally looked down at Rachel. Though her verdant eyes, rich as a dark pine forest, still danced with lingering sparks of fear and adrenaline, her golden skin seemed unnaturally pale.

Josh quickly shifted position so that he clutched her by both arms, right above the elbows. He hunkered down to her height, looking her straight in the eye. "Are you sure you're okay?" She nodded, but splayed her fingers over her pregnant belly and rubbed tiny circles there. Josh dropped his gaze to the fluent movement of her hands, immediately looking for signs of trauma to her abdomen. "The baby?"

Rachel's shoulders lifted with a sigh. A cleansing breath formed a foggy barrier between them, reminding Josh of the dangerously low temperature. "She's dealing with this better than I am. But she won't stop tossing and turning."

Feeling somewhat relieved, Josh straightened. "The stress and cold can't be good for it."

"For *her*." Rachel twisted her arms out of Josh's hold. She pulled her shoulders back into a stiff posture as she walked to the hood of the car to retrieve her bag.

Josh grinned at the indignant reprimand. Good. If Dr. Livesay had the energy to chastise him, she wasn't seriously hurt. "*Her* mom's a nice shot," he said, complimenting her snowball-tossing skills. "I owe you one. Thanks."

He knelt beside the car and pulled the tire iron from underneath.

"I'd say we're even. I'm not sure what I would have done if you hadn't shown up." She scrunched her arms together in front of her and shivered, though whether it was the cold air or the memory of David Brown's threats that shook her, Josh couldn't tell. "He could have killed you."

"He didn't."

Purposely keeping his breathing shallow to avoid undue pressure against his sore ribs, he bent over and released the jack. He lowered the flat tire to the pavement and began disassembling the jack.

"What are you doing?" Though he had his back to her, Josh could hear the suspicious accusation in her voice.

"Packing up." He straightened with the jack in one hand and the tire iron in the other. "Where are your keys?"

"In my pocket. What do you mean, you're packing up? I still have to get home tonight." She followed him around to the trunk of her car. "I'm not expecting you to stay around and change my flat, Mr. Tanner. Clearly, you've done more than I'd expect from any student. But—"

"I'll drive you home tonight, then come back and change it for you in the morning."

"I can change it myself."

Dammit! Josh whirled around, his patience frayed by her stubborn independence and his own instinct for survival. "It's two degrees out here. Wind chill puts the temperature below zero. Who knows how long you've already been outside. And Brown and his buddies might come back any minute—with more friends to back him up."

"I doubt that. They've spent their bravado for the night. I think they're smart enough to know not to try something that foolish again."

"Did it feel *foolish* to you, Doc?" Josh leaned in. Rachel Livesay was a fairly tall woman. Her tipped-up chin met his shoulder. But few people could match his height or brawn. Especially when someone told him he was doing the wrong thing.

Again.

"You should have been scared," he warned her. "*I* was."

"Of course I was scared." She lowered her challenging expression until she was staring at the front of his jacket. Her gaze darted from shoulder to shoulder, as if gauging the breadth of him up close like this and realizing for the first time just how big a man he was. "I think under different circumstances, David and I could have had a rational discussion about his grievances. With a little encouragement—"

"The only *encouragement* those hotheads need tonight is another beer in their bellies."

She flattened her hand at the top of her protruding stomach in an instinctively protective gesture, and retreated a step. Damn. Now *he* was scaring her. He tried to inject some reason into his voice. "Quite frankly, Doc, my fingers are growing numb and my side aches. I'm not leaving you here by yourself, and I'm not in the best of shape to change a tire or take those three on again. If you won't accept a ride for yourself, think about your baby's welfare."

That wide, green gaze was studying him again. The tiniest of frowns dimpled her forehead. "You *are* hurt."

In the space of three short sentences her tone had changed from lecturing him as a professor to debating her convictions as a therapist to expressing her concern in a soft, throaty voice that was all female compassion.

His aching body lurched in unwitting response to that gentle tone. Beneath Rachel Livesay's cool, professional demeanor, she was incredibly feminine.

Maybe it was her blossoming mothering instincts that had her running her gloved fingers along the ridge of his jaw, tilting his face from side to side to inspect for damage. But if he didn't know any better, he'd say the cool professor was checking him out. Why else would her hand linger on the jut of his chin? Why else would those rich green eyes be looking so deeply into his own?

She pulled away and raised her two fingers in a victory sign.

"How many fingers am I holding up?"

Then again, he could just be imagining that the attraction sparking between them was mutual.

Josh turned his face up toward the falling snow and exhaled a painful, impatient breath. "Two."

Typically, he prided himself on his ability to read a woman's moods. He had a mother and sister and three sisters-in-law who were as different in looks and personality as were any of the women he'd dated.

But Rachel Livesay was as confusing and unpredictable as they came. "I've had some advanced training in first aid."

"I'm okay." He looked down into her uptilted face and saw all three facets of her personality reflected there. Professor. Counselor. Woman.

David Brown and his juvenile thugs he could handle. But Rachel Livesay's mood swings? Maybe her hormones were out of whack. Maybe his were.

Maybe by their next class he'd have her figured out. After a long talk with his mother. Or his sister. Or anyone who could explain his fascination with a woman he had no business being fascinated with.

Right now, though, he'd settle for getting her someplace warm and safe so his conscience could have a rest. "Would you just unlock your trunk? Please."

She answered by pressing the release button on her key chain. The trunk popped open. Josh loaded the equipment inside and closed it. "Are you sure I don't need to get you to an emergency room?"

"I'm sure." His injury would prompt questions that might lead to a police report. And Josh couldn't afford that kind of attention while he was on this assignment. "It's just a bruise. I can doctor it myself."

"What about the police?"

When he looked down, her wide, full lips were pinched at the corners, as if she'd tried to hold the words back but couldn't. Explaining tonight's brawl to cops who didn't know he was undercover would prove pretty tricky, as well. Still, he wasn't the only one who'd been threatened tonight.

"That's up to you."

The pinched look relaxed, though she didn't smile. "I think I'd rather just forget about this for now."

He didn't stop to question a mature woman's motive for avoiding the cops. "Then, let's go."

He slipped his hand beneath her elbow and steered her across the slippery asphalt to the sidewalk. After a moment's hesitation, she fell into step beside him, hurrying to keep up with the brisk pace he set. "How far are we going, Mr. Tanner?"

"My truck's a block away. Where do you live?"

"Just south of the Plaza. About twenty minutes from here."

"I'll have you home in no time."

"Uh—" Her breath came in quick, short puffs in the night air as she seemed to rethink whatever she'd been about to say. "Good."

Josh immediately shortened his stride. She didn't sound good. "Don't worry. My heater works fast."

When they hit the light from the next streetlamp, Josh looked down. Rachel's chin quivered as her clenched teeth chattered. The north wind had already numbed his cheeks, and the tips of his ears and nose. Rachel must be freezing. He slipped his arm around her shoulders and snugged her close to his uninjured side, letting his big frame block the wind while offering what body heat he could.

For an instant he felt her lean in to him, turning her face and her belly toward the warmth and shelter he provided. But two steps later, she stopped and pulled away. "This doesn't feel right. I'm sorry. I should just call a cab."

"That's crazy. My truck's right there." He pointed to the red Dodge Ram parked fewer than twenty feet away.

The wind caught a strand of her sable hair and whipped it across her face. She shook her head as she reached up and tucked the errant lock beneath the brim of her red cap. "You don't understand. You can't give me a ride home."

"Why not?" Did every authority figure on the planet hold him to standards he had to fight to measure up to? "You're a hell of a lot safer with me than you were on your own or with David Brown."

"It's not that, Mr. Tanner." She patted the air with an open hand, placating his defensive outburst with a rational explanation. "You're a student of mine. It wouldn't be proper to accept a favor from you. It could be misconstrued as fraternization."

"Fraternization?" Was she for real? It was past midnight. He was a cop. It was his job to protect innocent people, including headstrong college professors whose sense of decorum could kick in at the damnedest times. He grabbed her hand and pulled her toward his truck. "I'm not asking for any favors in return. I'm just doing my—"

"Mr. Tanner!" She planted her boots on the sidewalk and jerked her hand from his.

Josh pulled himself up short. His frustration seeped out on a sigh of understanding. Of course. To Rachel Livesay, he wasn't a cop. He wasn't even Josh Taylor.

He was the smart-mouthed charmer who sat in the second row of her Community Psychology class. Her student. Her younger, less mature, more impulsive student.

"Sorry, Doc." Josh scanned the eerie snowfall that shut out the silent campus around them before shrugging his shoulders and curving his mouth into a wry version of a smile. She didn't have to know his real identity to accept a logical argument. "My ma taught me to always see a lady home to her front door. Not just out of respect for her family, but because it's just not as safe a world as it used to be. Do you see anyone else around here? You shouldn't be alone on campus in the middle of the night." He hoped he could sweet-talk her into letting him drive her home. "Look. After seeing those kids go after you, I'm not going to get any sleep tonight until I know you're safely locked inside your own place."

Rachel rubbed her hands up and down her arms, the chill or nerves or both evident in the shaking tips of her fingers. "Your mother is to be commended for instilling those values in you. But—"

"Next time you can call Campus Security to walk you to your car. Tonight I'm driving you home." He raised his hands in a gesture of conciliation. "Please."

She paused to consider his argument. "No sleep at all, huh?"

"Not a wink."

"I suppose it would take forever to get a cab here this time of night. And I do have to go to the bathroom."

He'd heard that frequent pit stops were a necessity for pregnant women. Maybe he could win this argument, after all. "We'll stop at the first facility that's open and well-lighted. I promise."

"I've already detained you long enough." She shook her head again and sighed, as if leaning toward a decision that went against her better judgment.

Flattering.

Josh pushed the sarcastic thought aside and waited as patiently as he could for her to speak. This was about her safety, not his ego.

"All right. I'll take that ride—"

Finally! He'd never had to work this hard to get a woman to share his company before—be it for business or pleasure or practicality. Josh pulled out his keys and unlocked the door.

"But don't think this is earning you any extra credit, Mr. Tanner."

Would it kill her to call him Josh instead of using that fake name over and over? But as he opened the door and helped her inside, he remembered the role he was supposed to be playing and laughed on cue. "Do I need any extra credit? I thought I was acing your class."

She laughed. "Not quite."

Definitely a hottie. When Rachel Livesay smiled, her eyes sparkled like polished emeralds and her full lips just begged to be kissed.

"I guess I'll have to work harder, then." Josh leaned into the truck, almost giving in to his body's natural instinct to press his mouth against hers.

Fraternization.

The thought sobered him up like a slap in the face. He pressed his lips together, trying to rub away the temptation that lingered there. Minding his manners and the part he had to play, he pulled out the seat belt and handed it to

Rachel, making sure his fingers never touched her eloquent hands.

Then he shut the door and cooled his libido in the night air as he circled the truck.

Once he had climbed behind the wheel, he started the engine and cranked up the heat. The confined area of the truck's cab quickly filled with the smells of winter dampness on wool and leather. Then his nose attuned itself to a more subtle scent. Something delicate. Like peaches and cream. The scent of Rachel herself.

He tightened his grip on the steering wheel. Oh boy.

"Did your mother also raise you to be this persistent, Mr. Tanner?"

"Josh. It's—" He turned and looked into her eyes, which flashed in stubborn contrast to the wind-whipped cold that turned her cheeks a rich, rosy pink. Whoa. He had completely lost perspective here. *Teacher,* he told himself. *Think teacher. Think dead Billy Matthews. Think undercover assignment.* He breathed in deeply. The sharp pinch of bruised ribs provided plenty of pain to clear his head and get him thinking straight.

"I'm the baby of the family. I'm used to getting my own way. It's one of my bad habits."

"You have other bad habits?" He heard more challenge than curiosity in her question.

He forced his thoughts away from those incredible eyes and double-checked that there were no signs of traffic before pulling out onto the street.

"Yeah. I never know when to mind my own business."

"WE'RE HERE, DOC."

Rachel stirred at the deep, seductively pitched man's voice. She snuggled deeper inside her covers, relishing the cocoon of warmth that enveloped her.

Something even warmer settled on her shoulder. Someone cleared his throat. "2415 Woodley, right?"

Rachel's eyes snapped open. The gentle weight on her shoulder was a man's hand. And she wasn't bundled up in her bed. She was wrapped in her wool coat, dozing in the cab of Josh Tanner's snazzy red pickup.

A jolt of adrenaline shot through her, waking every nerve ending and snapping her back to rationality. Oh God. How could she have dropped her guard like that? No wonder *Daddy* had been able to slip her that note. No wonder David Brown and his thugs could sneak up on her. Self-preservation instincts that had seen her through troublesome patients, a rebooted career and a painful divorce seemed to have shorted out.

She sat up straight and shrugged, shaking loose the caring prod of Josh's hand. "I guess I fell asleep."

"No problem." His wolfish smile beamed clear across the bench seat between them. "It's one in the morning. You're probably needing extra sleep, anyway."

"When I can get it. This little girl has a sleep schedule all her own." The baby stretched, right on cue, jabbing her foot into the tender spot near Rachel's ribs. She pressed her hand to her side and moaned. "There she goes again."

"Must be playtime."

"Must be." Rachel grinned, telling herself she was being appreciative of the knowledge that she'd been in safe hands on her ride home, and wasn't succumbing to the boyishly charming effect of Josh Tanner's easy smile.

Her ex-husband, Simon, had possessed a smile like that. Along with a worldly intellect and cultured speech. Coal-black hair and bright-blue eyes. She'd fallen under his spell easily enough. Unfortunately, so had a dozen other women.

"You said before it's a girl," Josh commented.

Rachel nodded, cradling her precious cargo. She gladly switched from thoughts of Dr. Simon Livesay to her favorite topic. "At my age, I've had to take some extra precautions with my pregnancy. During one of the amnio tests I found out I was having a girl. I've already decorated her room, in shades of peach and pastel blue."

"What do you mean, *your age?* You can't be that old." In the light reflected by streetlamps and snow, she could see the flush of color creep into his cheeks. "Sorry. I know you're not supposed to talk about a woman's age."

"Something else you learned from your mother?"

He shook his head. "Something I learned in the trenches. If you want to make an impression on a lady, age and weight are two taboo subjects."

"I'm thirty-seven." She made the admission with a touch of fatalism. Like a warning. Maybe speaking their age difference out loud would be enough of a reminder that Josh Tanner's old-fashioned chivalry and state-of-the-art charm were of no concern to her.

"Just right."

Oh God. Couldn't her student see that he was wasting that smile on her?

He turned off the engine and dropped the keys into his pocket. "C'mon. I'll walk you inside."

"That's not necessary."

"For me, it is."

With that, he climbed out and walked around the front. Even hunched down against the cold, he was a big man. Tall and golden and young. Too young and off-limits for her hormones and used-up girlhood dreams for her to be sitting up and taking notice of his broad shoulders and long stride.

And good manners.

His mother had taught him well.

Rachel had fished her keys out of her pocket by the time Josh opened the door for her. He offered a supportive hand as she clutched her bag and climbed out. She held on to him just long enough to find her balance on the freshly graded pavement. Then, before the solid strength of his forearm could imprint itself on her fingertips, she hurried toward the four-story brownstone across the street.

A blast of cold air hit her in the face, making her pick up her pace. Josh locked up and quickly fell into step behind her, near her right shoulder, blocking the worst of the moist arctic chill that blew in from the north.

With her key she opened the foyer door to her building. Normally, she would have stopped to pick up her mail. But there had been nothing *normal* about her evening, so she headed straight to the stairs. Josh had shown himself to be too much of a gentleman to leave before he'd seen her to her condo.

He waited until the entryway door had closed, then jimmied the knob himself to double-check that it was locked before he followed her upstairs. Taking the stairs two at a time in a long, easy stride, he caught up with her on the landing.

If the cold air hadn't shocked all thoughts of sleep out of her system, then her awareness of the big, golden Sir Galahad who followed in her footsteps certainly did. He had charged out of the darkness and put his life at risk to save her from three drunken bullies.

Her conscience told her she owed him something.

But thirty-seven years and a strict departmental policy about faculty fraternizing with students warned her she had no way to repay him.

So when she unlocked her condo at the end of the hallway, she turned in the open doorway to say good-night. "Thank you, Josh. I—"

Her keys slipped from her hand and landed with a *thunk* on the polished wood floor. She stooped to retrieve them, but Josh was already there.

She heard the hiss of pain from between his teeth as he straightened up. She saw the grimace before he masked his expression with a smile.

Rachel snatched the keys from his outstretched hand and tugged on the sleeve of his jacket. "You said it was just a bruise."

Thirty-seven years and departmental policy be damned.

She pulled Josh into her condo and closed the door behind them.

Chapter Four

Josh Tanner seemed to swallow up all the room inside Rachel's refurbished condo. Even after she'd taken his jacket and invited him into the high-ceilinged living room, his presence dominated the place.

Maybe she'd been on her own too long, had kept to herself too much since making the decision to have the baby. She hadn't even invited any of her colleagues over, once the nesting instinct had kicked in and she'd redecorated the place from top to bottom. Now that she finally had company, the home that had seemed just right for a single mother and her child had grown way too small.

Or maybe it was Josh himself who made her homey condo feel suddenly too cozy, derailing her weary body's attempts to remain emotionally detached from her rescuer.

All the fresh, feminine details of lace pillows, floral upholstery and pale yellow walls she'd chosen to decorate her ladies-only haven seemed to highlight the masculine details of her unplanned guest.

He was a handsome study in leather and denim and muscle. A dangerous mountain of strength and energy. A golden sheen of late-night beard growth hugged his neck and jaw above the brick-red sweater he wore. His electric-blue eyes sparkled with an apologetic expression as he situated himself on one of the love seats. The soft, faded denim of his jeans cupped and cradled each hard muscle of his long thighs as he continued to shift back and forth in his seat, as though worried the glazed chintz was no match for his considerable size and weight.

The tight pinch of his mouth as he reached behind him to rescue a crushed gingham pillow finally shook her from her fascinated stupor. She'd been trained to study people's expressions and reactions. And though he remained silent, Josh's face broadcast a hidden pain.

"I've had some first-aid training." She took the pillow from his hands and tossed it onto the opposite love seat. "Better let me take a look."

She pushed aside a stack of books and sat on the edge of the weathered oak coffee table across from him. Spreading her legs apart to accommodate the curve of her belly, she leaned forward and tugged at the hem of Josh's sweater. But her outstretched fingertips couldn't get a good grip from this distance. She leaned farther. He inched forward. Their knees bumped.

"Sorry."

Rachel scooted her leg aside, but his knee brushed along the inside of her thigh. Solid muscle and soft denim caught in the nap of her corduroy leggings and pressed into the tender skin beneath, giving her a stroke of pure electricity that arced up her leg into the very heart of her.

For an instant their eyes locked as if he'd been stunned by the same bolt of electricity.

"Oops." The deep voice sounded more teasing than apologetic.

Rachel almost laughed in response. Almost. Horrified to feel herself falling under his charming spell, she tore her gaze from his and jumped to her feet.

Her intention was to put a polite distance between them.

But when she turned to scoot the coffee table back, she stepped on his oversize boot and stumbled. Her long legs tangled with his. He reached out to steady her. But in a humiliating attempt to assert her independence, she pushed his hand away, awkwardly shifting her center of balance. She toppled to one side. She felt Josh's hand at her hip, but it was too late. She landed with an unceremonious *plop* in the middle of his lap.

Out of pure reflex, she pushed against his knee and shoulder, trying to stand.

"Easy, Doc."

A wheezing gasp echoed deep in his chest. His arms wrapped around her like twin vises, anchoring her in place. Rachel froze. She'd hurt him.

"I'm sorry."

He nodded, but the grim tightness at the corners of his mouth wasn't a smile. "Gimme a minute."

In that minute's time, Rachel held herself still, riding the slow, guarded rise and fall of his chest as he breathed through the pain of whatever injury he'd sustained.

In that minute's time, her body noted with stunning clarity the masculine details of his body. The way her bottom cradled intimately between his steely thighs. The way the heat of his body warmed hers. The way his mouth was centered with chiseled perfection beneath the straight, proud line of his nose. The way the smells of leather and winter lingered on his skin.

The way every feminine instinct in her body longed to answer those masculine details in some very elemental way.

Barely daring to breathe for fear of aggravating his injury, she whispered, "I didn't do that on purpose."

"I know." A healthy color returned to his pale lips as he began to breathe more easily. He loosened his grip at her shoulder and gave the spot a gentle massage. "I didn't mean to hurt you."

A muscle at the small of her back cramped with jealousy at the tender, healing stroke of Josh's hands. She needed to get out of this tempting position. Now. Before she did something stupid like burrow against his chest or press her lips against the bold line of his jaw that hovered in front of her eyes.

"You didn't hurt me. Is it okay if I move now?"

His hands stopped their massage. His bright eyes clouded over. "Sure. Just don't push against my left side."

Nodding, Rachel swung her feet toward the floor. But they didn't quite reach because she was wedged between Josh's legs. With her knees hooked over his thigh, she tried to pull herself up. But scooting uphill against the weight of the baby proved an impossible task. She reached behind her and pushed at his thigh, but that only thrust her up against his chest.

And here she was trying to avoid that type of contact!

Pushing against his torso wasn't an option. Feeling an embarrassing similarity to a beached whale, Rachel swallowed her pride. "A little help, please?"

Josh slipped his hands beneath her and lifted her as if she weighed no more than one of the throw pillows. As soon as she stood squarely on her feet, he released her, though she could still feel the brand of his hands on her bottom.

She shouldn't be feeling tinglings of awareness or rushes of pleasure, should she? She was old enough to be his big sister or his aunt, even his mother. She should be feeling maternal, not romantic. She should be feeling pregnant. Not…aroused.

"Oh God." She pressed a cool hand to her flushed cheeks.

"You're sure you're all right?" he asked.

No, she'd have to answer if she was being truly honest. *I'm hot and flustered and feeling hornier than any thirty-seven-year-old pregnant woman has a right to be.* But in this instance, honesty didn't seem like the best policy. Summoning the noncommittal smile that she'd worn through countless patient interviews, she chose a different answer. "You're the injured party. I invited you in to doctor you up. Now, let's have a look."

"I'll get it." He reached for the hem of his sweater and lifted it. But when his left arm stretched above the plane of his shoulder, he swore. He crushed the material in his fist and clutched his elbow protectively to his side.

"This is ridiculous," Rachel said, admonishing her own foolish hang-ups as much as Josh's effort to do the impossible.

The man was hurt. It was her fault. And now she was being so self-conscious about the possibility of impropriety that she wasn't even helping him.

Letting a choice word of condemnation slide from between her own lips, she pushed his knees apart and knelt on the floor in front of him.

"Doc—"

Before he could utter one more polite apology, she had his left arm pulled from the sleeve of the sweater and was untucking his black T-shirt from his jeans. Taking care to keep his left elbow well below his shoulder, she undressed the left side of his body, pushing both shirts up beneath his right arm and draping the excess behind his shoulder.

"Oh my God." For a moment, Rachel sank back onto her haunches. "He caught you with the tire iron."

''Tell me about it. It hurts a little.'' He managed a grin, though she suspected it was all for show.

''That hurts more than a little.''

Way more than a little. She brought the lamp from the end table closer and inspected the damage. A slender welt the length of her foot had raised itself along Josh's flank. At the center of the swelling, the skin had already turned a deep bloodred. The bruising webbed outward in fingers of blue-black and dark purple. The discoloration marred the taut skin of his belly and disappeared up beneath the burnished hair sprinkled across his pectoral muscle.

Rachel touched her fingers to the wound. She grimaced an apology at Josh's sharp intake of breath, but continued to inspect the swollen, feverish skin to ascertain the depth of damaged tissue and whether or not he had sustained any internal injuries.

''Looks like bruised ribs. If I were you, though, I'd get an X-ray in the morning. For tonight, I can wrap it to give you some external support and take the pressure off the muscles around your rib cage. It should make breathing easier.''

''I'll do that when I get home.''

''How? You could barely turn around to save the pillow.''

Rachel looked up and found herself bathed in a watchful gaze of vivid electric blue. Josh's eyes had an almost catlike quality to them, seeming to glow from the inside out. In a brief flight of fancy, she imagined those eyes peering into the dark and seeing things no mortal man could. Her longing for a home and family. Her determination to succeed on her own merits and not her ex-husband's name. The need inside her to believe she was special enough and sexy enough and woman enough to be loved.

The woman Josh Tanner loved would know his feelings with a single look. The unabashed intensity of that gaze reached out to Rachel like the caress of his hand. It quickened her pulse. Soothed her misgivings about helping him.

He incited all sorts of soft, womanly yearnings with that gaze, making her feel female and pretty and ten years younger, with just a look.

A sharp pain in the tender tissue beneath her own ribs broke the spell, and soft, womanly yearnings gave way to one of the painful realities of impending motherhood. "Ow." Automatically, she pressed the flat of her hand to the sore spot just below the juncture of her left breast and round belly, urging the baby to move her foot. "We're quite a pair."

"Is something wrong with the baby?" A shadow darkened those bright-blue eyes.

Rachel smiled and pushed herself up via the coffee table and Josh's knee, daring her hormones to ignore the potent combination of soothing comfort and sizzling awareness that touching this particular man seemed to trigger in her. "We're fine. She just decided to move. I have a clean old sheet I can tear up and some stretch gauze to cover the wrap."

She'd barely turned when he grabbed her wrist. "I don't want to put you to any trouble."

"Please, Mr. Tanner—" she extricated herself from his sure yet gentle grip "—Josh. You put your life on the line for me and my baby tonight. The least I can do in return is to rip up an old sheet." Rachel cringed as a thought hit her. She rubbed at the cramp in her back, seized with a sudden ache that had more to do with her abused heart and ego than with any baby pain. Maybe Josh's polite reticence to accept her help had nothing to do with his mother's bang-up job of raising him. What if her inept attentions were embarrassing him? "I'm sorry. Maybe you have someone at home you'd rather have help you."

Like a girlfriend. A live-in lover. Or—even though he sported all the signs of bachelorhood—a wife.

Josh smiled. There was something more like calm reassurance than charm in this particular version of his megawatt grin. "Not unless I go home to Ma. And she'd have a cow if I showed up with a bruise this size."

"So would a girlfriend." She was such a glutton for punishment. Simon's last conquest had been about Josh's age. The final "other woman" Rachel had endured had shared Josh's youth and vigor. She'd felt old and worn-out by comparison. But the rational side of her continued to push the point. *Was* Josh Tanner attached to anyone?

He shook his head. "I live solo in my bachelor pad, Doc. I have ever since I turned twenty and moved out of the house."

Which must have been all of two or three years ago, she mused. Though back in that abandoned parking lot, and just now when he'd held her, Josh had seemed much older than his student status would indicate.

"It's settled, then. I'll repay your chivalry by bandaging your wounds."

"Sounds medieval to me."

Rachel grinned to herself as she walked to the linen closet in the bathroom. She could certainly picture Josh Tanner in a suit of armor, charging in on his noble steed.

But she was no lady fair.

Simon's actions had told her as much.

The fanciful images drifted away in the face of reality. She'd better get Josh doctored up and out of here before she did something she'd regret. The attraction she was feeling probably had a lot to do with gratitude. And a little to do with loneliness. In her years of helping clients deal with problematic relationships, she knew gratitude could often be confused for attraction. She knew loneliness sometimes made people do uncharacteristic things.

Despite the vulnerability she'd been feeling ever since receiving that note from *Daddy,* she was smart enough to know not to confuse her emotions. She could objectively appreciate Josh's boyish grin and rugged good looks. She was an older woman, not a dead one, after all. And she *was* grateful for his timely intervention and insistence on seeing her safely home. But that didn't mean he could provide any other emotional support for her.

She knew how humiliating and soul-draining it could be to fall for the wrong man. She wouldn't let her common sense get carried away on a tide of ill-conceived feelings and misfiring hormones.

Josh Tanner was handsome. He was a hero.

But he wasn't hers.

By the time she'd retrieved the supplies she needed, shredded an old cotton sheet, and knelt in front of him again, she had her head on straight and her hormones firmly in check.

Right.

She propped Josh's hand on her shoulder to ease the strain on his sore muscles and reached behind his back to wrap the first cotton strip around him. The tip of her nose brushed against his bunched-up sweater and Rachel inhaled again the masculine scents of wool and winter and man. But she also caught a whiff of something distinctly more pungent.

Rachel leaned back and breathed in fresh air, clearing her sinuses of the unexpected smell.

Marijuana.

She wrapped the second band of cotton around his torso and sniffed again. The odor was very faint, but distinct.

Her imagined white knight just slipped off his horse.

"So, Mr. Tanner—Josh," she amended before he could correct her. "What were you doing out on campus in the middle of the night?"

Maybe she imagined the slight hitch in the muscles around his chest. She didn't imagine the uncustomary pause. Her smooth-talking patient was searching for words. "I was at a party."

A pot party. So many young people drank too much and smoked too much and abused their bodies in ways they shouldn't. David Brown and several of her clients leapt to mind. But Josh had seemed like such a fit, health-conscious young man. It surprised her to learn that her wounded hero took those risks. Or at the very least, associated with others who did.

"By yourself?" She leaned in again to pull the bandage tightly enough to offer support without constricting his breathing. She was close enough to feel the heat emanating from his bare skin. Close enough to hide the disappointment that must be reflected in her expression.

"I told you I was unattached. The party bored me, so I left." His deep voice had lost the humor that gave it that sexy, musical lilt. This tone was taunting, laced with danger. It rumbled at such a different timbre that it distracted her from his intent, until she felt the two fingers beneath her chin, tilting her face up to his. "What were *you* doing on campus in the middle of the night?"

Avoiding being home alone. Trying to spot the jerk who threatened my baby. His eyes were clear, crystal blue, reflecting no sign of drug use. Her relief at reaffirming he was clean was tempered by the unblinking concern in his gaze that demanded the truth. She offered one version of it. "I was working late."

He made no comment when she shifted her chin from his touch and resumed her doctoring. She wound the strip of cotton two more times before he spoke again.

"Why would David and his buddies want to attack you? It looked like more than a simple mugging to me."

"Drop the inquisition, Josh." She reached for the elastic gauze on the coffee table. "My business with David is confidential."

"Apparently so. Is that why you didn't want to call the cops?"

She looked up on her own then. Nailed him with a stern glare and a raised eyebrow. She fought the urge to put more than those few short inches of distance between them.

"You didn't want to call the cops, either. With the smell of pot on you, I'm not surprised." For an instant his expression hardened, giving her the fleeting impression of a man more weary of the world than that second-row hotshot who breezed his way through life would be. But he never responded to her subtle accusation. Rachel went back to work. "David's problem is an academic matter. It's being handled through the proper channels."

He nodded. "*A*, I don't do drugs. And *B*, I hope those channels work fast enough to keep you safe from any more drunken threats."

Believing his assertion about the drugs, she offered a bit of an explanation for her own actions. "I'm trying to keep a low profile right now. Dean Jeffers is looking to name a new assistant dean for the College of Arts and Science. Someone to oversee academic advising, work with alumni, that sort of thing. I'm one of the three final candidates."

"Congratulations. Who else is up for the job?"

"Curt Norwood. He's a psychologist from the Criminal Justice Studies department. Gwen Sargent from Theater."

"You'd get my vote."

Rachel clicked her tongue behind her teeth, her effort at masking a laugh making her sound unexpectedly matronly. "Your views are probably more liberal than Dean Jeffers'. He's still trying to figure out whether or not he approves of single parenthood."

Josh's eyes widened at her last comment, and again she wondered if she'd crossed the line from professional to personal by revealing her relationship status.

"He can't hold your pregnancy against you, can he?"

"Legally, no." Rachel shrugged and focused on Josh's injury instead of her worries over a possible promotion and the job security it would provide. "But the selection will probably come down to what kind of image we can project for the college. Alumni donors like to see their money supporting cutting-edge research and intellectual, moral teachers who can shape the leaders of the future. Their donations go to help the best and brightest of students. They want a good show for their money, not controversy."

"That's why you're being so strict about fraternization, aren't you?"

"It's not just for appearances, Josh. It's never right for a teacher to take advantage of a student."

"Or vice versa." The hand on her shoulder squeezed in a gentle prelude to the warning he was about to issue. "David threatened you. Even if he was drunk and not in control of his faculties, he's still accountable for his actions."

"I have bigger problems to deal with than David, believe me." She pulled his comforting hand away before she gave in to the urge to rub her cheek against it. She thought of the wadded-up note from *Daddy,* still buried deep in her coat pocket. If it had been nothing more than a prank intended to rattle her, it had succeeded. If it was intended as something more…

Rachel shuddered. But she pushed the thought aside and pulled away just as Josh's fingers began to close around hers. She concentrated on securing the self-adhesive gauze wrap above his waist without accidentally brushing her fingers against his warm, supple skin. Again.

She didn't need his comfort. Even for one evening, it was a luxury she couldn't afford to indulge in.

"Are you talking about raising a baby on your own? C'mon, Doc. You're one of the smartest, most capable women I've ever run across. You'll handle it just fine." She smiled, letting him misinterpret her reason for caution. "Where's the dad? Does he plan to help?"

Her smile flattened as she cut the last strip of tape. So he had taken note of her earlier confession to single parenthood. "*That's* where this conversation ends."

He immediately shifted his position on the couch, trying to tug his T-shirt down over his shoulder. The mummy-wrap that stretched from just below a flat male nipple to a latitude about an inch above his waist didn't budge. "I didn't mean to bring up a painful topic."

"Not painful, just personal."

She rose up on her knees and helped him into the sleeves of his T-shirt and sweater. He stood as she re-packed the first-aid supplies on the coffee table. When she had finished, his hand was there, waiting to help her up. Appreciating the practicality of his offer in lieu of repeating her embarrassing visit to his lap earlier, she folded her fingers into his palm. But as soon as she was on her feet, she released him, not wanting to analyze her body's swift, needy response to his strong, considerate care.

She brushed down the hem of her tunic and led the way to her front door. "You, sir, have a psych quiz to review for, I believe. I'd better send you on your way." She pulled his thick leather jacket from the peg beside the door. "Thanks for seeing me home."

"No problem."

Holding the jacket out in both hands to help him put it on, she had no chance to hide the big yawn that suddenly assailed her, stretching her chin almost down to her chest. Rachel shook her head, trying to stem off the overwhelming fatigue that followed right after, turning her muscles to mush.

"Nothing personal."

Josh grinned, his good-humored charm back in full force. He slipped his arms into the jacket and pulled it up onto his shoulders. "I'll get out of here and let you get some sleep."

She had no argument for him this time. Unlocking the door and holding it open for him, she gave her belly a gentle hug. "Thanks for keeping us safe."

"My pleasure, Doc." He waved at her stomach in a ridiculously touching gesture. "You, too, little one." He inspected the chain and dead bolt before walking out onto the landing. "Lock up behind me."

"I will. Stay away from those parties. And don't forget about the X-ray."

He nodded a response as he pulled on his gloves. "Sweet dreams, Doc."

"Good night, Josh."

She didn't hear him move until she had set all three locks. She rested her forehead against the door and listened to his footsteps fading down the stairs. Her energy faded right along with the sound. She was weary. She'd been on an emotional roller-coaster ride today. Fear. Anger. Longing. Lust. Confusion. Disappointment. And twice she'd been rescued by Josh Tanner.

Two times too many for her own peace of mind.

She'd better have a snack and turn in—and put an end to this long, long day. For her sake as well as the baby's.

But as Rachel pushed away from the door and faced the warm colors of her condo, she rubbed her hands up and down her arms, wishing the color scheme alone could provide a tangible rise in temperature. Because now her cozy little condo felt big and empty—and lonely.

Dismissing the fanciful conjecture as a by-product of her tired brain, she headed into the kitchen, where she poured some milk and fixed herself half a peanut butter sandwich. She had a feeling that tonight her dreams would be anything but sweet.

Moments after she'd taken her first bite and leaned her hip against the counter to slowly chew and savor the taste, the phone rang. Her gaze instantly slid to the digital clock on the microwave. 2:26…a.m.

Her blood pulsed through her veins in a feverish rhythm. While it rang a second time, she scanned the living room. Maybe Josh had forgotten something. But other than the first-aid supplies on the coffee table, everything was in order.

She drifted back into the kitchen on the third ring. Perhaps it was a patient. Lucy Holcomb had been spiraling toward depression during their last chat.

Taking a deep breath, burying her wary feelings and adopting her cool, professional persona, Rachel swallowed her sandwich and picked up the phone. "Dr. Livesay."

There was a beat of utter silence. Then the caller spoke.

His voice, barely audible, was a hoarse whisper, as if the man—judging by the low pitch—was talking through a wad of cotton. "This is Daddy. What are you thinking, fooling around with that boy toy while you're carrying my child? If you want to keep that baby, you'd better watch yourself."

Boy toy? "Who the hell—?"

Click.

Rachel jumped as if a gunshot had thundered beside her ear. For a moment she could only stare at the receiver, her mind numb with shock and fear.

Then the baby kicked. And a helpless anger flooded her veins. A need to protect. A need to strike back at the bastard who got *his* kicks by terrorizing a lonely pregnant woman.

He was watching her.

Tonight.

Now.

How long had he been watching her?

She slammed down the phone and paced to the living room windows. A surge of adrenaline fired up her brain and scattered all thoughts of peaceful slumber. She cracked the blinds behind a lace panel of curtains and peeked outside. Traffic was nil this time of night. And though the street was lined with parked cars, there were no lights. All seemed quiet.

Was he out there in one of those cars? Sitting in the dark with a cell phone? Watching her peer helplessly into the night?

Creeped out by the very idea, Rachel closed the blinds and backed away from the window. She turned to the door where Josh Tanner had just exited, wondering how many minutes had passed since he left. Five? Ten? Was his truck still parked across the street? But then she realized she couldn't bring herself to look out the window again. Besides, turning to Josh a third time wasn't really an option. Hell. He might even have been the man on the phone. With her track record of being drawn to the wrong man, she'd be wiser to question Josh's timely interventions rather than appreciate them. His help and comfort was off-limits, anyway.

Her problem needed to be handled discreetly. On her own.

The damn thing was, she didn't know how. Maybe tomorrow, in the light of day, she'd think of a way. But for tonight, feeling as raw and vulnerable as she ever had in her life, she settled for checking all her locks, unplugging her phone and lying down for a few fitful hours of sleep haunted by nightmares of a faceless man breaking into her home and snatching her baby.

Chapter Five

Josh pulled out his cell phone and dialed the number A. J. Rodriguez had given him.

He'd sat in his parked truck with the engine running, waiting until the light in Rachel's condo went out. She seemed to be taking an awfully long time getting ready for bed. Was she plagued by the same disturbing attraction that he felt? Or was he the only one whose equilibrium was being tested by forbidden urges?

Somewhere along the line tonight, his protective feelings and aesthetic appreciation for Rachel Livesay's finer attributes had gotten tangled up in a sexual tension that was at once irresistibly intriguing and damnably inconvenient.

She'd literally fallen into his lap. Scooted her curvy rump against his privates, eliciting a purely masculine response to her, despite the pain he'd been in. Then she'd half undressed him with a speed and finesse that had him thinking bedroom rather than hospital room.

His physical response had been tempered by the absolute awe of learning the elusive differences between her pregnant body and the body of any other woman he'd known. There was a vulnerability about a woman whose normal state of grace had been altered by the fragile miracle of life growing inside her belly. Everything about her seemed like femininity intensified. Fuller hips. Softer, porcelain-fine skin. And the unmistakable evidence of the woman's fertility mounding beneath that clingy green sweater.

He'd wanted to touch her belly, feel the life within her. He'd wanted to kiss her.

Her soft, beautiful lips had hovered so close to his while he held her. He'd felt her warm breath on his neck. It would have been so easy to simply angle his face and capture her mouth with his. So easy to pull her even closer, to run his hands along the ripe curves and long planes of her body.

Talk about blowing his cover!

He could tell the whole party scene he'd admitted to had disappointed her. It had quickly sealed the opening of any kind of relationship that might have blossomed between them. Maybe she'd lumped him in with David Brown and his drinking buddies.

If only she knew how hard he crusaded against young people using drugs. How he was putting his future as a cop and maybe even his life on the line in his quest to redeem Billy Matthews's death and get every drug off every street corner, and protect every kid from that kind of hell.

Josh laughed out loud, mocking his lofty ideals as he turned on his headlights and checked for traffic. In reality, he knew he couldn't save every kid. But he was a Taylor. He had to set his goals high.

He pulled out onto the deserted street and headed for his temporary apartment off 63rd Street near Swope Park. It lacked the history and personality of the City Market area where he'd grown up. But for now it was home. It was closer to campus and it had a bed. And at two in the morning, even that broken-down mattress would look mighty good.

A string of Spanish expletives greeted him after the second ring of his cell phone. "What?"

Apparently, the perennially cool Detective Rodriguez didn't like being awakened in the middle of the night.

"A.J., it's Josh."

"What's up?" A.J.'s tone changed in the time it took him to sit up in bed. He was all business now.

Josh had to admire the man's chameleonlike ability to change personas. "It may be nothing, but I need you to run some checks for me first thing in the morning."

He waited through a shuffle of noises. A.J. was probably reaching for a pen and notepad.

"Give me the names."

"David Brown. Lance Arnold. Shelton Parrish. They're UMKC students. I picked a fight with them."

"*You* started a fight." A.J.'s teasing bordered on incredulity.

"They were picking on somebody smaller than them."

"You really want that badass reputation, don't you? You hurt?"

Josh shrugged as if A.J. could see him, and immediately regretted the movement. The curse of pain between clenched teeth was answer enough.

"How bad is it?"

"Just some bruised ribs. I got 'em bandaged up."

"How?"

"I don't have to report *everything* to you."

The detective laughed. "You're the only man I know of who can take a beating and still come out smelling sweet. Is she pretty?"

"She's a knockout." Josh didn't bother to deny A.J.'s

intuition about his nurse tonight. He didn't bother to explain, either. "You gonna run those names for me?"

"You don't kiss and tell, huh?"

A kiss? His body heated up all over again just thinking about the possibility of pressing Rachel Livesay's sweet lips beneath his own. But she had a strict rule about not fraternizing with students. And he had a strict rule about keeping innocent parties out of harm's way.

"Yo, Josh." A.J.'s voice snapped him back to the issue at hand. "Forget the lady. How was the party?"

"It was a bust. They had marijuana in the back room, not meth."

"Don't sweat it. Ninety-nine percent of what we do is boring, setting up the groundwork for the big finish. Being there tonight should net you some contacts. At the very least, it legitimizes your cover as someone who's looking to score some action."

"If you say so."

"I do. I'll let you know when you really screw up."

Josh shook his head at A.J.'s subtle laugh. "If you don't, I'm sure Lieutenant Cutler will."

"Speaking of which—Cutler's been doing some research. He gave me another name for you to check out." Josh heard A.J. thumbing through pages of his notebook. "Kevin Washburn. He's an on-again, off-again freshman there. He's been picked up twice for meth possession. You make friends with him and maybe he'll lead you to his supplier."

Josh wrote down Washburn's dorm address and his home address in the ritzy K.C. suburb of Mission Hills, Kansas.

"Got it. He's not in any of my classes, but I'll find a way to make contact." Josh tucked his notebook inside his jacket pocket. This next request was off-the-record. "And A.J.?"

"Yeah?"

"Do one more thing for me."

"Name it."

Josh took a moment to change lanes and head for his turnoff. "I want you to find out everything you can about a Professor Rachel Livesay. She's in the Psych department."

"Is she a suspect?"

"She's the reason I got in the fight."

"*Madre Dios.*" A long silence followed before A.J. spoke again. A warning simmered in the detective's ultra-quiet voice. "You know you're not supposed to get involved with anyone while you're on a case. That puts them in danger, too."

"What was I supposed to do? Stand by and let them go after a pregnant lady?"

"Was it a robbery? A rape attempt?"

The image of Brown and his buddies putting their hands on Rachel made him queasy. His heavy sigh fogged up the truck's side window.

"Neither. But there was some serious intimidation going on."

"Stay out of it, Josh."

"Obviously, I can't report my involvement tonight." He wiped the window clear with the side of his fist, wishing he could see his way through his concerns about Rachel just as clearly. "But she needs to report what happened. If nothing else, get the guys' names on public record to establish a pattern, in case it gets out of hand and winds up in court."

"Let her report it, then," A.J. advised. "We can keep your name out of the record."

"She won't do it. She doesn't want the publicity, either."

"Then, that's her choice, man."

Josh shook his head. "The guy who went after her is a power freak. I don't think he'll let it go. She's not safe."

"All right—"

He could hear different noises in the background now. A.J. was up and moving. Someone else's good night's sleep had been shot to hell.

"I'll look into it. See what connections I can drum up. I'll post someone to keep an eye on her if the situation warrants it."

"It does."

"We'll see. I'll take care of the professor. You get your head back in the game." A.J.'s reprimand was as stern as any Josh had received from his brothers or Lieutenant Cutler. "You know, maybe that fight will work to your advantage. Prove you're a real bad boy on campus. Folks who are in the market to do business seem naturally drawn to a man with that kind of attitude."

"So if I can't charm my way into the meth ring, I'll just overwhelm them with my 'manly man' ways?"

"Something like that. Dealers can almost always use more muscle for protection."

"I'll see what I can do."

"But Josh?"

"Yeah?"

"Sometimes bad boys don't like competition. Look at Randall Pittman."

Josh closed his eyes and briefly pictured A.J. going down with a bullet in his shoulder. He'd come too close to losing a good cop and a new friend back in that warehouse. "Watch your back."

"Always."

He disconnected the call, fully intending to keep an eye on Rachel Livesay's beautiful back, as well.

"RACHEL! COME IN." Dean William Jeffers stood up from behind his imposing cherry-wood desk and greeted Rachel at the door to his office, welcoming her with a hearty handshake. "How are you?"

She smiled at his fatherly manner. "Fine, thanks."

Behind his wire-framed glasses, his pale-brown eyes squinted with concern. "My daughter is having her second child this April. Says she's having a devil of a time with swollen ankles. You'd better sit. Feel free to put your feet up on the ottoman."

He guided her to a Chippendale sofa and sat her down with the same care and caution he might use if she'd announced her water had broken and she was going into labor. She wondered if the delicate shadows under her eyes from the lack of a good night's sleep worried him. Or maybe it was just his old-fashioned way to treat a pregnant woman, as if she were a fragile piece of glass.

She needed to set him straight before he added health concerns to his list of reasons why she shouldn't be named assistant dean. "That won't be necessary. My doctor says everything is progressing healthily and normally." She patted her stomach beneath the navy sweaterdress she wore. "This baby has been good as gold. She hasn't affected my work at all."

Not counting the first few weeks of morning sickness. Or the next few weeks of sudden, intense bouts of fatigue.

Or yesterday's ominous threats from *Daddy*.

She closed down that train of thought and gave herself a bit of free press while reassuring her boss. "My article on post-partum depression and its effect on teenage mothers is scheduled for the next issue of the *Journal of Amer-*

can Psychology. I'm hoping to track the same subjects
as they enter their twenties and thirties.''

"Yes. That's wonderful. Publish or perish and all that.
Keep up the good work.'' He waved aside her comments
and sat in the wing chair opposite her. He unbuttoned his
sport coat and adjusted his tie while he spoke. "You know
I've never questioned your credentials, Rachel. And I appreciate that you've agreed to work right up to your delivery date. But your work performance and commitment
to the college are not why I've called you here this morning.''

Impromptu meetings with the dean generally meant a
crisis was brewing, or good news was ready to be shared.
She sincerely hoped it was the latter.

It was too soon for Dr. Jeffers to have made his decision on the assistant dean's position, though. Even if he
had decided on his nominee, he had to get approval from
a faculty committee first. Nervous anticipation vibrated
through her, threatening to wake the baby who was nap-
ping contentedly against something besides her bladder
for a change. "What's up, then? You said it was important.''

"Well, I've been looking ahead at the rest of the semester—'' A sharp knock at the door interrupted him. He
got up and hurried to the door, offering a conspiratorial
wink over his shoulder as he crossed the room. "I've
asked Curt Norwood to join us, if that's all right.''

"Fine.'' Curious as she might be about the reason for
the meeting, she wasn't about to protest. Dean Jeffers'
old-school charm and penchant for surprises masked his
true personality. The former economics professor always
had a plan. If he was up to something, he'd reveal it in
his own way, in his own time. Besides, she and Curt were
old friends from back in their graduate-school days in

Kansas. When she'd interviewed for the position here a
UMKC, he was already on the faculty and put in a goo
word for her.

She stood as Dean Jeffers opened the door. "Morning
Curt."

"Rache." Curt was a tall, lanky man—handsome in a
washed-out sort of way, with soft hazel eyes that reflected
considerable intelligence, and light-brown hair that he
cropped short to minimize the twin points of his receding
hairline and play up his sharply chiseled features.

He urged her to stay put when she would have risen
and sat beside her on the sofa. Rachel frowned at the
mischievous smile lighting his eyes. He knew something
Though she remained in the dark about the reason she'd
been summoned to the Dean's Office before her morning
counseling sessions, Curt knew what was up. She was the
only person out of the loop here.

Her ex-husband had also kept secrets from her. He'd
turned lying into an art form. And while William Jeffers
and Curt Norwood weren't lying to her, the effect of de-
liberately being kept uninformed was the same. She
pressed her hands together in front of her and steamed.

"Someone needs to tell me what's going on." Dean
Jeffers hiked his slacks up at the knees and sat across from
her. Was she in trouble? Had he called in Curt to offer
her some kind of moral support? Resentment turned to
anxiety in the pit of her stomach, but she didn't give it
time to turn sour. "Dean?"

The college chief cleared his throat and leaned forward
resting his forearms atop his knees. "Rachel, I know that
your baby is due next month."

She nodded. "March twentieth."

"Yes. And as I said, I know you'll work up to the last
possible moment, but I need to think ahead about your

eplacement. You'll be gone on maternity leave until the
all semester.''

Put on guard by his pacifying tone, Rachel scooted forward on the sofa. ''I thought the plan was to reassign my
clients temporarily, and have one of the graduate assis-
ants step up to take over my classes.''

''Initially, yes.'' The dean's face crinkled with an excited grin and he looked over at Curt, whose expression
could only be described as sheepishly apologetic.

Rachel looked from one man to the other. Her defensive
posture gave way to annoyance. ''What?''

Dean Jeffers sat up straight. ''This is such a wonderful
opportunity. And I really do have the best interests of the
college at heart.''

Not the most promising lead-in to the mysterious announcement. ''I never doubted that.''

''Curt has recommended a visiting PhD who could finish your semester and even teach over the summer session.''

The dean's excitement would be contagious if she
didn't have such a bad feeling about whatever he was
trying to tell her. ''Who is it?''

Curt shifted to the edge of the sofa when the dean nodded to him. He angled himself toward Rachel and scooped
her hands into his. Beneath the arch of one raised eyebrow, Curt's eyes were asking for understanding. Rachel
braced herself, hoping she could give it.

''Dr. Simon Livesay.''

For a moment, she simply stared at Curt. She looked
down at their lightly clasped hands and studied them as
if they were foreign objects. Then she blinked. She pulled
her hands away, tucking her fingers into her palms.
''Simon.''

She repeated the name out loud, testing the feel of it

on her tongue. She hadn't used it for so long. Her ex
husband's name.

Surprise gave way to a slew of other emotions, every
thing from amusement to anger to disbelief.

"You want to hire my former husband to replace me?"

Dean Jeffers raised his hands in front of him, placating
her in tone and gesture. "Temporarily. The position, o
course, will remain yours in the fall. But if he's available
it would be a wonderful coup for the college. And Cur
thinks he's interested in a short-term assignment. The pri
vate practice the two of you shared had a sterling repu
tation. That's why we snatched *you* up, after all. You
research was solid, innovative—the success rate of you
clientele was phenomenal." He swept his hands through
the air in a wide gesture, asking her to see the big pictur
the way he did. "I'm calling him this afternoon with ar
offer."

Rachel looked from one man to the other, feeling cor
nered. She'd cleaned up after Simon time and again, right
ing the devastation that—whether intentional or not—
seemed to follow in his wake. Was this an opportunity to
forestall his hiring? Ages ago she'd learned to shield he
heart from Simon's infidelities. She'd even salvaged a rep
utable portion of their joint practice so that she could con
tinue a successful solo career.

In the years since their divorce she'd come to look or
Simon as a mistake of youthful thinking. She'd once loved
him with all her heart, but had quickly discovered it was
too painful to love that way. Over the years she'd learned
to hold something back, until she'd trained herself not to
feel much of anything at all.

Maybe that was why having a baby suddenly had be
come so important. She needed to love someone uncon-

ditionally. She wanted to trust that her love would be accepted. Valued. Necessary.

Could Simon Livesay wreak havoc on her life a second time around? Did he still have the power to hurt her, even though she'd moved on with her life? Would his return ruin the self-sufficient independence she'd worked so hard to achieve? Or was this a chance to prove to herself that Simon no longer had influence over her life?

She wasn't sure what Dean Jeffers wanted from her. "Are you asking for my approval? Is this a background check?"

He shook his head. "I simply wanted to notify you about what the committee was planning. And to see if maybe you could give us an inside track."

"To hiring Simon?" Was he for real? She'd do a lot for her school, even more to support the dean. But this? Sarcasm bubbled up in her throat, raising the pitch of her voice and sending her hands dancing through the air in front of her. "You want me to sweet-talk him into saying yes to your offer? I hardly think that I'm—"

Curt laid a calming hand on her arm. "Dean, maybe you'd better let me handle this."

"Fine." The dean stood, clearly relieved to be passing this task off to someone else. "Just remember, Rachel." He strolled toward the door, signaling an end to his involvement in the meeting. "No matter what your relationship might be on a personal level, as a professional, Simon Livesay has few peers his equal."

As the dean opened the door, Curt slid his hand to the small of Rachel's back to help her up from the couch. "I'll discuss the same pros and cons with her that we did, Bill."

"Good. I'll talk to you both soon."

Curt was having private discussions with the dean? Calling him *Bill?* Smoothing things over with her?

Suspicion oozed from every pore. She pulled away from Curt's friendly touch and hurried out the door ahead of him. Once the door clicked shut behind them, she whirled around. "You're doing the dean's dirty work now? Are you trying to earn points toward the promotion?" she accused in a hushed voice.

He scanned the office to check that the attention of the two secretaries was diverted before bending toward her. "I'm trying to spare your feelings."

Then, his technique needed work. "By recommending Simon as my replacement?"

Curt's eyes narrowed to warning slits, sending a different message from that of the cajoling smile on his lips. "Why don't we discuss this over a cup of coffee instead of in the middle of the Dean's Office."

"I don't drink coffee anymore."

"Humor me." His hazel eyes softened to match his smile. "For old times' sake?"

Rachel threw up her hands, fully intending to drop the conversation until she'd figured out whether this was resentment or anger or hurt she was feeling. But her stomach grumbled with an unmistakable cue. Between the baby's needs and Curt's winsome smile, her emotional indignation faded. She touched her stomach as the baby stirred. "I could use some more breakfast."

"My treat," he offered, his smile firmly back in place. "I'll even drive."

He'd have to, Rachel remembered with a sudden rush of awareness. She'd taken a cab to work this morning. She hadn't even reached the parking lot where her car was parked before receiving the summons from Dean Jeffers on her cell phone. Then she'd gotten so caught up in her mixed-up feelings over the dean's new plan that she'd forgotten about her car.

Josh Tanner had promised to fix her tire for her this morning. But she hadn't given him her keys. She hadn't trusted him enough. She didn't want to trust him.

But independence was one thing. Rudeness was another. She should look up his number and try to call him. Thank him for his offer but tell him she would just contact a wrecker herself.

Thinking back to the young man's promise triggered a cascade of uneasy emotions. The sense of danger that emanated from his broad shoulders had made her feel at once nervous—and protected. He'd shielded her from the danger of last night's attack, but he'd gone beyond the tough, take-charge persona who had emerged from the shadows and had transformed into a stubborn, solicitous, sexy man.

She'd tended his wounds. He'd filled her condo and her head with images of confident masculinity softened with just the right tinge of humor and humanity. His stunning blue eyes had sought her out time and again—flirting, questioning, reassuring. And when he'd held her, they'd gone a deep, intense cerulean that had probed deep inside her woman's heart, giving her ideas about falling into his arms. About spearing her fingers through his short, golden hair and tugging his mouth down to hers.

After that horrible phone call, she'd wished he'd never left. Her momentary suspicions of him had been unfounded—borne of momentary panic instead of rational thinking. Josh Tanner was no villain. Something about his presence seemed to keep her fears at bay. Even if those electric-blue eyes and broad shoulders made her hormones dance in an illicit game.

If only she were ten years younger.

If only he were ten years older.

"Rache?" Curt's voice, mature and concerned, whispered close to her ear, dragging her from her speculations. "Are we on?"

She'd figure out her car later.

She'd put distracting thoughts of Josh Tanner completely out of her mind and focus on the more appropriate relationship she shared with an old school friend.

"We're on."

But somehow, it proved much harder to dredge up a smile for Curt now than it had been to conjure one for Josh last night.

TWENTY MINUTES LATER Rachel was laying claim to an empty table, while Curt stood in line for cappuccino, herbal tea and scones at the Bookstore Coffee House. She hung her coat over the back of her chair stool and tried to find a graceful way to climb up to the high table. The coffee shop was a hive of activity this early in the morning. Hopefully, the other patrons were too busy waking up or running to work and school to pay any attention to the awkward way the pregnant lady hooked the heel of one leather boot over the bottom rung, braced her hands on the table and chair, and lifted and twisted and plopped onto the vinyl seat.

By the time she had adjusted her slip, had pulled her dress down to her knees, and had crossed her feet at the ankles, she realized she was about ten inches away from the table, leaving a large enough gap to spill food or drink on her lap and belly. And she had no way of moving herself closer, short of climbing down, moving the chair and repeating the whole ungainly process all over again.

She also realized Curt had been standing there for several seconds, holding a tray in his hands and watching her squirm and situate herself in the chair, while he smiled with amusement.

She harrumphed in frustration. "You try negotiating the world with an extra twenty-five pounds of boobs and baby stuck on the front of you."

"No, thanks. You do it so well." He set the tray on the table and climbed easily onto the seat across from her. "Pregnancy makes you even more beautiful than you were before. If that's possible."

Rachel's embarrassment at the outrageous compliment manifested itself in a blush that warmed her from her face to her toes. "C'mon, Curt. Flattery was never your style."

He set her tea in front of her and handed her a paper napkin. "No, but I always thought that of you. Even back in grad school when you were dating Simon." He pushed a plate of scones and jam packets across the table. "He always did pick the lookers."

"Even after we were married." The sarcasm in her voice reflected more humor than bitterness. She'd enjoyed a few solid, happy months with Simon. And now her life—for the most part—was on an even keel once more. Still, those years of doubt and insecurity in between had been pure hell, leaving her with no desire to take a trip down memory lane. She spread a napkin across the front of her and picked up a packet of strawberry jam. "So, why don't you explain this morning's meeting to me. Why on earth would you recommend Simon as my replacement?"

Her nostrils and taste buds stirred as Curt opened his fragrant cappuccino and took a sip. "Marquee value. His reputation in the counseling world could bring lots of free press to UMKC."

She spread the jam on a scone. "His *reputation* in other

areas could be a huge embarrassment, as well. Does Jeffers know why we got divorced?''

"It's not set in stone yet, Rache. Bill asked for recommendations. Simon told me he's been looking to get into education. The coincidence was too good to pass up.''

"Isn't his private practice lucrative enough? Are you sure he's not just looking for a ready supply of young babes to hit on?'' She leaned forward, straining her neck in an effort to get her mouth as close to the tabletop as she could before taking a bite. She sat back and chewed slowly, savoring the sweet taste and looking forward to the renewed energy the snack would provide.

"Give the man a break. I know he treated you unforgivably. But he *is* a good psychologist. His track record with patients is impeccable.'' He set his coffee on the table and frowned into its milky depths before looking up at her again. "Simon told me that he's going through some financial trouble. I don't know if business is dropping off—''

"Or his reputation is catching up with him?'' she countered.

Curt smirked, acknowledging the gibe. Then his mouth formed a grim line. "He closed the Livesay Center Clinic, Rache.''

She stared into his rueful eyes as the shock sank in. "He closed the clinic? We worked so hard to get that up and running.''

Years of graduate research. Years of scrimping and taking chances. Years of young clients they'd worked with and fought for and fought with—all gone. The most successful chapter of her life that she'd signed over in the divorce settlement. Gone.

All she could ask was "Why?''

Curt shrugged. "He didn't elaborate. But the steady job at UMKC would look good on his résumé, as well as tide him over until he joins another practice or research staff."

Rachel sipped her tea and pondered the news. "I understand your wanting to help out an old friend. But Simon's never taught before. Do you really think it's a good idea to hire him?"

"Sure. Even without classroom experience, donors and students both will flock to see him. Increased revenues are always a boon for the college." Curt seemed sold on the idea of welcoming his old friend to the faculty. "Jeffers can hardly wait to sign him up."

She nibbled another bite of scone, wondering at the suddenly bitter taste on her tongue. "It can't hurt you, either. Landing Simon would be a big plus for you with the selection committee."

Curt choked on his sip of coffee. He coughed, set down the cup and flattened his hand over his heart, completing the picture of wounded ego. "Rachel. You know I have nothing but the college's best interests at heart."

She scoffed at his mock humility. "You can't tell me you don't want the assistant dean's job as badly as anyone else on the short list."

"Fine, I won't tell you." He laughed, their old camaraderie firmly back in place. "It wouldn't do you any harm, either, to prove you can work with your ex. I'll bet you'd cinch the promotion if you persuaded Simon to accept Jeffers' offer."

Rachel groaned at the suggestion in his tone. "What, you want me to prostitute myself for the college just so my lying lout of an ex-husband can get the glory of taking my place?"

"*Temporarily* take your place."

"Temporarily." She conceded the point with a wry grin.

She took a long sip of tea and cradled the warm cup between her hands. Closing her eyes, she tried to convince her palate that the flavor was just as rich and pungent as Curt's cappuccino. The jingle of the bell over the coffee shop's front door intruded on her taste buds' reverie.

A sudden prickling of hyperawareness across the back of her neck muted the bustling cacophony of chattering customers, hissing coffee machines and clinking glassware around her. Twin bores of imagined heat crept along her nerve endings, raising goose bumps on her skin beneath the warm knit of her dress.

The creeping sensation could only be explained one way.

She was being watched.

Instinctively, she slid her hand to her belly and shielded her baby from the unwelcome perusal. Since she was a woman of intellect and intuition, and not given to fanciful imaginings, she demanded a rational explanation. Keeping her face downturned, she glanced around the shop. Students. Faculty. Wait staff. Neighborhood patrons. Some she recognized. More were strangers.

Everyone seemed preoccupied with conversations and newspapers and customers. No one seemed to be focused on her. And yet...

The bell above the door jangled again, drawing her attention like a magnet to the tall, broad-shouldered man who came in with a rush of cold air and filled the doorway.

Josh Tanner.

Like a burnished beacon of light, he captured her attention. Their gazes met and locked. He tugged off his gloves and acknowledged her with a slight nod.

Her breath seeped out in an unconscious sigh of relief. The sensation of being watched faded beneath a very different type of awareness that flushed her skin with heat. Sir Galahad had arrived—minus the white charger and suit of armor, though looking no less imposing in worn denim and black leather.

Maybe she stared too long. Maybe her longing for a safe haven was reflected in her eyes. Almost imperceptibly, his bright-blue eyes narrowed, silently questioning her.

What's wrong?

Chapter Six

"Rache?"

Rachel blinked, reluctantly breaking the connection with Josh. Reluctantly pulling her wishful heart away from the safety he promised.

So, she was being watched. It was probably some student, amazed to see a teacher outside of the classroom. Or maybe someone *had* witnessed her comical climb onto the stool and he or she was still laughing at her.

Or maybe it was *Daddy*.

She shivered and glanced at Josh again. His assessing gaze was still locked on her, as if she was transmitting her fear to a tiny receiver inside his ear that he alone could hear and understand. When he took a step toward her, though, she shook her head. An imperceptible movement. But Josh Tanner read it and understood.

This was a public place. She had a reputation to consider. She couldn't allow a handsome student to walk over and sweep her into his arms and hold her until the chill of her own paranoia receded.

Still, she was disappointed when he dismissed her with a nod and went about his business. She didn't want to analyze the sudden thrill that had coursed through her at his arrival, nor her deflated energy when he walked away—leaving her feeling as abandoned and vulnerable as she'd been each time she'd discovered one of Simon's new infidelities.

"Rachel." The sharp voice called to her a second time, finally pulling her attention back across the table. Curt repeated the question he must have asked a moment earlier. "You don't still have feelings for Simon, do you?"

"No, of course not." Her hasty reassurance sounded false, even to her ears. She looked down into her cup of tea, not wanting Josh or Curt or anyone else to read the apprehension that had tightened her expression.

It wasn't that her heart still had any connection with Simon that she needed to justify. But she'd have a hard time explaining her fears about a nameless, faceless stalker. She'd have a harder time explaining away this inexplicable bond she shared with Josh Tanner.

She didn't even understand it herself.

"You know, you've never talked about the father of your baby. I thought, perhaps, you and Simon—" She watched from the corner of her eye as Josh got in line at the counter. She noted how he held himself stiff and erect, despite his easy stride, and wondered if he'd gotten that X-ray. She'd moved on to wondering whether he'd sustained any broken bones on her behalf, before she fully tuned in to Curt and realized where his conversation was leading. "Sometimes divorced couples reconnect—"

"Simon is not the father of my baby."

He held her pointed look. "Then, who is?"

93579. Daddy.

Rachel flinched as if the baby had just kicked her.

Instead of giving in to the urge to wrap protective arms tight around her belly, she flicked away the crumbs that had caught in the wool there. "Why don't we change the topic while you're still my friend." Hint, hint.

"I just don't want to see you hurt. I worry about you. A woman alone, bringing a child into the world." Curt was starting to sound almost…intimate. Less like the buddy she'd crammed with during final exams and more like a…date. "You know, if there's ever anything I can do, I want to help."

Oh, no. This was not a complication she needed right now. She twisted in her chair and leaned forward. She could stretch her fingertips just far enough to reach his where they rested on the tabletop.

Squeezing his hand, she smiled and appeased him in a clear you-and-I-are-just-friends tone. "Okay. I'll forgive you for bringing Simon back into my life. But my baby's parentage is *my* business. She and I will be just fine on our own."

Curt nodded, then leaned back in his chair, slowly pulling away from her touch. "Dean Jeffers would like to see you married."

"Dean Jeffers needs to get in touch with the new millennium. There are a lot of single mothers out there."

"Yes. But if you know the father, he should play a part in the baby's life. A part in your life."

Was he accusing her of sleeping around? Questioning her morals? "*If* I know the baby's father?"

"I'm just sharing the dean's concerns. It doesn't look—"

"Dr. Norwood." A young man, wearing a white apron and carrying an empty tray, dashed over to their table. With almost manic efficiency, he cleared Curt's empty cup and wiped the table in front of him. Still stewing from Curt's insinuation, Rachel snatched her cup of tea when he reached for it. Thwarted by that task, he straightened the basket that held packets of sugar and sweetener, and centered the plate with the last scone in the middle of the table. "We need to talk. When would be a good time to talk?" His gray eyes darted toward Rachel. "You're Dr. Livesay, aren't you? I know you."

On a winter's day when the temperature stood in the single digits, this twenty-something waiter had a sheen of sweat that made the tendrils of his short brown hair stick to his forehead. His skin had a pasty pallor beneath pink, chapped cheeks. He seemed familiar, though she didn't recognize him from her classes. Perhaps she'd seen him around campus or here at the coffee house.

Her temper cooled as her curiosity grew. "Yes, I'm Dr. Livesay. And you're—?"

"Kevin." Curt's smile didn't reach his eyes. "We're having a private conversation. Now isn't a good time."

The young man seemed visibly shaken by the rebuff. "But we need to talk. Last night didn't work out like you said. I need some money—"

Curt cut him off with a stern voice. "You're fine. Call my secretary and make an appointment for this afternoon or tomorrow morning. I'll fit you onto the list if I can."

"But, the money—"

"Hang tough, Kevin. You can handle this."

The young man named Kevin opened his mouth again, but spluttered into silence at Curt's uncompromising expression. He blinked his wide gray eyes several times in rapid succession and then nodded. "I'll call."

Then he disappeared from their table as quickly as he had arrived, zipping over to clear another table before carrying his tray back behind the serving counter. Curt's grim mouth dimpled into an apologetic smile. "Sorry about that."

"I take it he's one of your students?" Now that it was safe to do so, she set her tea on the table. Curiosity had given way to concern. Clearly Kevin was in some kind of distress. "Are you counseling him with tough love?"

"He's dealing with some issues. But it's time he moved past them."

"Doesn't the patient decide when he's ready to move on?"

"I'm his advisor, not his shrink."

Rachel sat back in her chair, feeling the sting of his sarcasm. "He didn't look well. Physically, I mean."

Curt shrugged off her observation. "He's been battling the flu. Missed over a week of classes. He's having a hard time catching up and is worried about losing his scholarship."

Maybe. Rachel studied Kevin's frantic pace as he waited on a customer. A person with the flu would be battling fatigue, not imitating the Flash.

He jumped, then froze as someone called his name. Rachel's gaze drifted to the customer who had spoken. Josh. Though she couldn't hear the words, she could detect the low hum of his voice. Almost like a lullaby, the bass-deep words calmed her worries. The soothing intonation seemed to be having a similar effect on Kevin. Rachel smiled at the kindness. *Go, Josh.*

"While we're on the subject of troublesome students—" Curt cleared his throat. "I'd like to talk to you about David Brown."

The name alone jolted her from her silent observations. She must have given some sort of tangible reaction—a soft gasp, perhaps, or a shifting in her chair—because she immediately felt Josh's eyes on her again. Their gazes met and locked. That psychic connection between them sizzled. There was no question in his eyes now. For an instant, something distinctly predatory and utterly protective glittered in the blue depths.

"Oh God," she murmured, tearing her gaze away. Maybe she did have an overactive imagination. Seeing things that weren't there. Wanting things she shouldn't. She was shaking her head in disbelief when she zeroed in on Curt's dull gaze. *"You're* David's advisor?"

"'Fraid so." There was no softness to his tone. This was no old friend talking. This was the criminal psychologist, the expert negotiator who worked as a consultant from time to time with KCPD. Rachel set her cup down and raised her guard. "He says you're going to report him for plagiarism."

"I am." *She* wasn't interested in negotiating.

"David's really not a bad kid. But he's got nothing at home to support him. Maybe he did make a bad choice with his paper." Curt gave a bare-bones version of what could have been a sob story about David's past, and how he was trying to "save" David by steering him toward police work. "With his background, I think he could make a real difference in law enforcement."

Rachel felt the warmth behind her before the large shadow fell across the table.

"I didn't realize this was a recruiting office for KCPD." Josh Tanner invited himself into the conversation, setting his coffee down and pushing Rachel's chair up about six inches to a spot where she could comfortably reach the table. The subtle courtesy this morning touched her as much as had his heroic rescue last night.

"Doc." He acknowledged them both with a half smile. "Professor Norwood."

"Excuse me, son. We're having a private conversation here."

Son? Curt couldn't have provided a more tangible reminder as to why she shouldn't be having these feelings—any feelings—for Josh.

"I won't be long," he answered without batting an eye at Curt's dismissive tone. He turned that casual, heart-stopping grin directly on her. "I just wanted to stop by and let you know I got your car fixed."

"But I have the keys. How did you…?"

"I called a friend with a tow truck. We replaced the valve stem and reinflated your tire. He didn't seem to think there was anything wrong with the tire itself."

He'd kept his promise. No, he'd gone out of his way to keep his promise.

"You called a tow truck? You shouldn't have." Rachel twisted around on her seat, trying to reach her bag, which she'd looped over the back of the chair. "How much do I owe you?"

He touched her elbow and stilled her search. "Nothing."

"Josh." The call alone could cost twenty or thirty dollars—extra money that most college students wouldn't have on hand. Not to mention parts and labor. "That's too much."

She braced her hands on the table and chair, hooked her heel around the bottom and pushed herself up, reversing the comical process of sitting down. But this time, Josh's big hand snagged her beneath the elbow, offering balance and support, allowing her to climb down gracefully.

"Rachel." Curt stood, as well, moving a step closer, clearly eyeing Josh's hand where it lingered on her arm. "We need to finish our talk."

Without calling attention to it, she pulled her arm from Josh's grasp and reached for her coat. But his chivalry would not be denied. He took the coat and held it open for her. Choosing practicality over decorum, she turned and let him help her wrap up to face the cold weather.

Curt's washed-out gaze seemed to take note of her every movement. Shrugging into her coat. Pulling on her gloves and hat. Taking her bag from Josh and smiling her thanks. She threw back the same compassion he'd shown for Kevin. "Call and make an appointment. I have business I need to take care of and then a counseling session."

"Rache—"

"Old friend or not, you won't change my mind." Not about reporting David Brown, not about marrying for the sake of the baby or her reputation, not about leaving with Josh Tanner right now. "Goodbye, Curt. We'll talk soon."

"Bye, Dr. Norwood." Josh added a more cheerful farewell and followed her to the door.

She felt the brush of his fingertips at the small of her back as he opened the door for her and ushered her outside. Rachel hunched her shoulders against the blast of cold air. Automatically, Josh wrapped his arm around her shoulders and snugged her to his side. The man was a living, breathing furnace, and for a few moments, she let herself savor the good smells and sheltering warmth that surrounded her.

But then she noticed the other people on the sidewalk. Whether they wore suits for work or jeans for school, the men and women cuddling together for warmth against the damp, frigid air were all the same. Couples. Deep in conversation or exchanging silent looks or bravely moving forward together—the pattern was the same.

Man and woman. Boyfriend, girlfriend. Husband, wife. Lovers.

With her nose turned into his coat to protect it from the bite of wind, and his arm falling possessively around her back, she and Josh could pass for a couple. Despite the difference in their ages, certainly no one would mistake them for mother and son. And with her obviously pregnant belly leading the way… What if someone thought that she and Josh…?

Rachel shrugged off his arm and stepped to the side, putting a good foot of space between them. "Maybe you'd better not do that. Someone might misinterpret your actions."

"Someone?" She couldn't tell if Josh's snort was one of frustration or a testament to the wintry air hitting his lungs. "You mean Dr. Norwood?"

She recognized his cherry-red pickup from the night before, parked a couple of vehicles away. "I mean anyone." Without Josh to shield her, the wind whipped her coat around her legs and chilled her through and through. She appreciated his gallantry, but he had to understand her situation. "Look. This is a tricky time for me at work right now. The dean is more excited about my replacement while I'm on maternity leave than he is about naming a new assistant dean."

"They're going to replace you?"

"Temporarily." She kept saying the word, but she was starting to feel like someone was trying to get rid of her permanently. "At any rate, I can't afford any hint of scandal right now."

"Putting my arm around you is *scandalous?*" They'd reached his truck, but she couldn't read his face as he stretched in front of her to unlock the passenger door, so she couldn't tell if he was offended or making a joke.

She appealed to his sense of reason to make herself clear. "The fact that I'm pregnant and I haven't told anyone who the father is, raises suspicion. Everyone from the dean down to the building custodian has speculated about the father's identity. If they see you and me being friendly, then a natural conclusion might be that you and I, a student and a professor—''

He turned to face her, startling her with the intensity of his bright-blue eyes. ''—slept together?''

Even as the north wind swirled beneath her coat, Rachel grew hot. The very idea. She and Josh…in bed. An unbidden image sprang into her rational mind. Josh—golden and naked, gloriously aroused—rolling her beneath him and taking her with all the power and tenderness of a knight, home from a dangerous quest, claiming the love of the lady he adored. She swallowed hard, choking down the lump that rose in her throat at the erotic, romantic image.

''Yes.'' Her voice was barely a squeak. She put her fist to her lips and coughed. With a stronger voice she added, ''Yes. Someone might think we share more than a student–teacher relationship.''

He opened the door and reached out to help her inside. With outstretched fingers, he waited patiently for her to take his hand. ''Scandalous or not, I'm not going to have you fall and hit the sidewalk.''

That said, she laid her red-gloved hand in the middle of his black-gloved palm and used his strength to step up inside the truck. ''Thank you.''

He pulled up the seat belt and handed it to her. ''Why don't you just tell the dean who the father is—even if it didn't work out between you—and end the speculation?''

Sitting up high like this put her at eye level with Josh. She looked deep into his eyes, willing him to understand. ''It's not that simple.''

He studied her without a glimmer of comprehension, but with something more like disapproval or disbelief stamped across his clean-shaven features. Then he closed the door and circled the truck. He climbed in behind the wheel and started the engine and the heater before asking a pointed question.

"You *do* know who the father is? Right, Doc?"

"Sort of."

He squeezed the steering wheel in a grip tight enough to snap it in two, before turning his skeptical expression on her. "I don't believe for one minute that you're the type of woman who has so many lovers she can't keep track of them all."

She pulled her shoulders back, affronted by the accusation. "I'm not."

"Then, you're protecting someone. A married man?"

"No."

"Someone on the faculty?"

"No!"

"Another student—?"

"A sperm bank!" She pressed her fist to her mouth, feeling as if she had somehow betrayed her baby by sharing their secret. She hugged her arms around her belly and whispered in apology. "I was artificially inseminated at a sperm bank."

Josh's breath rushed out along with hers, the anger of accusation and defense spent between them. "Why don't you tell them that?"

"Because it's none of their business. It's none of yours, either. But I need you to understand why you can't keep coming to my rescue, or touch me—no matter how impersonal it is. Someone might think that you—" she pointed to her swollen belly "—that you're the father."

He nodded, conceding her point but saying nothing.

"Now do you understand my concerns about improper conduct? You've been a good Samaritan to me, and for that I'm grateful. But it can't be anything more. Once you drop me off at my car and I give you a check, I don't expect to see you again. Except in class.''

He threw the truck into gear, glanced over his shoulder and pulled into traffic. "It's not all impersonal, Doc.''

She thought the matter was settled. "What's not?"

"You're gonna tell me you don't feel this connection between us?"

"What connection are you talking about?" Lusty animal attraction? She hoped not. It had better be something like *You've inspired me to become a teacher,* or *My bruised ribs give me an empathy for the pains a woman must experience during pregnancy.*

She wasn't expecting "Something spooked you back at the coffee house. You were shaking.''

"I was not.'' She knew it was a lie, but she didn't want him to make this point.

"You turned to *me.*" His eyes stayed focused on the road and the traffic. "You had another man sitting at the table with you, yet you sought me out of the crowd.''

"I—''

He stopped the truck at a light and looked at her with eyes that dared her to contradict. "You *connected* with me.''

Oh God. He felt it, too. But he shouldn't. This wasn't right. They shouldn't feel anything for each other.

Momentary panic fueled her blood pressure, and the baby chose that moment to shift. Rachel seized the opportunity to tear her gaze from those compelling blue eyes and adjusted her posture in the seat. She pretended not to understand what he was talking about. "Having all those pretty young coeds throwing themselves at you has given you an oversize ego, Mr. Tanner.''

She purposely used his surname, avoiding the intimacy of being on a first-name basis.

The light changed and he turned his attention back to driving. Instead of defending himself or calling her a liar, he asked, "So what spooked you?"

She rode for several blocks in silence, watching the bare, dark trees, speckled with patches of snow that had settled into each fork and cranny and on each horizontal limb. A black and white, colorless world, broken only by dirty winter vehicles and gray, concrete buildings. It all looked about as bleak and unfriendly and devoid of color as her own world these past twenty-four hours.

Except for Josh.

And whether sharing her fears with him was appropriate or not, the same stark chill that had rippled down her spine at the coffee house assailed her again. Josh Tanner might be the only friendly face who could understand her paranoia.

"I felt like someone was watching me. It felt…unnerving." She dared a look at Josh's profile to gauge his reaction. "Maybe David Brown is following me."

"I looked around. I didn't see him." To her surprise, he reached across the seat and squeezed her hand. He held on when she tried to pull away. Rachel decided to relax in his grip and accept the comfort he offered. Comfort wasn't against the rules. The other feelings—longing, lust—were off-limits. But comfort was okay. And Josh Tanner had that in abundant supply.

"It plays with your head, doesn't it," he went on. "When you feel someone's watching your every move? Silently judging you?"

His understanding surprised her. Almost any other college student would have thought she was a kook. She clung to his fingers, grateful to hear someone put into words what she'd been feeling. "I'm just a silly pregnant woman, I guess. All those extra vitamins I'm taking have made me paranoid.''

He didn't laugh at her weak attempt at humor. ''Don't discount your intuition. Could there be anyone else who might be following you? Maybe for a legitimate reason? A courier? A student with a question about despondent youth?''

Only one person had any reason to follow her. Only one. She pulled away and gently rubbed her belly, silently reaffirming her promise to protect her little girl.

Josh's gaze followed the movement. ''You're a woman with a lot of secrets, Doc.''

''No, I'm not.'' Her wistful sigh bespoke her gratitude as well as her regret. ''You're just not the person I can share them with.''

She had the feeling of having come full circle, both literally and emotionally, as Josh pulled into the faculty parking lot. ''Here we are.''

He parked his truck right behind her Buick and set his blinkers, since all the parking stalls were full. True to the manners his mother had taught him, he swung his long legs out of the truck and hurried around to open her door and help her climb down from her perch.

Her car looked as if last night's flat tire and scuffle had never happened. Josh walked around the perimeter of the car with her, explaining what his friend Freddie had repaired, including a couple of scratches on which he'd used touch-up paint. ''One of us might have dinged it with a belt buckle or a zipper from our coats.''

Rachel smiled. ''I'm just glad no one was seriously hurt.'' Embarrassed she hadn't checked sooner, she asked, ''Your ribs aren't serious, are they? Did you get an X-ray?''

He nodded. ''Nothing but a big, nasty bruise.''

She set her leather pouch on the trunk of the car and dug down to the bottom to retrieve her wallet. Ignoring Josh's protests, she quickly dashed off a check for fifty dollars and handed it to him. "Here."

"Doc—"

"Make sure your friend gets paid. If there's anything left, you can put it toward your tuition."

Reluctantly, he folded the check in half and stuffed it into his back pocket. "All right. I'll pass it along to Freddie. Make sure you have an escort walk you to your car when you leave. Especially if you're working late again tonight."

She replaced her wallet and slung her bag over her shoulder. "I will."

"All right, then. I guess this is…well…goodbye. I mean, until class tomorrow."

Rachel extended her hand. "Goodbye."

He eyed her gloved hand for a moment, then swallowed it up in his big paw. "Bye, Doc."

He held her hand longer than was necessary. Long enough to turn their handshake into something secretly intimate.

Long enough to distract her from the excited shouts that got louder and louder, until the person shouting ran right up to her.

"Dr. Livesay! Dr. Livesay!" Josh stepped back as Lucy Holcomb threw her arms around Rachel's neck and hugged her tight. The impact knocked her bag off her shoulder and scattered the contents at her feet.

"Lucy." Rachel pushed the bouncing chestnut curls out of her face and pulled back to study Lucy's beaming face. "What is it? What's happened?"

Lucy practically clapped her hands. "I'm pregnant."

Rachel's jaw dropped open. The cold air on her tongue

reminded her to snap it shut. This was the last thing Lucy needed right now. "Are you sure?"

The girl nodded. "I took one of those home tests this morning. It was positive. We're going to be pregnant together!"

She braced herself as Lucy launched herself into her arms again. This was the manic side of Lucy's manic-depressive personality. Rachel patted the girl's back, unable to find the words to congratulate her. Lucy hadn't recovered from her recent miscarriage yet. Yesterday, she'd admitted to the ongoing problems she and her boyfriend were having. This wasn't good. They needed to talk.

Rachel freed herself and gave Lucy her counselor's smile. "Do you have a few minutes? I think we should talk more about this."

"Sure. I was on my way to pick up my notes from my last class. I skipped it because I knew I just couldn't concentrate this morning. But I'll meet you in your office. Okay?"

"That sounds great. See you in a few minutes."

While she watched Lucy dance off toward her classroom, Rachel realized that Josh had come to her rescue yet again by stooping down to retrieve her things. "That's not news you wanted to hear, I take it?"

"Not at all." He stood and handed her her bag. "Thanks."

He still held something in his hand. A paper with writing that was obscured from view by Josh's long fingers. But as he scanned the paper, the natural humor drained from his expression, and she had an idea which piece of paper it might be. Hadn't she thrown that thing away? Had she really gotten it out and read it time and again last night when she couldn't sleep? She'd forgotten that she'd finally had the sense to stuff it, out of sight, into her bag.

When Josh lifted his clear, probing gaze to hers, she knew. "Who's *Daddy?*"

Oh God. She snatched the cryptic note from his fingers and stuffed it back in her carry-all. "I'll thank you to mind your own business."

"Is that guy for real? Or is it some kind of sick joke?"

"Goodbye, Josh."

"He as good as said he was going to take your baby."

"Good. Bye."

"Doc?"

She emphasized the end of their nonexistent relationship by turning away from him and hurrying toward the sanctuary of her private office.

Letting Josh Tanner share her burden was a luxury she couldn't afford. Curt Norwood already had his suspicions about her relationship with Josh. Who knew how many others had seen them together and misconstrued the bond between them.

Josh Tanner was not an option.

She needed to deal with *Daddy* all by herself.

She just wished the idea of *all by herself* wasn't such a frightening prospect.

Chapter Seven

Josh slouched on the bench outside the biology lab, wait-ing for the afternoon session to get out so he could take his undercover assignment to the next level.

Make a buy.

Kevin Washburn had come through for him sooner than he'd expected. The poor kid had been desperate to find a friend this morning. He'd been coming down off whatever high he'd been on. Josh had talked to him the same way he'd calm a frightened animal, and gradually Kevin had opened up. Yeah, he knew a few of the names Josh had dropped into the conversation. Discovering mutual ac-quaintances had apparently been enough for the young man to put his faith in Josh.

He'd watched the kid talking to Rachel and Dr. Nor-wood. Had seen the crestfallen expression on Kevin's face when Norwood rebuked him. Just like a kid who wanted approval from a father figure. Just like a kid whose father wasn't there for him.

Just like all the kids Josh shot hoops with at the com-munity center.

When a kid went looking for something to give his life meaning, he'd better find it. Or else the drugs were always there waiting for him. Providing the illusion of meaning in his life, when in reality, the drugs simply stripped away the need for anything aside from the drugs.

Josh shifted his position, crossing his right ankle over his left knee, fighting the urge to pace up and down the length of the hallway. He was supposed to be Josh Tanner, the king of ultracool. Laid back and looking for fun.

He drummed his fingers against his knee and did his pacing inside his head. All Kevin Washburn had needed that morning was a word of encouragement from Curt Norwood. That positive reinforcement might have given Kevin the strength to fight his way through today clean. But combining that disappointment with whatever other troubles plagued him had made Kevin desperate enough to call Josh—a virtual stranger—and make a deal.

I'll connect you with the meth if you buy a sample for me, too.

Josh tasted the bitter guilt in his mouth. A cop buying drugs for a junkie. It sure didn't feel much like he was saving the world today.

And then there was Rachel Livesay.

She should be making plans for her baby's arrival, not dealing with scum like David Brown and that insensitive excuse for a man, Curt Norwood. He decided he didn't like Norwood much. He wouldn't help a lady sit in her chair. He wouldn't make the time to assist a needy kid. And he'd been holding hands with Rachel. Across the tabletop. Where anyone, including Josh, could see. And she hadn't protested *that* public display of affection one little bit.

Nope, he didn't like Curt Norwood much at all.

And what about that sick note that had fallen from Rachel's oversize purse? Josh's skin crawled with frustration. He couldn't do anything about that threat, either.

I want what's mine.

Who the hell would want to scare Rachel like that?

David Brown? After last night's fight, Josh doubted the subtle approach to intimidation was David's style. Of course, David sober was a much more calculating piece of work than David drunk.

But who else might have a grudge against soft, sexy, prickly, proud Rachel?

She'd told him there was no father. And he believed her. The admission had been too painful for her to have made it up.

But a test tube didn't say things like *I'm watching*.

He'd been a little surprised at first to learn there wasn't a man around that she'd been intimate enough with to create a new life together. But then he'd been secretly pleased. Because there *wasn't* a man around she'd been intimate enough with to create a new life together.

And wouldn't he love a shot at being that man she *would* get intimate with.

Josh shifted again, trying to find a position where the bandages around his ribs didn't pinch and the muscles beneath them didn't ache.

He was a sorry overachiever. He had a meth ring to crack. A lieutenant to butter up. A kid in trouble he wanted to put into a rehab unit. A beautiful professor he wanted to take into his arms and protect.

But the drug dealers were hiding out. The lieutenant thought he was a hotshot. Kevin Washburn wanted more drugs. And Rachel Livesay thought he was too young.

Holding *his* hand in public would be too scandalous.

Kissing her would be downright illegal.

And no matter how many times he charged to her rescue, no matter how many times she turned to him for comfort, she just plain straight wasn't going to let any magic happen between them.

A high-pitched chirp saved Josh from the introspection that was eating him up inside. He pulled the cell phone from his jacket and checked the unmarked number. *A.J.*

Josh punched the on button and put the phone to his ear. "What do you got, A.J.?"

"My day's going fine, thanks. And yours?" The accented inflections in A.J.'s voice teased him out of his foul mood. At least trading quips with Detective Rodriguez gave him something new to focus on.

"Sorry. *Buenos dias, amigo.* How's it hanging with you today?"

A.J. laughed. "Your Spanish sucks. I liked you better when you woke me up at three in the morning."

"It wasn't three. It was more like 2:58."

"Ah. That makes all the difference in the world." The tone of A.J.'s smooth voice altered slightly. "Seriously, *amigo.* I've been tracking down information for you since before dawn. Lieutenant Cutler keeps walking past. I think he's going to bring a razor next time and order me to clean up my act if I'm going to be sitting behind a desk."

"Sorry, man. I know you'd rather trade places with me."

"What, and miss out on all this quality time with the lieutenant?"

It was Josh's turn to laugh. He caught his side and groaned, immediately regretting the impulse. "Better tell me what you found out. I'm meeting a kid in a couple of minutes who said he'd set me up."

"Right. Here's the short version." He could hear the shuffle of papers as A.J. went through his list. "David Brown had a sealed juvie record. I had Merle Banning dig into the computer files and get me the details. Vandalism. Petty possession of narcotics. Assault. Aggravated assault."

"Terrific." Josh's stomach churned at the idea of Rachel facing off against David and his goons last night. What might have happened if he hadn't come along when he did? "He's a real Boy Scout."

"He's been arrested twice since he turned eighteen. Two counts of possession. Both times the charges were dropped."

Maybe Josh did need to get closer to David. The creep seemed like a natural suspect to lead a ring of drug dealers on campus.

The door to the biology lab swung open and the first of the hundred-plus students began to file out. "Make it quick, A.J. It's time for my appointment."

"Shelton and Parrish are clean. Probably recent recruits." Josh stood, listening to A.J. turn another page. "And your Dr. Livesay." Josh's full focus zeroed in on the voice on the phone. "Age thirty-seven. Divorced. She and her former spouse, Dr. Simon Livesay, had a groundbreaking counseling practice working with teens and young adults. I haven't read the articles, but they've been written up in medical and psychology journals across the country. She's big news."

"Any enemies?"

"An unsatisfied customer, maybe? I haven't had time to dig deep yet. But I can tell you this—"

Kevin Washburn popped out of the classroom. Josh doffed a salute and the dark-haired kid headed his way, checking every classmate who passed him with a darting glance. "What?"

"Her ex, Simon Livesay, is in financial trouble. Apparently he got sued by one of his female clients for sexual harassment. They settled out of court and the guy retained his license. But he had to declare bankruptcy. The plaintiff's attorney threatened to use some of your Dr.

Livesay's divorce deposition against him. The guy's a
player.''

''Interesting.'' Another suspect with a motive to stalk
Rachel? ''Let me know if you find out anything else. And
thanks.''

''Just doing my job. You do yours.'' A.J.'s tone
switched from one of superior officer to one of comrade-
in-arms. ''Watch your back.''

''Always.''

Josh disconnected the call and pocketed the phone as
Kevin approached him. ''Hey, Kev.''

''Josh.'' He jammed his fingers through his oily hair
and fiddled with the strap of his backpack. ''Friend of
yours?'' he asked, nodding toward the phone.

Josh smiled and thumped Kevin playfully on the shoulder. ''You're my friend right now, Kevin.'' He steered
the young man toward the outside doors and fell in step
beside him. ''Let's go meet that special friend of yours.''

RACHEL'S LIFE had gone from bad to worse.

''Simon.''

Of all the people she'd expected to find waiting outside
on her front stoop, her ex-husband wasn't one of them.
He looked as impeccably handsome as ever, despite the
fact he was shivering inside his tailored, double-breasted
suit.

''Rachel.'' He clasped her by the elbows and kissed her
on her cheek. His lips felt like ice against her skin. He
leaned back and looked at her, his gaze sweeping from
the top of her red hat to the soles of her brown boots.
''You look absolutely gorgeous. Pregnancy agrees with
you.''

Too stunned by his appearance to respond to the compliment, she stepped out of his grasp and asked, ''Don'

you have a coat? It *is* winter in Missouri. I'm sure Armani makes one in your size.''

"Witty as always—''

She wondered how she had ever found his hollow flattery charming.

"My coat's at the hotel. I'm meeting with your Dean Jeffers tomorrow. But I wanted to surprise you and take you to dinner tonight.''

Rachel glanced at the cold-shrouded sun still high in the sky, then pushed back her glove and checked her watch. "It's three in the afternoon.''

His smile dimpled in mock apology. "I hoped maybe we could talk first.''

This visit still didn't make sense to her. "You could die of exposure out here. How long were you planning to wait for me?''

"Oh, I've only been here a few minutes. I called your office. Your secretary said you'd just left, so I called a cab to bring me here. I'm staying at Crown Center, so the trip didn't take long.''

Crown Center, eh? One of the finest, most expensive hotels in the entire city. Simon always did everything first-class. How he ever thought he'd be happy on a professor's salary dumbfounded her.

"I was coming home to take a nap. I didn't get much sleep last night.''

"Is the baby keeping you up?'' he asked.

"That's after they're born, Simon.''

He nodded and then sneezed. "So may I come in?''

He sneezed again, pulled out his handkerchief and dabbed at the pinkened tip of his nose. Great. He'd made this grand gesture to impress her, and now he was going to get sick. If he expected her to take care of him this time, he was wrong.

Linking arms with him, she unlocked the foyer door and escorted him inside. "Let's get you out of the cold before you catch something."

Ten minutes later she had a pot of tea brewing and a cup of forbidden coffee heating in the microwave. Even though it was instant, the aroma was heavenly. The first thing on her list once she had given birth and weaned her baby from nursing was to sit down with a cup of freshly brewed coffee. French vanilla roast mixed with dark Colombian beans. She closed her eyes and inhaled, using her imagination to turn the freeze-dried crystals of coffee into a rare treat for the senses.

"Pregnancy has changed your behavior, I think. That's the second odd thing you've done since I've been here. The first was that whole belly-rubbing thing you did after you took off your coat."

Simon's observation upon returning from the bathroom echoed the subtle criticisms that had finally made her give up the fight to save her marriage. Maybe if she'd thought he found her as attractive as he did his mistresses, she might have tried harder to reform his wandering ways. She'd wanted a home and a future. He thought she was an old fuddy-duddy.

Rachel opened her eyes and faced him. She didn't have to listen to his ego-eroding comments anymore. "I rub my belly to get the baby to move. Sometimes she's wedged against a bone or muscle and it hurts me."

He sat at her table and shook his head. "I still don't see why you'd want to put yourself through pain like that. The sex between us was always good, wasn't it?"

The sex between them had been nonexistent after that first year. After that first affair. After she'd immersed herself in her work so that she wouldn't know her husband wasn't at home anymore.

"Why are you here, Simon?"

The microwave dinged. She served him the coffee and poured herself a cup of tea. When she joined him at the table, he finally answered.

"I want to know what kind of money you make. What your work hours really are in school. Will I have time to pursue my own interests?"

That was brassy. "What I earn is private. Dean Jeffers will probably offer you the starting salary and some kind of bonus."

"Bonus. I like the sound of that."

She sipped her bland tea and wished for coffee and better company. "As far as the hours go, remember when we were in grad school?"

"Of course."

"I'm about that busy."

Simon frowned. "What about your social life?"

Social life? This baby was her life. "I make time for it as often as I can. But I usually spend my evenings at home."

A distracting image of Josh Tanner eclipsed the coffee fantasy in her mind. Sitting on her couch, half-dressed. Looking down at her with those amazing blue eyes. That would be a home life she'd crave. A darling baby in her arms. Herself cradled in Josh's arms.

There she went, wishing for the impossible again. Even if Josh Tanner wasn't her student and the powers-that-be accepted their relationship, she didn't know if she could trust that fantasy. Josh was young. Handsome. Stunningly sexy. And he had a heart and compassion any woman would love.

Any woman.

Josh would tire of her soon enough, just as Simon had.

Maybe even more quickly as the novelty of being with an older woman wore off.

Rachel took a hasty drink of her tea and nearly scalded her tongue. But the pain was a sharp reminder that spinning fantasies about her golden Sir Galahad was pointless. She couldn't become involved with a student, no matter how tempting he might be. And she wouldn't become involved with a younger man.

"I think I'll state a minimum amount I'll accept for the bonus. And request specific time off from my duties." He was completely oblivious to her miserable discomfort. "Do you think your dean will agree to that?"

So he'd come to pick her brain about the perks of *her* job. Right now she had bigger concerns than Simon's financial future and happiness. She had a baby to protect.

She pointedly glanced at her watch and rose to carry his cup to the sink. "I have a doctor's appointment in half an hour. Was there anything else you wanted?"

"A doctor? Are you all right?" He shot out of his chair and crossed the kitchen as if his concern was real. He wrapped his fingers gently around her elbow. "You look fine. Except for the pregnancy thing, of course."

"Pregnancy *thing?*" She pulled away from his unwelcome touch.

"You know what I mean." He followed her back to the table. "We have history, Rache. If there's anything wrong, I want to—"

"It's just a business meeting at the Washburn Clinic." She wanted nothing from her ex beyond a quick exit from her condo. "I'm fine. Our history shows that I'm the responsible one, anyway. If anything *was* wrong, I'd handle it without your help."

Instead of taking the hint and leaving, Simon perked

up at her announcement. "*Andrew* Washburn? Will you be seeing him? How is the old coot doing?"

Forget about bad to worse. Her day was about to go all the way to worst. "How do you know Dr. Washburn?"

"Why, I donated sperm to his clinic, of course."

SURELY SIMON wasn't 93579.

Wouldn't that be the ultimate irony? The man who adamantly claimed that children would slow down his life and mess up his house ending up as the father of her child. Rachel clutched her stomach. The possibility made her as nauseated as she'd been those first few weeks of morning sickness.

But later, as she paced the plush, wine-colored carpet of Andrew Washburn's office, the idea almost made sense. With Simon's ego, she wouldn't put it past him to somehow ensure that he was the one who impregnated her. It'd be the ultimate testament to his virility. Giving every woman—including his ex-wife—what he thought they wanted most. Himself.

Rachel stopped in front of the broad picture window and looked out across the snow-covered grounds of the Washburn Clinic. With each well-trimmed evergreen bathed in an icy sea of white decorative lights, the place looked like a fairyland at night. A wonderful place where miracles happened.

She hugged her own miracle.

Simon saw children as impositions, not miracles. Why would he threaten to take hers? Unless it wasn't about the baby at all.

How badly did Simon want her job? How permanently did he want to stay on at the university? If he was behind the note and the phone call, then he must be more desperate for money than Curt had indicated. Maybe Simon wanted to scare her enough that she'd pack up and leave Kansas City. Dean Jeffers wanted to hire him. With her out of the picture, a short-term replacement could become a full-time employee.

But Simon had once claimed to love her. *Unfaithful* and *inconsiderate* were words she'd always used to describe him. Never cruel.

She pressed her fist to her lips. How the hell was she supposed to figure this all out? "Damn."

"I'm working as fast as I can. These damned computers never cooperate." Andrew Washburn's frosty gray eyes nailed her above the half-lenses of his glasses. Those shrewd eyes softened as he realized her curse hadn't been directed at him. His snowy-white mustache twitched as he worked to control his burst of temper. "Sorry. Was there something else you wanted to ask?"

Since he wouldn't give her the answer she wanted most—the identity of her baby's father—she shook her head and let him return to his computer search. He'd been scrolling through a file on his screen, reading his data on the mysterious 93579. She'd settle for any information she could get about the father, even if it wasn't his name.

"Looks like he was only with us for a short time. He made regular donations for two months and then he left us."

"Is that unusual?" she asked, crossing around his desk and sinking into a red leather chair to give her tired feet a rest.

He traced his mustache with his thumb and forefinger in a habitual gesture that revealed nervous frustration. "Not necessarily. Every case is different. Though most of our donors do stay with us for one to four years."

"Four years?"

"Some of our donors see it as a way of preserving their place in the future. For others, it's a steady income."

Four years. Rachel sat forward in her chair, wondering if the timespan was a coincidence or a clue. "Do college students ever donate their sperm?"

"Of course. They're some of our best customers. They can always use the extra money, and we like them because they tend to be healthier than older men." He frowned as a new thought struck him. "You don't think you've been contacted by one of your students, do you?"

Now, there was a disturbing thought. Though she could think of one blond student who would make excellent father material.

Andrew Washburn had been clearly concerned by her report that her sperm donor had made contact with her. She'd left out the details of just how unsettling his form of contact had been. In an effort to help her—and to protect his clinic from liability—he'd stayed late and answered every question he legally could.

He'd promised to call 93579 himself and remind the donor of the privacy clause in his contract. He'd sorted through records, both on-screen and in the hard copies he stored in manila folders. He mostly told her the facts she already knew. The father had brown hair. He lived in the Midwest. He had a high I.Q.

"What about mental illness?" She was grasping at straws now. "Could the father have some kind of disorder that would make him forget the rules of his contract or lay claim to my baby?"

Dr. Washburn removed his glasses and steepled the ear-pieces between his hands. He shook his head, his mouth creased in an apology that was nearly hidden by his thick mustache. "The father has no mental problems on record. Either in the donor himself or in his family line."

He rose and circled the office, stopping in front of her and sitting one hip on the edge of the desk. He leaned forward and took her hand, sandwiching it between his. "I am so sorry this breach of trust has happened, Rachel. Believe me, the Washburn Clinic will do everything in its power to rectify the situation."

Her mouth crinkled into a wry smile. "Except tell me his name."

He inhaled a sharp breath before patting her hand. "Except tell you his name."

Dr. Washburn stood and pulled Rachel up along with him. "The hour is getting late, dear. Could I take you to dinner as a small recompense for the anguish we've caused you?"

Anguish? He didn't know the half of it. "No, thanks, Doctor. Right now, I think I just want to get home and get some sleep."

"I understand." He released her hand and headed toward a small room at the back of his office. "Just let me get my coat and double-check that everything's locked up, then I'll walk you out."

The room in the back turned out to be a private washroom. While Dr. Washburn went in, Rachel pulled on her coat. As she buttoned up, she drifted closer to the massive walnut desk. Though the doctor had made a point of keeping 93579's file hidden away, she couldn't help but glance down at the open folders on top of his desk.

Most of the information she skimmed. It was a meaningless collection of pertinent physical facts, personality profiles and donation records. But one item leapt out at her with gut-twisting clarity. A tiny photograph, no bigger than a matchbook. Rachel pressed her lips together to keep from crying out.

David Brown.

Forgetting all ethics when faced with finding the truth about her baby, she quickly scanned his file. The number listed on the folder was 90422. Not a match. Unless the report was mislabeled.

She glanced up to check that Dr. Washburn was still occupied in the washroom before reading the rest of David's file.

He'd been donating sperm for almost two years now, from the middle of his first semester at UMKC to the present. According to the payments listed, he'd earned enough to buy his books each semester and maybe pay rent for a month. Beyond his health report and a current address, the details here were pretty thin. There was no family tree. No hobbies or talents were listed. No information at all about his life before UMKC.

She wasn't sure what the gap in information meant, but she'd file it away in her memory and sort through it later.

First Simon. Now David. Were there other men in her life with a connection to the Washburn Clinic? Men who'd have a reason to hurt her?

Or was she still looking for some anonymous donor who simply didn't think she was fit to be the mother of his child?

RACHEL DROVE HER BUICK around the curves of Brush Creek Boulevard on the south side of Kansas City's Country Club Plaza, objectively admiring the dramatic lines of the Mediterranean-style architecture. Even without the million-plus colored lights that decorated the red-tile rooftops during the holiday season, it bespoke wealth and old-world elegance.

Many of the shops had closed for the night, but there were still several tourists and locals walking about, visiting one of the trendy restaurants or window-shopping.

Some of them were dressed to the nines, others hurried along in jeans and tennis shoes. But they all moved about together. They all belonged to someone. They all felt safe and carefree enough to go out and enjoy each other's company.

Rachel was alone.

She wondered when she, too, would feel safe.

And with all the questions running through her mind in her search for logical explanations, it would be a long time before she'd feel like celebrating anything again.

She turned north and drove past the Nelson-Atkins Art Museum, finally heading toward her empty condo. She'd dined alone on salad and pasta at a chain restaurant. And though she'd been very disciplined about following the rules of her O.B.'s prescribed diet, she'd indulged a craving by buying two scoops of coffee ice cream.

She pulled into the parking unit behind her building and punched the remote to open her garage door. *Woo-woo,* she thought sarcastically. Was this the same kind of excitement, the same kind of fulfilling life her daughter had to look forward to?

Oh, how she hated these mood swings. They bothered her even more than the morning sickness or raging appetite or weight gain had.

She was a psychologist. She should be stronger than this. She'd spent years studying how the human mind functioned. Her recent research had specialized in how a pregnant woman's mind worked. And while she didn't suffer from any clinical or chemical depression, she still had to deal with these bouts of self-pity that turned her from a mature, rational human being into a sad, lonely woman who pigged out on ice cream and cruised the Plaza wishing she had someone to share her joys and responsibilities with.

"Get over it!" she chided herself out loud. Before she'd let this funk become debilitating, she'd chase it away with anger. She pounded the steering wheel once for good measure, then shut off the engine and reached for her bag.

Still fuming, and finding strength in the cleansing emotion, she slammed the car door and walked outside, heedless of the pair of eyes that followed her every movement.

Armed with the mace on her key chain, she closed the garage and headed for the front door at a brisk pace. She followed the cleared sidewalk around to the front of the brownstone, then hurried up the front walk, just as the crunch of snow behind her registered.

Rachel had her key ready for the lock and let herself in, barely breaking her stride.

That's when the charging figure leapt over a snowbank onto the stoop. The big man braced one huge, black-gloved hand against the door before she could close it, and shoved his way inside.

In one awkward motion, Rachel jumped back and raised the can of mace and sprayed. In a flash of gold and black, the man ducked.

"Doc, it's me!" He snatched her wrist and twisted it down to her side, pushing her against the row of mailboxes and trapping her there with his body. "Where the hell have you been?"

The voice cut through her fears long before her vision could make sense of what she saw. Josh Tanner. Gold hair. Black jacket. Low voice.

Without a trace of humor in it right now.

Remnants of fear mixed with anger, giving her the audacity to punch him in the shoulder. "Dammit, Josh, you scared me."

As rationality pushed its way past emotion, she realized

that he hadn't hurt her. The grip on her wrist was firm, but gentle. Only her shoulders touched the wall behind her. He'd had the presence of mind to protect the baby by angling himself to the side and pinning her with just his arm.

But gentle consideration didn't equal an explanation. "What are you doing here?"

"Waiting for you. You're late." That electric-blue gaze flashed with sparks like a downed power line sizzling and leaping about with an unleashed power.

Though he quickly released her and stepped away, Rachel kept her back pressed to the wall, feeling some of that same loose energy coursing through herself. "I thought I told you goodbye. I thought I made it clear that we can't be seen together outside of class."

"That was before *Daddy* popped up and penned you that note." He yanked off his gloves and jammed them into his pockets, giving her the impression that he wasn't about to willingly turn around and go home.

Rachel planted herself squarely and stated her position very carefully. "I'm not your responsibility. Now, get out of here."

She whirled around and marched up the stairs, hoping a warning look and a turned back would drive her message home.

But Josh fell in step behind her, following her with his bulk and heat and hardheaded determination. "Somebody needs to be responsible for you. You take stupid chances and put yourself in needless danger."

She stopped halfway up and turned, expecting to glare down at him. But standing just a step behind her put him at eye level. She refused to be daunted. "What are you talking about?"

"Walking from your car down that blind driveway, for

starters. Walking from your office to your car by yourself, even though I warned you not to.''

"Excuse me?" She tugged her hat off her head and swatted him with it. "Are you following me?"

"I'm keeping an eye on you."

"Don't." She turned and stormed on up the stairs. "I already have someone who's taken up watching me for a hobby."

"Exactly." In two long strides, he'd joined her on the landing. "You get to me more than any woman I've met in a long time. Maybe I can't hold your hand in public, but, by damn, I'm going to see that you stay safe."

"You *are* following me." She spun around and glared up into those sparking eyes. "How does that make you any different from *Daddy?*"

He recoiled as if she'd struck him. For one endless moment in time, she stood there staring at the changing emotions playing across his handsome face. She felt guilty. She'd hit him way below the belt. She'd accused him of something she knew in her heart could never be true. She wanted to apologize. But, dammit all, he'd scared her. He refused to take no for an answer. He refused to let her suffer alone.

"Different?" His entire body suddenly went still. Rachel backed away a step, then another, distancing herself from a man who was suddenly years older, suddenly much harder, suddenly much more potent than any student she'd ever taught in any class. "You mean from the creep who sends you sick notes about taking your baby? This is how I'm different—"

Without further warning, he reached out and grabbed her by the shoulders, quickly closing the distance she'd put between them, and brought his mouth down to cover hers.

Josh's kiss was raw and wild, full of an intensity and passion she'd never experienced before. This was so wrong. So dangerous to her peace of mind.

So intoxicating.

No! She pounded the heels of her palms against his shoulders and twisted her hips, trying to escape the assault on her senses.

But she was no match for his strength. His arms swept behind her back, lifted her onto her toes and pressed her closer to the hard, fiery heat of his body.

She was no match for his passion. Her beating hands stilled as his lips began to work a magic on hers that woke long-untouched parts of her body and made her achy with desire.

She was no match for his need. She breathed a heavy sigh and surrendered to the hunger that filled her woman's soul.

Opening her mouth beneath his, Rachel returned his kiss. She dug her fingers into his jacket, clinging to Josh and pulling herself into his kiss.

He was her hero. He was her baby's hero. His gallantry had kept them both safe time and time again. There was no threat from this man. And the way he was holding her now, the way he was kissing her—he was very definitely all man.

And her curves and planes that hadn't felt sexy for so long reveled in the sweep of his hands on her back and bottom. Lips that hadn't been touched for so long yielded to the heady force of his kiss. She tasted the unique male contours of his mouth. Brushed her tongue along the warm salt of his skin.

A fire sparked low in her belly, below her baby's precious home, filling her with an erotic heat that pulsed between her legs and tingled at the tips of her sensitive breasts.

Rachel hung on to Josh's powerful shoulders and gave herself over to the stirring needs in her body and heart. The need to be held. The need to be cherished. The need to feel sexy and pretty and desirable. The need to be all a man could ever want—even if it was just for a few, short, stolen moments in time.

Chapter Eight

Josh had died and gone to heaven.

The sexual hunger that had drawn him to Rachel time and time again, when the world around them kept telling them it was wrong to feel this way, exploded in an embrace that left him hard and shaking.

He speared his fingers into her hair, soft as the sable it resembled in color, and let the thick tresses tease his palms. Her body was a treasure of abundant curves. And her mouth?

Soft and supple. Giving and gorgeous. More delicious against his than any fantasy he'd imagined from the second row of her class.

He'd simply intended to prove his point. To remind her that he was here because he cared. He'd watched her condo for her return because she wasn't safe. And he desperately wanted her to be safe.

He'd kissed her to prove that he was a better man than she gave him credit for. Worthy of her trust. Deserving of her notice.

But this was wild. This was one kiss that was getting out of hand.

This was the way it should be between a man and a woman.

He slipped his hands inside her coat, trying to move impossibly closer. The clingy dress she wore hugged every curve, giving his palms a chance to enjoy her sensuous figure—

Something thrust against his stomach. Something as soft and fleeting as a love pat.

"Whoa."

The unexpected touch startled him, though his throat could barely produce the husky reaction. He tore his mouth from Rachel's and leaned back. They still clung to each other, linked together, belly to belly.

Josh looked down and studied the juncture where their two bodies touched. He breathed heavily in and out through his nose and mouth, trying to make sense of what had just happened.

The flat knit of Rachel's dress cupped her pregnant belly like a second skin. A moment later, the blue knit moved, stretching outward, then receding—like watching a heart beat.

"I saw it." He was awed, and it cooled the heat that fired in his loins and kindled a brand-new fire closer to his heart. "That's the baby, right?"

But when he lifted his gaze to Rachel's face, he could see she didn't share his excitement. The beautiful flush of passion on her skin, the telltale signs of a man's possession around her mouth, meant little compared to the flat, impenetrable wall of withdrawal in her eyes.

She let go of his jacket that had wrinkled in her grasping fingers and pushed back against his hands. "That's the baby. Anne-Marie Livesay. *My* baby."

Josh released his hold and watched her put a good three feet of touch-me-not distance between them. He shrugged in disbelief, ignoring the pinch of pressure against his sore ribs. "You don't want anyone else to share in all the cool wonders of bringing a new life into the world?"

"I don't want to share anything with you, period."

You don't measure up, Taylor. In his mind he could hear Lieutenant Cutler's voice, condemning, in much the same tone as Rachel had used. *You have to prove to me that you're your own man. That you're not just riding along on your family's history with the department.*

He hadn't surrendered to Cutler's challenge without a fight, either. "What just happened here, then?"

"A mistake."

Deep in his gut he knew that was a lie. That no matter what the rules of society said, he and Rachel were dynamite together. Two people didn't connect on a physical level like that unless there was something deeper that already existed between them.

But Rachel was determined to deny those feelings. She smoothed her hair where he'd mussed it with his greedy hands, then overlapped the front of her coat. She held it in place by splaying one of her long, expressive hands across her belly. Was she protecting her baby? Or hiding her from his curious gaze?

Damn, but she was stubborn. "I'm not going to apologize for kissing you."

"No, but I'm going to apologize for kissing *you*." She reached into her pocket and pulled out her keys, essentially dismissing him by turning her back on him and walking to her door. "That shouldn't have happened. It won't happen again."

From where he stood, he watched her profile, set in stone and refusing to show any emotion. He watched her trembling hands grow steady as she unlocked the dead bolt and the doorknob.

He felt like a chided schoolboy or rookie cop, though

his blood was still pounding through his veins like a man who was her equal. He'd accomplished his goal. He'd seen her safely home, and now he would respect her wishes and leave.

She opened the door and disappeared inside without another word. Josh shoved his hands deep inside his pockets. He was too embarrassed to admit how many women had made a play for him. Even the girl Kevin Washburn had introduced him to that afternoon had offered to sell herself as well as the methamphetamine if he was interested in buying. He wasn't.

The one woman who tore him up inside seemed to be the one woman who wouldn't have a thing to do with him.

That was some sort of crazy justice for being a flirt all his life, he supposed.

Josh turned and headed for the stairs. When he talked to A.J. tonight, he'd ask him to post that tail on Rachel. There was just no way he could keep her safe without winding up getting hurt.

And a blow with a tire iron wasn't nearly as painful as what he suspected lay ahead of him if he continued his involvement with Rachel—

The scream from Rachel's condo turned his blood to ice.

"Doc!"

Josh flew down the hall. He shoved open the door and slammed into Rachel. He would have sent her flying if he hadn't cinched his arms around her and pulled her close.

"Josh?" She'd been running toward the door herself. "Oh, Josh." She clutched up handfuls of his jacket, buried her face in the leather and sobbed.

"Shh, Doc," he soothed her with a hushed voice. He held her tight with one arm, automatically reaching for the gun at his side, silently cursing the universe when he remembered it wasn't there. Her heart pounded ninety miles a minute against his chest. She was shaking in his hold, murmuring something unintelligible against his chest. Enough. "I've got you. C'mon."

He cupped the back of her head, pulling her with him, backing out of the condo, away from whatever had terrified her.

"I want you to wait out here." He propped her against the wall in the hallway, stroking a fall of hair from her face as he hunkered down to look her in the eye. "I'm going back in to check things out, make sure everything's okay."

Though shiny with tears, those emerald eyes were bright and focused. "I'm going with you."

Josh straightened, intending to argue the point. But then he realized she meant to go back in herself, with or without him. "All right."

He clutched her hand where she linked it around his forearm, and they went back inside. He scanned everything. The lock looked clean. The condo itself looked spotless, just as neat and tidy as it had the night before. The curtains hung straight, indicating the windows were closed.

Her fingers bit into his arm as she squeezed. "In the baby's room."

A feeling of darkness and foreboding pooled in his stomach. He angled Rachel slightly behind his shoulder and peeked inside the small bedroom.

Josh swore, a vicious, damning curse that couldn't quite convey the sense of anger and violation that swept through him. Rachel turned away, one hand pressed to her mouth, the other holding her rounded stomach.

He gave her shoulder a reassuring squeeze then moved

in closer to examine the hideous gift that had been left for her.

All the stuffed animals that had been stored in the baby's crib had been shredded and tossed about. And hanging from the flowered light fixture in the center of the room was a stuffed rabbit, its head nearly pinched off by the noose tied around its neck. The pink fur on its belly had been slit open and filled with some kind of red liquid that resembled blood. A note was tacked to its foot with a diaper pin.

You failed the test.
I'll be waiting for you in the delivery room.
One way or another, I want what's mine.
Daddy.

Josh didn't bother swearing this time. He wrapped his arm around Rachel's waist and guided her out to the kitchen. Beyond the line of sight of that ugly, twisted message. He sat her in a chair and poured her a glass of water. Then he pulled out his cell phone and punched in a familiar number.

"Who are you calling?" she asked.

"A cop."

"But…what about—?"

Not that marijuana thing again. He cut off her protest. "It's okay. I'm clean."

He knelt down beside her and pressed a kiss to her temple. She willingly leaned her head against his shoulder when he pulled her close.

Undercover or not, he was going to make the bastard pay for threatening Rachel.

He waited impatiently for the phone to pick up. He'd

skipped A.J. this time and gone directly to the cop he needed most right now.

One more ring and a familiar, gravelly voice identified the speaker. "Detective Taylor."

"Mac? It's Josh. It's time for you to repay a favor."

RACHEL STOOD OFF TO ONE SIDE and watched forensic expert Mac Taylor from the Kansas City Police Department turn her little girl's nursery into a science lab. He'd pulled all manner of tools from his aluminum suitcase. A camera. Giant tweezers. A magnifying glass. Some sort of infrared scope. Plastic evidence bags.

He wore gold-framed glasses that didn't quite mask the fact that he was sightless in his left eye. But she had the feeling as she watched him work that his good eye missed nothing. No detail, no possibility went unexplored. She somehow found his scientific precision very comforting. If there was a clue to be found that would lead them to *Daddy,* Detective Taylor would find it.

What she found more oddly unsettling was the way he kept seeking out Josh and asking questions. About the crime scene, certainly. He'd asked her the very same things. *How long were you gone from the condo? Were the doors and windows locked when you arrived? Does anyone have a reason to threaten you this way?*

But the two men had inspected her condo together, going from room to room and chatting about things *sotto voce.* She only caught snatches of words and phrases— something about a "case," the name "Jules"—and she swore she heard, "Ma doesn't need to know."

Why would Josh be friends with a cop?

Curious.

She thought she detected some similarities between Josh and Detective Taylor. But Mac Taylor had too many scars on his face to verify a physical resemblance. He had gray eyes as opposed to Josh's blue ones, yet they both had burnished highlights in their hair. Their body builds were different—Mac's, tall and lanky, Josh's, big and broad. But their demeanors were similar. They both carried themselves in a deceptively casual way. Josh's sense of humor hid a fiercely protective nature, she knew. And she guessed Mac's quiet manner hid a perceptive intellect.

She wasn't quite sure what her speculations meant. But she was trained to be an observer of people, after all. She'd figure it out sooner or later. Besides, she'd go out of her mind if she didn't do something more than just stay out of their way, brew tea and wait.

She could have handled the police by herself, she supposed. She could have called a friend like Curt to stay with her, or even Dean Jeffers. But she'd asked Josh to stay. Common sense had given way to the very human need to feel safe. And the only place she'd felt safe lately was with him.

It made no sense to her, really, this "connection," as Josh had described it, that the two of them shared. His kiss had been like nothing else she'd ever experienced. It had been the purest form of passion, an elemental meeting of bodies and souls. Physically, he'd made her feel things she hadn't in years, things she'd never expected to feel again.

Emotionally…?

Rachel sighed and sipped her tepid tea. She wasn't ready to explore what had happened to her needy heart during that kiss. His grasping hands and seductive mouth had done far more than feed her ego and make her feel attractive, and even sexy. His determination to bind them together in that way had nourished her parched woman's soul. For those brief, mindless moments, it hadn't mattered that he was the wrong man for her—that she was the wrong woman for him. All that had mattered then was that it felt right.

Thankfully, reality had intruded, reminding her that her growing feelings for Josh weren't appropriate.

Teacher, student.

Older woman, younger man.

Set in her ways mother-to-be, bachelor with his whole life ahead of him.

Josh looked up from where he and Mac kneeled together over some marking on the carpet. It was as if he knew her doubts were creeping back in, ready to destroy the tenuous bond they'd created tonight. But when he smiled at her, she couldn't help but smile back. There was something endearingly boyish in that smile, something that begged her to give him a chance.

And for tonight, at any rate, she was feeling too exposed and vulnerable to deny him that chance.

"Well, it doesn't look like anything's been tampered with outside of the baby's room." Mac pushed to his feet, raising his voice loud enough to include her in the conversation.

Rachel nodded, debating whether she found that reassuring or not. The intruder hadn't violated her in any other way, but it shook her down to her core to sense all that hatred directed specifically at her child. "Thank you for cleaning up the nursery."

"Not a problem." Mac put on his coat and pulled a business card from the inside pocket. "Here. Call me if you find anything else that seems out of order. Or just if you have any questions."

She took the card and tucked it inside her purse on the coffee table. "I will."

Mac picked up his case. "I've bagged everything and

taken the pictures I need. I'll have the lab run the items for further analysis and call you if I find out anything.''

"Please do.'' She encouraged his quest for answers. Josh followed behind her as she escorted Mac to the door. "Maybe there will be something there that will give me enough evidence to get a court order for Dr. Washburn to open up his files and tell me who the father is.''

Mac's hesitation put her on guard. "You don't think that's possible?''

"I don't think it's probable,'' Mac said.

Josh spoke over her shoulder. "You don't think the threat to Rachel is real?''

Mac shook his head and clarified his suspicions. "I don't think this looks like the work of an anonymous donor who's suddenly decided eight months later he wants his kid.'' He dropped his gaze to Rachel, his sighted eye filled with a grim truth. "I think this is the work of someone who knows you personally. I think he or she could care less about the baby. Their main interest is attacking you where it will hurt the most. Somebody is trying to punish you for something.''

It had felt personal enough. From the very first message she'd found on her car.

She felt herself swaying, her mind and body exhausted by stress. But then she felt Josh's hands at her shoulders, sharing a dose of his strength and support. "That's just a theory, right, Detective?''

"Right. Dr. Livesay. Mr. Tanner.'' Mac turned the doorknob and opened the door. But the doorknob itself seemed to remind him of something. He shrugged an apology as he faced them again. "Look. There's no sign of forced entry at the window or the door. Whoever came in here has a key. Whether you gave one to someone you thought you could trust, or—''

Rachel shook her head. "I'm the only one with a key."

"Then, someone had the opportunity to make a copy." His friendly warning seemed to encompass both Rachel and Josh. "That tells me it's someone you're close to. Someone with whom you come into regular contact. I'd suggest varying your schedule. And I'd have the locks changed as soon as you can."

Meaning *Daddy* wouldn't hesitate to come back to terrorize her again.

"I'll take care of it first thing in the morning," she promised.

"Will you be safe tonight?" Mac asked.

Josh's grip tightened on her shoulders. "She'll be safe."

Her response to his resolute promise was a thrill that cascaded down her spine and trickled out to the tips of every appendage, exciting her and frightening her at the same time. It would be too easy to give in to his strength. She needed to find a way to deal with this on her own. She wouldn't put Josh in danger. She wouldn't set herself up for the heartache the morning light would bring, when Josh had to leave her and she was on her own once more.

So she pulled away from his possessive, protective touch and shook hands with Mac Taylor. "Good night."

"'Night, ma'am."

She closed the door behind him and set the dead bolt, even though she now knew the one person she wanted to keep out could easily find his way in.

Ma'am. Rachel almost laughed at the reminder that she could never have a real relationship with Josh. She turned around to thank him for giving up his night for her, intending to send him on his way, as well, but he had disappeared.

"Josh?" He strode out of the kitchen, carrying one of

the padded oak chairs she used at the table. "What are you doing?"

He set the chair on the floor next to her, tilted it back and wedged it beneath the doorknob. "I'm adding another lock to the door."

"But you need to be on the other side of the door when I do that."

He stood, straight and tall. "I'm not arguing with you on this. I'll keep my distance, if that's what you want. I'll make sure nothing else *personal* happens that'll upset you. But I'm staying."

To emphasize his decision, he proceeded to untuck the flannel shirt he wore from his jeans. He unbuttoned the shirt and stripped down to a plain white T-shirt that molded itself to the powerful contours of his upper body. He folded the plaid flannel into a bundle as he crossed to her floral chintz sofa. Then he moved all the throw pillows to the matching love seat and set the shirt on the arm of the couch.

Then he unhooked his belt. When he sat down and began untying his boots, she knew she was in trouble.

Half fascinated by the fact he was undressing in her living room, it took her a moment to make her feet move toward the linen closet. "Wait. At least let me get you a blanket and a bed pillow."

"If you insist, Doc—"

A boot thumped on the floor behind her and she turned. She could tell by Josh's smile that she'd been suckered into this one.

"I'd be happy to stay."

RACHEL ROLLED OVER in bed and looked at the glow-in-the-dark numbers on her alarm clock. 1:46.

She'd been trying to fall asleep for nearly two hours.

"Damn."

Maybe she couldn't sleep because she was too hot. She tried to kick off her covers, but they'd gotten twisted into a knot between her legs from all her tossing and turning.

"Double damn."

She rolled onto her side to push herself into a sitting position, then reached down to untangle her legs from the covers. She fluffed the sheet and two blankets, folded them neatly at the foot of her bed and lay down again.

She stared up at the ceiling, noting how the night-light from her bathroom cast a glow on the cobweb that had gathered between the light and ceiling fan. She hadn't been able to climb up and dust it this past month.

Could she use a triple damn?

Rachel rolled onto her side and wrapped her arms around the long body pillow she'd bought to help support her stomach and back. She knew the real reason why she couldn't sleep. Because of those nightmares that had haunted her dreams last night. *Daddy* had come too close to making those nightmares come true. He'd been in her home. He'd been in her baby's things.

Someone she knew. Maybe even someone she trusted had been here. Why would someone want to torture her like this? Why would someone want to taint what should be the most precious time of her life?

Rachel punched the pillow and sat up again. She'd already been to the bathroom twice. Maybe she needed a little snack, a small cup of cereal, perhaps. The milk would make her sleepy and the cereal would prevent that early-morning hunger. Cereal. That was the ticket.

She swung her legs off the bed and stepped into her slippers. She pulled her pink flannel robe over her cotton-knit pajamas and tiptoed out toward the kitchen.

"Couldn't sleep, huh?"

Josh's voice, as dark as the moonless night outside, didn't even startle her.

Maybe she hadn't come out here for cereal, after all.

She heard a *click* and held her breath as the lamp on the end table came on. Josh had turned it on to its lowest intensity, and the dim circle of light cast a muted glow over his naked shoulders and chest.

He was so broad. So strong. A thatch of golden curls clung to the bulges and hollows of his magnificent chest. Just looking at him, sprawled across her sofa, his blue eyes hooded, made her blood race a little faster in her veins. Made her stomach do little flip-flops that had nothing to do with the baby or hunger.

His smile crooked with a gentle humor that warmed her clear across the room that separated them. ''I couldn't sleep, either.''

When he sat up, her breath whooshed out in a gasp. The light hit lower on his body now, revealing jeans that were unsnapped at the waist—and the horrific bruise that covered his left flank.

''Josh.'' She dashed to his side for a closer look. The color was less intense, but the size of the bruise had grown as the blood from the injured tissue rose to the surface. She reached out, but didn't touch. Her fingertips hovered close enough to feel the heat off his skin, but she couldn't bear the thought of touching it and causing him more pain.

''It's not as bad as it looks,'' he joked, clearly trying to alleviate her concern.

''You lie,'' she accused, sitting on the coffee table across from him. They were facing each other just as they had last night.

He cupped her jaw with his hands and angled her face to look at his. ''I'm okay. Don't let worries about me keep you up.''

"I thought you went to the hospital yesterday morning." Her hands needed a place to go, and it seemed only natural that they should end up resting on his knees.

"I did. The doctor said I could take the bandages off when I sleep."

She squeezed her hands ever so slightly. "I'm sorry you got hurt on my behalf."

"I'm the one who's sorry." He leaned imperceptibly closer, stirring her bangs with a long, steady breath. "I'm sorry I didn't protect you from what you had to see tonight."

"No." She slipped her hands up to cover his. "I'm glad you're here. Tonight. I…" She squeezed her eyes shut as the memory of that bloodied fake animal snuck its way past her defenses. His fingers massaged her scalp, anticipating her thoughts and offering comfort. "I keep seeing images of a knife plunging down. I…I can't even think of where it ends up."

Josh's hands left her. Her eyes snapped open at the loss. But then she was weightless, being lifted into the air. And then she was in his arms. Snug in his lap, her head tucked beneath his chin.

"That's not going to happen." She felt his kiss on her forehead, heard the anger rumbling deep in his chest. "The man who's doing this is a coward. He thrives on your terror. But he's afraid to confront you face-to-face."

That sounded like the sort of character analysis she might do. Rachel tipped her head back and saw the fierce certainty on his face. "How do you know that?"

"It fits the profile."

"Profile?"

The spark of something flashed in his eyes. But before she could study its meaning, he tunneled his fingers into her hair and guided her cheek back against the warm skin at the base of his throat. "It's something Detective Taylor said."

"I don't like being afraid, Josh."

He rubbed gentle circles up and down her back. "I know."

The baby fluttered inside her, as unable to settle into a comfortable spot to sleep as she'd been. She remembered Josh's awestruck reaction when he'd seen the baby kick. She also remembered how vehemently she'd told him the baby was none of his business.

Anne-Marie shifted again and Rachel suddenly knew the best way to apologize.

"Here." She opened her robe. She pulled Josh's hand from her hair and guided it to her belly so he could feel the baby kick. His long fingers spanned the curve of her lower abdomen, cradling her precious cargo in a shield of warmth. With his hand anchored beneath hers, Rachel whispered, "She doesn't like being afraid, either."

Right on cue, Anne-Marie pummeled the target provided by Josh's hand. The big man jumped, startled by something so tiny packing such a punch. "She does that to you all the time?"

Rachel grinned at the amazed expression on his face. "She sleeps a lot, too."

Like a big kid delighted with a new toy, Josh pressed his hand gently against her again. Maybe Anne-Marie instinctively found Josh as irresistible as her mother did. The baby stretched and rolled, giving quite a performance.

Josh skimmed his hand across her belly, following the movement with utter fascination. "Wow." Josh looked up, his face mere inches from Rachel's. A calm serenity darkened his eyes to a rich shade of azure. It was as if all the conflicts and aspirations that clouded a young man's mind had vanished. He was a man secure in himself. A man secure in this moment with her. "Thank you."

He closed the short distance between them and kissed her tenderly, all the while holding the baby. It was a kiss that was achingly slow and thorough. The possessive warmth of his hand and the coaxing heat of his mouth created a viscous fire of sweet contentment that licked slowly through her bloodstream. Rachel returned the kiss, taking her time to explore the textures of strong, pliant lips and sandpapery beard stubble and moist, smooth heat.

It was a kiss that cut through the barriers of fear and insecurity, a kiss that chased away doubts.

A kiss that stamped something new and unexpected on Rachel's heart.

Rachel pulled away before the revelation inside her could take form and substance. It was a reverse strategy to what she often told her clients. If she didn't acknowledge the feeling, she wouldn't have to deal with it.

Josh didn't seem to mind her subtle withdrawal. He leaned over her tummy, turning his attention to the baby. With his mouth split wide in a lopsided smile, he talked to the little life inside her. "If you're half as stubborn as your mom is, little one, you're going to be just fine. In the meantime, I'll do all I can to keep both of you safe. Now settle down and let your mom get some rest."

Rachel laughed at Josh's order. But in the very next moment she was teary-eyed with overwhelming emotional pleasure. Impulsively, she kissed him on the cheek and hugged him tightly around the neck.

"I haven't shared that with anyone. Feeling her kick. Talking to her. I didn't think anyone would understand…what a miracle she is."

"I'm honored."

She hiccuped a sob against his throat. He eased her

away and tipped her face up to his. That's when the first hot tear trickled down her cheek.

"Hey," he said gently.

"It's hormones."

"It's fatigue."

He brushed away a tear with his thumb. "Come with me."

Josh lifted her and set her feet on the floor. He reached over and turned off the lamp before standing up beside her. Then he took her hand, pressed a kiss to her knuckles and started walking backward, leading her toward the bedroom.

"Josh," she protested, tempted to go with him, but knowing she was too confused and vulnerable right now for this to be a good idea. "You've been wonderful tonight. And I know that during a healthy pregnancy, it's okay as long as you take certain precautions. But I don't think I'm ready for—"

He shushed her with a finger. "I'm flattered, Doc. And maybe one day I'll take you up on your offer." His teasing smile told her she had misread his intentions. "But protecting you means taking care of your health, too. And I won't be much good to you if I don't get some sleep."

This time she followed him willingly as he led her to the edge of her queen-size bed. He took her robe and sat her on the side of the bed to remove her slippers. At his urging, she laid down and he pulled the sheet and blankets up over her.

Then he lay down on top of the blankets beside her and gathered her into his arms. Rachel burrowed up against his heat, resting her head on the pillow of his shoulder. "Are you sure you'll be comfortable this way?" she asked, carefully laying her hand on the side of his torso away from his bruised ribs.

"I'll be fine." He kissed the crown of her hair. "That couch was too short, anyway."

She giggled against his chest, as strengthened by his humor as she was by his sheltering arms. Somewhere tonight she had crossed a line she never should have gotten close to. In the morning she would try to figure out how to get their roles back to what they were supposed to be.

But that was the morning.

Right now she needed Josh's strength and comfort to keep the nightmares at bay.

Snug in each other's arms, Rachel drifted off to sleep. As always, her last conscious thoughts were of her daughter. And how Josh had already fallen asleep with his arms around her and his hand on her belly, protecting them both.

Chapter Nine

"Doc, don't do this."

Rachel looked across the cab of the idling truck to the man sitting behind the wheel, his intense blue eyes conveying a mix of anger and regret.

Feeling like a coward, but knowing it was the only way she could get through this, Rachel stared out the side window at the prismatic sparkles of sunlight reflecting in the snow on the UMKC quadrangle. "It's what I want, Josh. I agreed to let you drive me to school this morning, but now we have to go our separate ways. You can come to class, of course, but we can't have any other contact. There's nothing between us."

His strong hand closed around her chin, turning her back to face him. "Look me in the eye and say that."

She steeled her nerves and lifted her chin from his grasp. "There's nothing between us."

He settled back behind the wheel with a sound that was part scoff, part pout. "What time do you get off work today?"

"Three-thirty." She'd fallen for the sly manipulation. "No. You—"

"I'll pick you up at three-thirty."

She scooted forward on her seat, adamantly waving her

hands in the air. "Don't think I'm not grateful for your support last night, but I have a reputation to consider. You—"

He merely turned his head. "I'll kiss you right now, in the middle of this parking lot, if you don't tell me you'll be waiting for me to drive you home this afternoon."

Rachel's words caught in her throat, shocked into silence by his tautly articulated promise. She looked through the windshield at the hundreds of people on campus around her, dashing to and from their morning classes.

What a thrilling temptation it would be to let him kiss her. What a fool she'd be to let him try.

"Fine. You can drive me home."

Without looking at him again, she opened the door and climbed out of the truck, not waiting for his assistance.

"Keep Anne-Marie safe, too," he called after her.

Rachel whirled around in the open doorway and warned him with a heated whisper. "You can't use her name in public. I haven't told anyone about it yet." Oh God. She'd just admitted to the emotional intimacy they'd shared last night. Rachel pulled back and said apologetically, "I'm trying to avoid trouble. Please. This is the way it has to be."

He pointedly ignored her comment and shifted his truck into gear. "I'll see you at three-thirty."

When she closed the door, he pulled away. She stood in the middle of the parking lot until his cherry-red pickup turned right and disappeared around the corner. Only then did she rouse herself enough from her wishes and regrets to pull her hat down over her ears and hike over to the sidewalk.

Inside her condo in the middle of the night, she and Josh had been a couple. Sleeping together with arms and legs entwined. Sharing a drowsy good-morning kiss. Last night had been a fairy tale, a reckless fantasy she'd indulged in for a few short hours.

But out here—in the real world, in the clear light of day—Rachel couldn't believe in fairy tales.

And though in her heart, she longed to stay in her dark, cozy condo with Josh and her baby, in her head, she had to live in daylight. She had to be strong, independent. She had to set an example for her students and her child. She had to respect the rules of the university. She had to leave Josh and last night behind, and pretend the bond that was forged between them had never happened.

As she walked up to the psychology building, she sensed she was about to get a harsh dose of that reality. Curt Norwood, dressed in a field coat and thick wool gloves, with the receding points of his uncovered head turning pink with the chafing wind, stood on the first step, talking to a student in a black nylon parka.

"Good morning, Rachel." Curt looked up from his conversation and smiled.

"Good morning." She'd recognized Joey King by his omnipresent coat, even before he turned around. "Joey."

Though his face was angled toward the sidewalk, he raised his shy brown eyes to greet her. "Dr. Livesay." He shuffled nervously on his feet, then shifted his focus back to Curt. "Thanks for the tip, Dr. Norwood. I made rent this month when they paid me. Well, I'd better get to class. See you in a few minutes, Dr. Livesay."

He hurried on inside without looking her way again. Curious. Joey had never been much for conversation, but he'd always been polite. Today, he actually seemed embarrassed to be talking to her outside of class. Oh, well.

She smiled at Curt. "I didn't know lining up jobs for our advisees was part of the job description."

His smile had vanished. "Clueing my students in to an

opportunity to make some extra money is a lot more appropriate than dating them.''

Rachel hoped she hadn't just heard the ring of judgment in his tone. ''Excuse me?''

''We were talking, Rache. You and me. Yesterday at the Bookstore Coffee House.'' He dipped his head closer to hers and whispered, ''You left with him. And now I see you with him again? Did you get another flat tire?''

She had no illusions as to who ''him'' was. She tapped her fingers on Curt's chest and pushed him back a step, out of her personal space. ''You're out of line, Curt.'' He might be closer to the truth than he knew, but he was still out of line for suggesting it. ''There's nothing inappropriate going on between Josh Tanner and me.''

''Are you sure?'' A gust of wind whipped a lock of hair across her cheek. Curt reached out and tucked it behind her ear. His hand lingered beside her neck, making the gesture feel more than friendly. ''Simon was an idiot for what he did to you. I don't want to see you get hurt again.''

The wool of his glove itched against her earlobe and she stepped away. ''I'm a big girl, Curt. I can take care of myself.'' Snatching at the easiest excuse to get out of this conversation, she checked her watch. ''I need to run. I'll be late for class.''

She hurried up the stairs and into the building. But when the second set of glass doors closed behind her, she stopped. A crawling sensation raised goose bumps across her back.

Not again.

Turning slowly at first, she glanced over her shoulder to see if anyone had followed her into the building. A handful of students excused themselves and scurried past her. But the sensation of being the specimen on the slide of some hidden giant's telescope remained.

She turned around completely, pushed open the glass door and retraced her steps to the outside entrance. Curt was gone. There seemed to be no one else out there standing still enough to be watching, no one else facing her direction.

Rachel pulled her hat off her head and shook her hair loose. This feeling of being watched was getting old. Maybe Josh was right, that the man stalking her was too much of a coward to show his face. He got his kicks from simply tormenting her.

Perhaps no one had been watching her at all. Maybe she was just creeped out by Curt's awkward attempt at affection. She shook her head and headed down the hallway to her office. In truth, she was worried that Curt Norwood might have a valid point about her recent behavior.

She was beginning to feel more like Mrs. Robinson from movie fame than staid psychology professor Rachel Livesay.

And the former was an unhappy role that could ruin her career and break her heart.

JOSH HAD PARKED around on the opposite side of the psychology building from the faculty parking lot where he'd dropped off Rachel. With his backpack slung over his shoulder, he strolled down the hallway toward the lecture hall, trying to talk himself back into the role of Josh Tanner, easygoing college student.

But in his heart, he was Joshua Sidney Taylor, twenty-eight-year-old, red-blooded American male who was falling in love with Rachel Livesay and her unborn little girl.

For the first time in his career, he wished he didn't live and breathe being a cop. He wished he hadn't been so obsessed with wanting to be a better cop. If he weren't so gung-ho on saving the whole world, he might have a shot at saving one woman and her baby.

He wanted to tell Rachel the truth. That he was a grown man, not a grown boy. That he was a professional law enforcement officer, not an uncommitted major wasting his student loan money so he could party full-time.

But there was one small catch to telling the truth. Exposing his cover could get him killed.

As he neared the classroom, he saw two students standing on the backside of one propped-open door. What he saw, and the angry clutch in his gut that the scene inspired, reminded him why he had lobbied so hard to get this assignment.

Kevin Washburn, the poor kid who needed a friend but would settle for a fix, was talking to David Brown.

Josh slowed his pace and studied the interchange between the two of them. David, cocky and cool in his baggy jeans and ivory turtleneck, flashed a little plastic package in the palm of his hand before burying the item deep in his pocket. Kevin, his clothes rumpled as if he'd slept in them, his skin a pasty beige color, pulled out a wad of bills and unfolded them in his hand.

Josh wanted to shout. He wanted to scream a warning to Kevin and knock David's lights out.

What he did instead was stop for a drink at the fountain, hiding his face and timing his arrival on the scene for just after the buy. He turned in time to witness the exchange, then sauntered down the hall in their direction.

"Hey, Kev." The kid jumped at Josh's friendly greeting. Kevin's glassy eyes were framed by dark circles when he looked up. He blinked and stared as if he didn't recognize Josh.

Then he muttered a "Hi" and darted on past.

Josh watched him over his shoulder until he disappeared inside the rest room. When he turned around, David was smiling up at him.

"Mr. Tanner—just the man I want to see."

Josh pretended there was nothing strange about David hanging around outside a classroom he was banned from. He'd go with this conversation and see where it led. Brown might just be a small-time peddler. But if his instincts were on the money, David Brown was into something much bigger than nickel-and-dime bags.

"Where are your goons?" Josh taunted.

David braced his hands in front of him in mock surrender. No tire iron. No drugs. "I'm thinking you and I got off on the wrong foot."

"I think we understand each other perfectly. I have a thing about men threatening women."

"I was drunk. That was a mistake." He paused to check the last few students who were trickling into class. When he spoke again, his voice was hushed. "I have a business proposition for you."

"Really." That sounded skeptical enough.

"A friend of mine—Kelly—says you bought something from her yesterday afternoon."

News traveled fast. "Maybe."

"If that's your thing, I know we can help each other." David sounded like he was Josh's best friend.

"I'm listening."

David pulled a business card from one of his voluminous pockets. "Here's my card. Meet me at that address tonight at nine."

A college kid with a business card? Either he was being set up for some major payback from their fight, or David Brown was about to deliver Josh to the methamphetamine

store. Though his heart pounded in his chest with anticipation of a major bust, he didn't let it show.

"This is downtown. You want me to walk into some
old abandoned building with you?"

"It's a dance club. There'll be plenty of people around
to watch your back."

"And just what's your proposition?"

"I can promise you a steady supply of what Kelly's
selling. In exchange, I need a bodyguard. Lance and Shelton weren't working out, but I think you're just the kind
of guy who understands the demands of getting the job
done right."

He had no idea.

"Why are you offering the job to me? You have to
want something more in return than a little muscle."

David grinned. "See? I knew you were smart. What
I'm looking for is this…I need someone with your—"
he thumbed over his shoulder to Rachel's classroom
"—'connections,' to sweet-talk a certain professor for
me."

THREE FORTY-FIVE.

"Where are you, Doc?" Josh drummed his fingers
against the steering wheel of his truck.

So David Brown wanted him to convince Rachel to
forgive the plagiarism and let him back into Community
Psych class. Hell. If Rachel Livesay was the kind of
woman who could be *sweet-talked* into anything, he
wouldn't be here right now, parked in the faculty parking
lot, waiting to chauffeur her home.

If she could be sweet-talked, he'd have her sequestered
in a safe house, surrounded by a police guard. And he'd
have her wrapped in his arms, doing all kinds of wicked,
wonderful things to that beautiful mouth of hers.

But Rachel didn't want a personal protector. She didn't want *him* for the job, at any rate.

But he'd volunteered. Her stubborn independence and rules of decorum could just learn to live with the fact that he wasn't going away. Not until they knew who *Daddy* was, and the bastard was locked up behind bars.

He checked the clock on the dashboard. 3:48.

Josh peered out through the windshield, trying to determine whether or not the lights were still on in her office. But with the afternoon sun reflecting off the exterior of her window, it was impossible to tell.

He'd give her another couple of minutes before he stormed inside and hauled her out of there himself.

Since he didn't appear to be going anywhere for at least two minutes, he decided it was a good time to call in. He punched in the number on his cell and waited for A.J. to pick up.

"Rodriguez."

Josh laughed. "You're not any friendlier in the daytime than you are in the middle of the night."

"I'm stressed out from baby-sitting you, Taylor." A.J. gave it right back. "What's up?"

"You hear anything from my brother Mac?" The forensic expert who'd combed through Rachel's condo last night was Josh's second eldest brother. He'd cornered Mac as soon as he came in and put him on guard about his cover. They'd talked like strangers in front of Rachel, but on their own he'd asked his brother to call in every favor the family owed him, to help track down the identity of *Daddy*.

Just like A.J., Mac had warned him about mixing personal life with an undercover op. Just like A.J., Mac had been told to stick it. Rachel didn't have a family like the

Taylors to turn to in times of trouble. Right now, all she had was him.

And whether or not she believed it was proper, he intended to come through for her.

A.J. relayed what info he had. "Mac doesn't have his full report in yet, but he said the red stuff on the toy was stage blood. The perp could get it at any costume shop or even the theater department there on campus."

As in Gwen Sargent, theater professor? Could one of Rachel's rivals for the Assistant Dean's position be trying to scare away the competition? Maybe he should have A.J. run a list of students enrolled in both Psych and Theater classes.

And maybe his speculations were getting him nowhere.

"Well, that narrows it down to about anybody."

"The note was clean, no prints anywhere. However, and he's not sure what the significance is yet, he says the paper the note was printed on was a high-quality vellum—whatever that is—probably business stationery from somebody with money."

Only Mac's penchant for detail would allow him to come up with a clue like that. "Sounds pretty thorough for a report that isn't done yet. I wonder if Rachel knows any high-class actors."

"She does run with a wealthy crowd, though."

"What do you mean?"

A.J. read from his notes. "Your professor is a client at the Washburn Fertility Clinic. I thought 'fertility clinic...' *Daddy.* Maybe somebody there—on the staff or a client—could be your stalker."

Rachel had said her baby was created at the clinic with one of her eggs and the sperm of an anonymous donor. "What do you think my chances are of getting a court order to unseal Washburn's medical records?"

"What do you think my chances are of getting you to focus on the campus meth case?"

Josh's heavy sigh echoed over the phone. "Don't worry. I've got my priorities straight. For your information, I'm meeting with a kid named David Brown at the Thunderbird Dance Club tonight at nine." He gave A.J. the address. "I don't know if he's the big man on campus or just a lieutenant. He says he wants to recruit me. Thinks I have a natural talent for distribution security."

A.J. didn't laugh at Josh's sarcasm. When it came to the job, Detective Rodriguez was deadly serious. "I'll get there about a half hour ahead of you, then. I'll bring in another detective familiar with how undercover ops work—Ethan Cross."

"I know him. He's a friend of Mac's."

"Good, then you'll recognize us. We can be a second set of eyes for you, and we'll get you out of there in one piece in case it's a setup."

"I wouldn't have it any other way." A familiar red hat caught Josh's attention. Finally. 3:55. "Something's come up. I gotta go."

As he tucked the phone inside his coat, he realized that Rachel wasn't just walking out of the building. She was running.

At least, she was running as fast as a pregnant woman with a cell phone to her ear could go. Josh opened his door to go meet her halfway and see what he could do to help, but she left the sidewalk and ran straight for the truck, waving him back inside the cab.

He reached across the seat and opened the passenger door.

"What's wrong?" By the time she'd climbed in beside him, he could hear her deep, raspy breathing, aggravated by exertion and cold air. Something had her in a panic. "Dammit, Doc, did *Daddy* contact you again?"

"No, Lucy," she was saying into the phone. "Keep your distance from him if you can."

"Doc?"

She turned and met his gaze. Josh could see her eyes were full of worry, not fear. She was safe. His pulse slowed closer to its normal rate. This was something else.

"I'm on my way." Rachel turned off the phone and buckled herself in. "A student of mine...the girl from yesterday..." She pressed a hand to her heaving chest and one to her belly, catching her breath. "Lucy Holcomb. She went to tell her boyfriend she was pregnant. She says he's throwing a fit and is out of control. I'm afraid he'll hurt her."

Domestic violence. Oh boy.

"Then, call the cops."

She shook her head. "She's so fragile right now. If they take her boyfriend away without any sort of resolution, she could become suicidal. Will you take me to her?"

Rachel had never asked him anything but to leave her alone. Now there was such a genuine plea in those wide green eyes that he couldn't refuse. "Where to?"

"Just across the state line in Mission Hills, Kansas." One of the finest old-monied suburbs of town. "I'll give you directions."

Josh put the truck into gear and steered toward the exit.

"What's the boyfriend's name?"

"Kevin Washburn."

A dime-bag of meth from David Brown.

Josh swore. He slammed his foot on the accelerator and sped out of the parking lot.

FROM THE EXTERIOR, the Washburn mansion was a testament to class and gentility and several generations of money.

But the interior could have been any seedy back alley where drunks and dopers had given up the fight to stay sober.

Not that the place wasn't filled with designer furniture and priceless antiques. But once people started slashing up seat cushions and artwork, breaking mirrors, and hammering the life out of a grand piano, a place lost its elegant charm.

"My God, it looks like a war zone." Rachel surveyed the devastation on the black and white marbled entryway. A chandelier lay dented and broken in the middle of the floor, the glass from hundreds of bulbs shattered and strewn beneath their feet. "Where is everyone?"

She and Josh had let themselves in when no one answered the front door. "If we're lucky, it's the maid's day off. If not—"

"Don't even think that." She had no trouble envisioning a servant being injured or worse by the young man who had caused such damage. She had no trouble envisioning Lucy Holcomb as an innocent victim, either. "Lucy?"

"Kevin!" A loud crash and a hoarse, croaking cry led them through the archway on the right into a long dining room. Lucy stood at one end of a polished mahogany table that seated at least twenty people. She clutched her arms around her middle and sobbed.

Kevin stood on the center of the table, stomping about on his precarious perch, shouting triumphantly about the shards of broken glass that had once been a mirror above the stone hearth. "You take that, you son of a bitch!" He waved a long brass candlestick in his fist. A matching candlestick lay on the hearth amidst the glass. "I never want to see your face again!"

"Lucy?" Rachel called to her in a soft voice, not wanting to draw Kevin's attention.

"Dr. Livesay?" Lucy turned her red, swollen eyes to her and ran straight into Rachel's arms. "He's so angry. Why is he so angry?"

Rachel offered the girl the hug she needed, then pulled away to demand some answers. "Are you all right?"

The girl, exhausted from endless crying, could barely lift her shoulders as she sobbed. "Kevin hasn't hurt me. He just keeps breaking things. Anything that has a picture of him or shows his reflection."

"I hate you!" Kevin yelled at his image on the polished tabletop. Wielding the candlestick like a club, he pounded the table at his feet in a strike so powerful, the walls and floor shook around them.

She felt Josh's steady hand on her shoulder. "I'm calling the cops and an ambulance."

"Let me try to talk to him first."

"I don't think so, Doc. That kid's wired."

Lucy sniffed and looked over Rachel's shoulder at the tall, wary man behind her. "Who's he?"

Just how did she explain Josh without upsetting Lucy further? "A friend of mine. His name is Josh."

"I'm a friend of Kevin's, too."

Thank God. Even though his defensive presence was imposing, Josh's tone was hushed and gentle.

"He's never mentioned you," said Lucy.

Josh was looking around the room, taking careful note of their surroundings. "I'll bet Kevin doesn't talk about much of anything anymore, does he?"

"No." Confused by Josh's amateur speculation, Lucy looked to Rachel. "Not since our baby died."

Kevin struck the table again, swearing at his reflection

there. Josh had shifted his attention to Kevin. "That's probably what pushed him back to the drugs. It's hard to cope with tragedy when you're an addict."

Enough. With Lucy tucked beneath a protective arm, Rachel turned and challenged Josh. "Just how well do you know Kevin?"

"I only met him a few days ago. But I know his type."

"His type?" she parroted with incredulity. "How do you know he's an addict?"

"Because I saw Kevin buy a pack of meth this morning. I'm guessing he's already smoked it. And judging by his reaction, either the drug was tainted or he came close to ODing."

"Kevin?" Josh's stark assessment of Kevin's violent behavior sent Lucy into another bout of tears.

"Will you be quiet?" she cautioned Josh. Though she didn't run a drug rehab program, she had worked with clients who were recovering from various addictions. "I may be able to help. I'll see if I can talk him into giving up the weapon. Then we can call the cops."

Josh's hands were splayed at his hips, extending the expanse of his chest and shoulders and, if possible, making him look even more imposing. "If I leave, you're coming with me."

Lucy tugged on Rachel's sleeve. "Will somebody please just help Kevin?"

She and Josh both spared a moment from their personal debate to comfort the distraught girl. Josh relented first. He exhaled loudly. His mouth was set in a straight, grim line. "Give it a shot. But be careful. I'll take her out to the truck and then I'll be back. I'll be gone one minute tops. I'll stay out of sight, but I'll be right here on the other side of this archway. Understand?"

Rachel nodded.

"Keep your distance. One minute." It was both a reminder and a reassurance.

He wrapped his arm around Lucy and took her out of the dining room. Rachel removed her gloves and wiped her sweating palms on her coat. She just had to get Kevin talking. If she could get him to talk, she could quiet him down.

She took a steadying breath and crossed to the end of the table where Lucy had stood. "Hi, Kevin. I'm Dr. Livesay."

His hair was a wild, scraggly mess, his eyes, unfocused. "My dad's a doctor. *I'm* a loser."

"That's not what I hear, Kevin."

For the next ten minutes, Rachel talked. She knew Josh was close by. Supporting her. Protecting her.

Kevin shouted and mumbled. But in between the delusional spells, she gathered a great deal of information. Kevin was an unhappy young man. He didn't measure up to his father's standards. He didn't make friends easily. He liked to write poetry, but his father wanted him to go into medicine. He'd given up the battle to stay clean and sober.

And he blamed himself for the death of Lucy's baby.

Kevin crossed his legs, pretzel-style, and sank on top of the ruined table. Rachel pulled out a chair and sat as well. She didn't want him to see her as being on a superior level and feel threatened. "Why do you say that, Kevin?"

He was on the downward spiral of his manic high, though his dilated pupils indicated the methamphetamine still had a powerful control over his system. "I didn't make the baby strong enough. He was weak. Like me."

"What do you mean?"

"He didn't live."

"But you're alive, Kevin."

"I'm not very good at it. I want to be better."

His gentle soul tugged at Rachel's heart. There were no small problems here. Nothing she could help him fix in a few minutes' time. But for this minute, she could keep him from self-destructing. Keep him from hurting anyone else.

"I'm glad you're talking to me, Kevin. It makes me feel good, knowing—"

The front door slammed. A deep, cultured voice demanded, "What's going on here?"

Kevin's head snapped toward the sound. "Daddy's home."

Daddy?

A frisson of familiar panic tightened Rachel's hands into fists. She hid them in her lap, not wanting to feed the tension she could read thrumming through Kevin's posture.

She heard Josh's footsteps heading toward the front door. "Sir, I need you to stay with me."

"This is my house. I'll go where I damn well please. Now somebody tell me what's going on. Have we been robbed?" She recognized the sound of Andrew Washburn's voice. "Kevin?"

Kevin jumped to his feet and swung the candlestick back like a baseball bat. "I hate you!"

He hit the table hard, splintering the wood. Rachel shoved the chair back as the table collapsed, scrambling to her feet as Kevin crashed to the floor.

"Doc!"

She spun around at the violent fear she heard in his voice. Fear for her. "No," she warned. "Don't come in. You'll set him off again—"

"Doc?" Josh charged in through the archway, the look

on his face as fierce as on the night of David's attack. He backpedaled to a halt at the pleading gesture of her outstretched hands.

"I'm okay."

His eyes darted to the left, warning her a split second before the crack of breaking wood behind her made her turn. Kevin had risen to his feet. The candlestick dangled from his fist.

"You lied to me."

He leveled the accusation at Rachel.

She shook her head. "I didn't."

"Doc!"

Kevin hurled the candlestick. Rachel ducked. She hit the chair and tripped, crashing to the floor as the heavy chunk of brass caromed past her head with the sonic roar of a missile shot.

Josh leapt through the air and tackled Kevin. Though she heard the sounds of a struggle, she knew it would be an unfair match. Josh was sober. Josh was bigger. And Josh was protecting her.

She rolled onto her side and saw a flurry of arms and legs, and heard a stream of curses and shouts. In a matter of seconds it was done. Josh had Kevin pinned, facedown, to the floor.

"Oh my God. Kevin."

Dr. Andrew Washburn walked into the room a blustery, powerful man. He took one look at the destruction around him and his son in the middle of it all, and transformed into a pale, stooped figure who had aged way beyond his sixty-something years.

Taking pity on the beleaguered father, Rachel sat up. She clenched her teeth against the sudden pain at the small of her back.

Josh, however, had his hands too full to mess with pity. "Help her," he commanded.

Dr. Washburn seemed to see her for the first time. He blinked once, then stooped to help her. "Rachel?"

"I'm okay." He eased her onto the chair. Lucy ran to her side, knelt beside the chair and hugged her.

"Now, can we call the cops?" Josh asked, using his greater weight and a headlock to pin Kevin's flailing body to the floor.

Shocked and disappointed and more worried about the twinge in her back than she cared to admit, Rachel nodded.

Chapter Ten

"You hungry, Doc?"

Eyes closed as she leaned back against the headrest, Rachel shook her head. "You can't take me to dinner, Josh."

"Maybe that wasn't an invitation. Maybe I was just asking a rhetorical question."

She opened one eye a slit and gave him her staunchest teacher's glare. But she couldn't help smiling at the teasing in his voice when it was accompanied by that not-so-innocent boyish grin of his. She let her eye drift closed again as the smooth ride of Josh's truck lulled her toward sleep.

"A rhetorical question, huh? That's a mighty big word for you. Were you planning to debate the finer points of hunger?"

"If it'll make you smile like that again, then, yeah."

"Josh." But she really was too tired to reprimand him for his gentle flirtations. This afternoon's run-in at the Washburn mansion had drained her both physically and mentally.

"Tell you what. I'll just hit a drive-thru somewhere and get some sandwiches. You can heat yours up later."

Though rest was a priority for her right now, his suggestion was a practical one. A big man like him probably needed to eat as often as she—a pregnant woman eating for two—did.

"Go for it," she agreed, sinking back into the seat and letting the stress seep from her weary muscles.

She'd been frightened for Kevin and Lucy. She'd been frightened for herself. She was grateful Josh had been there, not just to physically subdue Kevin until the paramedics and police arrived, but to provide that same shield of protective strength that had helped her get through her encounters with the mysterious *Daddy* who tormented her.

It had been a long, long day. She'd spent hours talking to Lucy, reassuring her that Kevin's rejections were a by-product of his chemical dependency. She'd talked at length with Andrew Washburn, a despairing father and physician who'd known of his son's addiction but hadn't been able to help him. She knew the hospital would counsel both him and Kevin about rehabilitation programs and support groups.

And though she still believed Lucy and Kevin were too young to become parents, she hoped the new life they were creating might be the motivation that could finally help Kevin stay in treatment and heal their ravaged lives.

The afternoon had been trying for *her* baby, as well, apparently, because Anne-Marie had been sound asleep inside her for well over an hour. She should eat, for the baby's sake. But the Livesay women were exhausted.

She faded out as Josh tuned in a quiet music station on the radio, and trusted him to drive her safely home.

She came to with a startled gasp as a sharp twinge of pain clamped its fist around her abdomen.

"Doc?"

Something warm and comforting covered her left thigh. She blinked her eyes open, recognized Josh's hand, and quickly tried to orient herself after being shocked into wakefulness.

"Where are we?"

"Heading east on Ward Parkway. The turnoff to Volker Boulevard is just ahead." He took his gaze from the road for an instant to study her expression. "Are you okay? You're white as a ghost. Did you have another nightmare?"

He turned back to the road, though his supportive hand lingered on her thigh. "I don't think so. I wasn't asleep long enough."

"Maybe the baby kicked," he suggested.

Maybe. But Anne-Marie's kicks and punches had been as soft as butterfly kisses compared to— "Ow-w, oh!" Rachel grabbed her stomach as the pain shot through her again.

Josh's hand tightened on her leg. "Did you get hurt at Washburn's? You fell."

Rachel shook her head, replaying her tumble off the chair in her mind. That pain had been in the small of her back. A pulled muscle, perhaps. "This is inside."

She felt a straining band of tissue in her lower abdomen, like a wide elastic band being twisted tighter and tighter. She unbuttoned her coat and rubbed her hand back and forth across the stretch of her belly, trying to soothe the tension there. She felt the cascading ripple of muscles expanding and contracting beneath her hand the instant before another cramp seized her.

"Oh God."

"What? Talk to me."

Rachel doubled over, then pulled up straight, desperately searching for a position to ease her discomfort. She didn't breathe again until the cramp released her. Her lungs filled and emptied on a cleansing breath.

"Doc?"

Her breath caught again, this time in fear. "I think I'm in labor."

Josh had both hands on the steering wheel now. "Did your water break? My sister-in-law said that's what happened to her."

"No. *Ow!*" The ride got bumpier as the truck picked up speed, but she barely noticed. "They're contractions. Hard ones. Down here."

"Are you sure?"

"I've never done this before!" she snapped at him. Then the pain receded and she could think and speak more rationally. "Josh, I'm not due for another month."

"I'm taking you to the hospital." The truck was really moving now.

"Yes. I should call my O.B."

She reached for her purse and her phone on the floor, but another cramp clutched at her belly, surrounding her baby with its frightening talons. She sat up again, pressing her back into the seat, seeking a reprieve, praying for her baby's life.

"Breathe." Josh's voice sounded as panicked as her own. "You know, in, out—breathe through the contraction—something like that."

When the pain receded, she could think clearly. This couldn't happen. This *shouldn't* be happening. Not now.

And Josh couldn't help her deal with this.

"No."

"Look, I'm not an expert on this. But I remember something about breathing from basic training and TV shows."

"I mean, no, you can't take me to the hospital."

He reached across and gave her thigh a gentle squeeze. He was trying to help. He was trying to do the right thing.

"I don't know where your doctor is. I'm taking you to the closest ER I can find."

"No." She dug her fingers into his hand, demanding that he look at her. When those blue eyes met hers, she made herself clear. "I mean *you* can't take me."

"Oh, that is bull—" He released her and lurched around a corner, steadily increasing the speed of the truck as he hit a clear stretch of road. "You're pregnant. You're hurt. I'm not worried about what anybody else thinks right now."

"But I have to be."

"You have to think about that baby right now. Anybody else can go screw themselves."

Miraculously, a tall, sprawling, gray and white building appeared around the next corner. Josh spun into a parking lot. They hit the curb and the truck bounced, timing the jolt with the next contraction that seized her.

"Ow! God!"

"I'm sorry, Doc."

"Where are we?" She panted out tiny breaths now, trying to apply what she'd learned in her birthing class.

Josh steered the truck up under a concrete canopy, screeched to a stop and killed the engine. "University Hospital."

He unhooked his seat belt and leaned over to undo hers. He snagged her bag from the floor, hooked the strap over her arm and plopped it onto her lap. As she fought to find enough breath to tell him to stay put, he jumped out and ran around the front of the truck, yelling something at the sliding glass doors that marked the emergency entrance to the building.

He slung open the passenger side door and reached for her. Rescuer or not, she pushed him away. "No, Josh.

You can't come in with me. Just drop me off. I'll be okay.''

"I am not dropping you off. I'm going to make sure you see a doctor."

She batted at his hands, refusing to let him grab hold of her. She latched on to the sleeves of his coat, willing him to look at her, begging him to understand, wanting him to know that this was hard for her to say. "You can't stay with me. Everyone will think you're the father."

Fire sparked in his eyes, but the frigid evening air that turned his breath into cloud puffs matched the ice in his voice. "And that's such a horrible possibility that you don't want anybody to believe it?"

She pounded his chest with one weak fist. "You're my student!"

He leaned across her lap and shoved his key into the glove compartment, unlocking and pulling it open and reaching inside in a series of precise, powerful movements.

She spotted the leather holster with the black steel pistol. "Oh my God." She tried to wrench away as she saw the leather come out, but another contraction gripped her and the pain held her in place. She nearly wept as fear mixed with pain.

"Josh, don't hurt me."

"Hurt you?" He slammed the glove compartment shut. "Dammit, Rachel, I'm a cop!"

He straightened and shoved a badge in her face. A shiny brass badge held in a leather wallet that matched the holster.

Hearing her name in that deep voice shocked her as much as did seeing the badge and realizing she was safe. She was too stunned to think, too stunned to protest. She could only watch the flexing line of his mouth and let the words he was saying sink in...to be dealt with and understood later.

"I'm a cop," he repeated, pocketing the badge and locking the gun in the glove compartment once more. "Officer Josh *Taylor*. Not Tanner. KCPD. I'm working an undercover case on campus. I'm twenty-eight years old, not twenty-two. And I'm sure as hell not going to dump you off and let you deal with this on your own!"

With that, he picked her up, wrapping her and her baby in strong, protective arms. He carried her inside and set her down in the wheelchair that an attendant had brought out for her. Then he gripped her hand tightly in his as they rushed inside to save her baby.

THERE WERE LITTLE WAYS a man could screw up his life that were fixable with an apology or a bit of extra hard work.

Then there were *big* ways a man could screw up. Ways that could kill a man inside by destroying his dreams, or the dreams of others who were counting on him.

He wondered where falling in love with Rachel Livesay fit on the scale of mistakes he'd made.

He'd been on campus for a month and a half now, silently lusting after Rachel Livesay from the second row of her classroom. Three days ago, he'd appointed himself her personal protector. And now, just as things were beginning to break on the meth case, he'd made an unforgivable rookie mistake.

Lieutenant Cutler would jump at the opportunity to say *I told you so*. He'd stick Josh in a blue suit and send him back to his beat as a uniformed officer. Josh had botched his assignment big time by getting involved with a civilian. A pregnant civilian, no less. Let's put the two most vulnerable people he could find in danger. Oh yeah, Cutler would love that.

And, Josh had blown his cover. He'd stood at the entrance to one of Kansas City's largest hospitals and publicly admitted that he was a cop.

Because Rachel was too damn pigheaded to accept his help.

And he loved her too much to see her suffer because of it.

Now she was resting quietly in a curtained-off recovery area near the hospital's emergency room. Braxton-Hicks, the doctor had called it. Damn fancy name for the fake contractions that women sometimes experience later in their pregnancy. As far as Josh could tell, there hadn't been anything fake about the pain Rachel had been in.

He leaned his hip against the counter at the far end of the recovery area and waited out of the way of the female doctor who was giving Rachel a report on her health and on little Anne-Marie, who'd snoozed through the whole ordeal and was now apparently awake and doing her nightly exercise routine.

Josh couldn't help but grin. Anne-Marie was going to be just as pigheaded as her mother. He imagined she'd be just as smart and just as beautiful, too. And he figured he loved her just as much as he loved the unborn baby's mother.

Rachel lay on a hospital bed, propped up by pillows and covered with a sky-blue thermal blanket. She rested her right hand protectively atop her swollen belly while the amply figured ER nurse with short blondish-brown curls of hair removed an IV from her left hand.

A healthy flush of color had returned to Rachel's cheeks, and the bright, shiny intellect of her wide eyes was focused on what the doctor was saying.

"Severe Braxton-Hicks contractions aren't all that unusual, especially when you tend toward mildly high blood pressure the way you have during your pregnancy." The doctor turned to Josh and waved him over. Her smile was more welcoming than Rachel's guarded expression. "I like to include the father whenever I talk about the mother and baby's care."

At the mention of the word *father,* Josh felt two pairs of eyes lock on him with shock and surprise. Rachel's and the nurse's. But he wasn't going to be the one to correct the doctor's assumption. He had a stake in what was going on here. And if pretending to be Anne-Marie's father was the only way he'd get to stick around and ensure Rachel's well-being, then he'd go ahead and play the part.

If Rachel let him.

This was her call. She had every right to tell the doctor that he was an impostor. He'd had no part in the conception of her child. He had no part in her life.

She could call him her student and jeopardize her own career. She could call him a cop and jeopardize his life.

She could call him a stranger and jeopardize his heart.

He didn't realize he'd been holding his breath and waiting for a second invitation to join them, until Rachel moved the hand from her belly and reached out to him.

Straightening from his perch, he walked over to the bed. He picked up the hand she offered, raised it to his lips for a kiss, and then cradled it lovingly between both his hands.

"Julia." The doctor spoke to the nurse. "Why don't you go ahead and get the paperwork processed. I'm ready to release Professor Livesay as soon as it's done."

Rachel, for some reason, had decided not to correct any *misconceptions* about the baby's parentage. And a silent request that Josh exchanged with the nurse warned her to do the same.

"Yes, Doctor." The soft-eyed nurse with the knowing smile gathered her things. "I'll be back in a few minutes, Mr....*Tanner.*"

Ah yes. Sisters-in-law could be such fun. He trusted that Mac's wife, Julia Dalton-Taylor, would keep his identity secret. For now. But he knew there'd be a slew of curious phone calls waiting for him on his answering machine as soon as he got home.

He'd deal with his family's questions and concerns later. Right now, his focus was on Rachel. "What do I need to do for her, Doctor?"

"The treatment is simple." The doctor smiled up at Josh across the bed. "Her elevated blood pressure was probably induced by stress or not enough sleep. All we need to do is keep her quiet and well-fed. I think she'll be able to resume her regular activities in the morning."

"I'll put her to bed as soon as I get her home," Josh said. He just hoped Rachel would let him keep that promise.

The doctor continued. "And the baby's fine. Her heart rate is right where it should be. The Braxton-Hicks are a discomfort to the mother, not a threat to the child. They can be frightening if you haven't experienced them before. But just remember, they are a false alarm." She broadened her smile to include Rachel. "Your pregnancy is still progressing just the way it should be."

"Thank you, Doctor," said Rachel. As soon as the doctor closed the curtain behind her and they were alone, Rachel pulled her hand free from Josh's. She rolled over onto her side and curled into a ball, facing away from him. "We don't have to keep up the charade any longer. But I'm glad you brought me in."

She didn't sound glad.

Josh shoved his hands into his jeans. Judging by Rachel's withdrawn reaction, this was one of those screwups on a grand scale. "False alarm or not, I wanted to tell you the truth about who I am. I just couldn't before. I shouldn't have now."

"Why not?"

"It's not my call to make. The whole idea of working undercover is that no one knows who you really are. *No one.*" He wasn't quite sure what she wanted to hear from him. He didn't know how to make this right. "Once the case is over, I'd be happy to talk to the dean or anyone else and explain what I was doing. I don't want my job to ruin yours."

"Maybe my job isn't worth all the trouble I've gone through."

"Don't say that." He was the one who'd risked her position at the university by presuming to have a relationship with her. "I've seen you in the classroom. I've seen you work with kids and adults and make a real difference in their lives—that's all I'm trying to do, too. Our methods may be different, but our goals are the same. We both want to improve people's lives."

His words were absorbed into silence. Josh looked all around at the white walls of the sterile hospital environment, wishing he could find better words to heal her shattered trust.

An audible sob shook her shoulders. He swung his gaze around to the soft sound of distress.

"Josh?"

He ran around to the other side of the bed, took her hand and knelt beside her, face-to-face. "I'm right here, Doc."

Unshed tears brightened her eyes. "I was so scared."

He brushed a strand of sable hair off her temple and tucked it gently behind her ear. "I know. Me, too."

Her fingers tightened around his. Her eyes searched his for a promise. "I can't lose my baby. She's all I have. She's the only thing I know is mine in this world."

"You won't lose her."

He continued to stroke her temple, soothing her as tenderly as he knew how, until her face relaxed and her eyes drifted shut. Without releasing her hand, he pulled up a nearby stool and sat, keeping watch over her.

Several minutes later, on her next bit of energy, her eyes popped open. Josh was right there.

"Are you really a cop?"

He smiled at the childlike tone of her question. "Really, really. You can't tell anyone that, though."

"That nurse seems to know."

"That's Jules. She used to be my next-door neighbor growing up. Now she's married to my brother Mac."

"Mac?" Rachel was too observant not to remember names. "The same Mac I met?"

Josh grinned. "The forensic specialist who came to your condo last night is my big brother. I helped him and Jules out once, before they were married. He needed a little off-the-record police support on a case. I figured he could be equally discreet about helping you. And there's not a smarter man on the planet when it comes to piecing together clues. I am a little biased, of course."

"Of course." She fell silent again, breathing deeply in and out as if she was gathering her strength. She didn't look at him when she spoke again. "Are there any other secrets you want to tell me?"

How about *I love you?* How about *I can't see the rest of my life going by without you?*

"No. I think I already spilled all the basic information."

When she did make eye contact again, her expression seemed to hold nothing more than curiosity. "Is your job dangerous? I mean, I know police work is inherently dangerous, but, your assignment on campus—does that put you at greater risk?"

He massaged his thumb along the curve of her palm. "I can take care of myself. And I have friends watching my back."

She wrapped her fingers around his thumb, stopping the caress. "You didn't answer my question."

The woman wasn't easily fooled. "Yeah. Working undercover can be particularly risky. The cops don't all know you're a good guy, and the bad guys...well, once they find out you're a good guy, they—"

She held him tighter. "You mean *if*. You said 'once they find out,' you meant *if* they do, right?"

Maybe Rachel did have some feelings for him. Or maybe her questions about his safety stemmed from her compassionate nature. Either way, he wanted to ease her concern.

He smoothed her hair along her temple. "Right, Doc. I meant *if*."

"Would they kill you?"

"I think these people would."

"Then, don't let them find out."

He laughed at her commonsense solution. "It's not on my to-do list."

She still hadn't smiled yet. Hopefully, it was just fatigue that left her in such an introspective mood.

"Are you really twenty-eight?"

So she wanted to explore every tangent of the deception he'd been forced to play on her.

"Yeah. But my baby face lets me pass for someone younger."

"You're still nine years younger than I am."

"I'm an adult, Rachel." Hadn't his badge and ID proved what his actions alone apparently couldn't?

"It sounds funny when you say my name. You usually call me Doc."

"I didn't think we should be on a first-name basis in public. And *honey* seemed out of the question. I guess the nickname kind of stuck."

She yawned and closed her eyes. Josh assumed she was drifting off to sleep.

When would he learn never to assume anything with this woman? "Is it easy for you to lie, Josh? I had a husband once who was good at telling lies."

"Being good at it and liking it aren't the same thing." He stroked her hair one more time, wishing she could open her eyes—and put aside her stubborn sense of right and wrong—and see him for the man he was. The man he wanted to be for her. "I wish I could have told you the truth in the beginning."

"Me, too."

She pulled her hand from his and tucked it beneath her pillow. Beyond his reach.

He didn't want to read any underlying meaning in the weary gesture.

"Knock yourself out."

Bad double entendre, thought Josh. The brassy-haired waitress with the unnaturally large boobs pressed herself close as she set the beer in front of him on the high-topped table.

Josh pulled a five-dollar bill from his pocket, winked and told her to keep the change.

He now had a friend for life. Or, at least, a friend for the night, if he was interested.

He wasn't.

He watched her slow sashay back to the bar, ostensibly accepting her unspoken invitation to watch her butt. He kept himself from laughing out loud by trying to decide exactly how much peroxide and hair spray it took to achieve that particular hairstyle. As soon as her attention was diverted to the next customer, Josh looked away and blew out a breath so heavy it buzzed his lips.

The girl might not be half bad if she left her hair its natural color and dressed in clothes that actually fit her. Of course, then she might look all of eighteen. About three years too young to be legally serving the drinks at the Thunderbird.

The irony was rich. Rachel thought he was too young for her, and yet he felt like a dinosaur among this mostly college-aged crowd.

The dancing customers filled the center floor like a tightly packed box of puppets. They moved through the blaring hip-hop number as if they were doing an aerobic workout. How could a man take a woman in his arms with that many people thrashing around on all sides?

He spotted Ethan Cross, one of his undercover backup detectives, dancing on the floor. His long hair flew around his shoulders with every twist and jump, making him seem like the perfect partner for the skinny brunette he was dancing with.

A.J. was at the bar, making time in his hushed Latino way with a redheaded bartender.

Why couldn't he be home with Rachel and her naturally dark, lustrous hair and beautiful breasts and perceptively knowing eyes? He'd left her sleeping in her condo, with his brother Mac and sister-in-law Jules to keep her company. Why couldn't he be watching over Rachel's unborn baby instead of watching the young twenty-somethings on the dance floor who were looking for fun or action or maybe a little bit of meth?

Why the hell did he have to be here?

"Tanner. I wasn't sure if you'd show or not."

That was why.

"David."

The drug lord wannabe still wore the same ivory turtleneck and baggy jeans he'd had on earlier. But tonight he'd accessorized with a tall, auburn-haired coed on his arm. He had the whole big-badass, man-on-campus routine down cold. The kid's supreme arrogance in acting like the world owed him something curdled in Josh's stomach.

And this kid—this mobster in a schoolboy's body—had had the temerity to threaten Rachel?

Josh carefully schooled the resentment from his expression and stood. He slowly stretched himself up to his full height, propping his hands on his hips to emphasize the bulk of his upper body. The kid supposedly wanted to hire him for his intimidation factor. Why not make the most of it?

"Your proposition sounded interesting."

David pulled out a twenty and handed it to his girlfriend. "Go buy yourself a drink, babe. I need to talk business for a few minutes."

When they were alone, David sat and gestured Josh to the seat across from him. "So you can set me up?" Josh asked. He didn't want this meeting to last any longer than necessary.

"You're in too good shape to be a user, Tanner, so I'm guessing you resold yesterday's purchase and made a profit. I can tell you and I are both shrewd businessmen."

The charm of David's winning smile was lost on Josh. "I can make you rich."

"I'm listening."

David pulled a thick stack of twenties from his pocket and laid it on the tabletop. A visual aid for this recruitment speech. Josh had seen bigger flash wads of money before. But for someone as young as David, the six hundred or so dollars he set on the table was a fortune.

"As you can see, I'm a man of some means. I'm good to the people who work for me as long as they're loyal to me. That's where you come in."

"To ensure employee loyalty?"

"I won't pretend I like you, Tanner. But you're one hell of a fighter. I've seen you charm the ladies in class, too. I have a feeling you're able to get your point across one way or the other." He slid the stack of twenties across the table in front of Josh. "I'm looking for someone to run interference for me. A man who can keep track of my…"

What, dope dealers? Drug peddlers? Kid killers?

"…my employees."

"Where do you get your runners—the students who actually distribute the product to the buyers?" Josh leaned back on his stool, a signal to A.J. and Ethan that the meeting was going well and they could keep their distance. "Aren't the cops suspicious that there are suddenly a dozen newly wealthy dudes running around campus?"

"That's the beauty of the plan. We—I mean, *I*—recruit runners for research projects."

The small slip of a pronoun had filled in a key question for Josh. David was just a lieutenant—a student leader of the worst sort. There was someone else in charge who outranked him in the meth distribution ring. If Josh joined the team, he'd have a better chance of uncovering the leader's identity.

But David wasn't done bragging about the genius of his system. "Students get paid a small stipend for participating in everything from personality surveys to sperm donations. I just sweeten the paycheck for them a little bit when they make deliveries for me."

Was that how Kevin Washburn had gotten hooked on meth? Was he a recruit who had sampled one of the deliveries and then become a customer?

Josh had heard enough. He took the twenties and stuffed them into his pocket. "I'll take the job on a trial basis. If the money's good, I'm in."

"You're either in or you're not."

David's unforgiving look resembled the face he'd worn when he was swinging a tire iron. Josh's hands balled into fists beneath the table. But this was all about taking out the scum that supplied victims like Billy Matthews and Kevin Washburn with their drugs, not about the personal satisfaction of pounding David Brown's arrogant face into dust.

So he went against his instincts and lowered his gaze in unspoken submission to his new employer. "Then, I guess I'm in."

"Good." David waved to his girlfriend at the bar and invited her over, a clear signal that the business meeting had ended. "Your first task is to do me a personal favor. Prove *your* loyalty, so to speak."

"What's the favor?"

"Get me back into Rachel Livesay's class."

JOSH STOOD IN THE DOORWAY to Rachel's bedroom, watching her sleep.

Mac and Jules had stayed with her until after midnight

when he'd returned to the condo. Physically, Rachel was fine, according to Jules. "But I think she had the scare of a lifetime, Josh. Give her some time and space to figure out where her head's at."

Time and space.

They'd had so little time together. And yet he knew he could spend an eternity with this woman. What he didn't know was if there was time enough in the world for him to earn her trust.

I had a husband once who was good at telling lies.

Josh had lied about his last name, his age and his occupation. Simon Livesay's infidelities had rendered any lie an unforgivable sin in Rachel's black and white view of the rules of life. She'd never let herself care for a man she didn't trust.

Space.

If he got too close to her, her career would be in jeopardy. Unless, of course, she decided to reveal that the student who'd been seen all around town with her—including at her condo—was actually a cop.

In which case he couldn't stay close enough. He didn't think David Brown and his boss would make any distinction between an undercover cop and the woman who kept his secret.

And, of course, there was always *Daddy.* If Josh stayed too far away, her stalker would find a way to terrorize her once more.

Torturing himself with *what-if*s and *want-to*s wasn't getting him any closer to making things right with Rachel. Josh stripped off the chambray shirt and T-shirt that reeked of the smoky smells of the Thunderbird Club and brushed his teeth. Yet he found himself right back at Rachel's doorway when he should have headed straight for the couch.

She was the picture of wholesome beauty, her soft hair falling in a halo across her pillow, her long legs tangled in the covers, her lovely hands cradled in a protective shield around her belly. His body tightened in response to her beauty and vulnerability, but he didn't go to her.

Rachel and her baby represented everything good he wanted to protect in the world.

But in his misguided attempt to help her, he'd only exposed her to more danger.

"Forgive me, Doc."

He wasn't sure he could forgive himself.

Chapter Eleven

"You want me to what?" Rachel demanded. Surely Josh had misspoken.

"I need you to drop the plagiarism charges against David Brown."

The request didn't sound any better the second time she heard it. She rose from the kitchen table and carried her empty cereal bowl to the sink. "I don't want to see that creep again, ever. Now you want me to invite him back into my classroom three days a week?"

"KCPD needs your cooperation."

She heard his chair scrape the floor behind her. When he joined her at the sink, she grabbed the dishcloth and moved away. She was still too unsure of Josh and what she expected of him to risk confusing her senses with the inevitable pull of his gentle strength.

"My cooperation, eh? Do I really have a choice?"

"You always have a choice, Doc."

He wasn't her student anymore. Josh Tanner—correction, Josh Taylor—wasn't off-limits. He was no longer that forbidden fruit that rules and society said she couldn't be involved with.

But instead of freeing up her guilt, Josh's confession had mixed up a whole new set of troubles for her. Josh was kind, funny, caring, sexy, handsome, a dynamite kisser, a fearsome protector.

And almost a decade her junior.

Rachel wiped down the ceramic stovetop and put away the tub of butter sitting on top. He stood across the room from her now, leaning one of those trim, denim-clad hips against the sink. His eyes followed her with a deceptively lazy gaze while he sipped a mug of that instant coffee she craved as badly as she did the man himself. Well, almost.

Hadn't she just exchanged the impropriety of turning to him again and again for safety and comfort and illicit desires, for a whole new problem?

He was too young for her!

She turned her attention to the shelves inside her refrigerator. She'd always been neat by nature, but in recent months she'd been cleaning like a fiend. She took the milk when Josh handed it to her, and put it away. But then she moved on to the outside of the fridge and began wiping that.

She couldn't discount that he had truly been there for her throughout this whole ordeal with *Daddy,* but she did know a thing or two about young men. Attractive young men. Virile young men.

They liked women. They liked freedom. They liked exploring something—or someone—new and different whenever the mood hit them.

Simon had been in the mood for her for about a year and a half. Then he'd been in the mood for Denise. And Beverly. Edie. And so many other women that Rachel couldn't remember their names.

She stacked the bowls and spoons inside the dishwasher, then rinsed out the dishrag and washed down the front of the dishwasher.

Josh needed her right now. To protect his cover for his

case. And his mother's good training had him dashing to her rescue again and again because that's what a gentleman did for a lady. She even believed he was curious about her pregnancy and the baby. He was a man with good intentions.

But love her? Commit to her?

He'd already proved he could lie. Couldn't he cheat just as well?

"You should be arresting David Brown, not giving him a break." She wiped the table next. "What kind of message does that send to all those other students out there who are debating whether or not they should cheat?"

"Not a good one, I know. But it will secure my cover with the meth ring. I'm sure David thinks that if I can handle you, I can handle anything."

"Is that supposed to be a joke?" He wasn't laughing. The strained pinch around his usually smiling mouth made her think he was as uncomfortable with this request as she was. Maybe he *was* as uncomfortable with this whole situation as she was. Maybe he was already tiring of her. She was being an old-fashioned stick-in-the-mud about standing up for the university and her own expectations.

Rachel turned her attention to the countertops and started cleaning there. "You're asking me to choose between a plagiarist and a drug dealer."

When she reached for the toaster, Josh snagged her wrist and pried the dishcloth from her hand. "The rest of the world doesn't always function with one right or wrong answer the way you do, Doc."

"Then, how am I supposed to teach my daughter who the good guys and the bad guys are? How am I supposed to know which one *you* are?"

"Do you really doubt me?"

She twisted free of his grip and walked out of the kitchen. Josh was beside her in half the number of strides.

"You're scared, Rachel." He caught her by the elbow and spun her around, easily overpowering her. He pulled her belly flush up against his, wrapped his arms around her and absorbed the halfhearted pounding of her fists on his chest. "You've made yourself your own pretty little world. Just you and your baby. You've made the goals that suit your needs. You follow the rules that you think keep you safe."

The warmth of Josh's body sank in, surrounding her, calming her, seducing her. She spread her palms flat against his chest. His heartbeat was strong and steady beneath her hand. "That sounds smart, not scared."

"It sounds lonely to me." He dipped a finger beneath her chin and tipped her face up to his. She felt the warm fan of his breath across her cheek and lost herself in the depths of his eyes. "You don't know what to make of me, do you? You're attracted to me but you can't explain why. You need me, but it doesn't make sense to you. I came into your life and busted up your little plan, didn't I? Because I don't play by your rules."

He lowered his mouth to hers and kissed her, a chaste, lingering kiss that gave her permission to either pull away or deepen the kiss. When she didn't immediately respond, he moved his lips to the apple of her cheek. To the soft bend of her brow. They were gentle kisses. Soothing kisses. Rachel let her eyes drift shut as she succumbed to his seductive magic.

"If I played by your rules—" his lips grazed the tip of her nose, and when she laughed in response, he stopped up her open mouth with a kiss "—we never would have met."

His tongue wet the bow of her lips and she trembled in response. "Josh…?"

"Tell me what you want." He nibbled her mouth. "Forget the rules and tell me exactly what you want."

She felt herself melting into his touch. "I…" She tilted her chin back and stretched her neck, trying to catch her breath and a sane thought.

"There?" He pressed his lips to the long column of her throat. "Do you want me to kiss you here—?"

His tongue dipped into the hollow at the base of her throat, and Rachel moaned as an invisible line of warm honey gathered in the spot and lapped outward in a gentle, consuming heat.

"You like that, hmm?"

She felt him smile against her tender skin, felt a matching smile form on her own lips. "Josh?" She was an expert at relationships and communication. She knew the first rule was identifying her feelings. Admitting them. "I *am* scared."

He was busy unbuttoning the top of her tunic, pushing the knit aside with his nose and kissing each new revelation of bare skin. But he stopped and looked at her, nestling her snugly in his arms. "Are you scared of me?"

"I'm scared I'm going to get hurt when all is said and done."

"Not by me." He leaned back and spread his left hand across the curve of her belly. "I swear on this baby's life—not by me."

She covered his hand with both of hers where it rested. She believed the quiet promise in his voice, the sincerity in his eyes. She believed the gentle grin on his mouth. Now she just had to believe in herself.

"Kiss me, Josh."

His grin flashed into that devilishly irresistible smile. "If you insist."

He bent down and claimed her lips. It was a slow, thorough, painstakingly mind-blowing kiss of promise. Of reassurance. Of need and desire.

Rachel let her hands slide to his shoulders, and she hung on as he moved the seduction along her jaw and down her throat.

A funnel opened inside her and the languid, liquid heat he ignited inside her tumbled down to the achy juncture between her thighs. "You have such beautiful skin," he praised her. His tongue stroked the shadowed valley between her breasts. "You smell like peaches. Peaches and cream."

His hands had slid down her back to cup her bottom. He squeezed and lifted her onto her toes, slipping his thigh between hers. When he rubbed against her down there, Rachel's fingers clenched. Her thighs clenched. Her entire body clenched with the sudden, potent possibilities he was making her feel.

"Why, Josh? Why are you doing this?" She framed his face between her hands and brought him back up to eye level.

His eyes were a deep, midnight blue, drowsy with passion. He smiled and his magic lips moved closer to claim hers. "Because you're a desirable woman. Because I've been wanting to do this for weeks." He pulled back just far enough to watch her eyes. "And because you want it, too."

Rachel was nodding. "I do." She leaned forward and kissed him. He grinned at her bold initiative. "I'm afraid of how much I do." She kissed him again. He caught her to him and lifted her right off the floor.

By the time he had her sprawled in his lap on the love

seat, the gentle seduction was gone from their kiss. At her willing invitation, a clutching, needy passion blazed between them. "Take off your shirt."

His fingers bumped hers as they raced to undo buttons. They untucked, pushed sleeves off shoulders. "Now yours," he demanded.

They kissed at every opportunity. Searing, slaking, pulsating kisses. Quick. Slow. Eager.

"Touch me," she begged.

"I need you," he said hoarsely against her mouth.

Her tunic hit the floor and then his hands were on her breasts. Big hands. Gentle hands. Hands that cupped and squeezed and kneaded the full, aching tips through the lace of her bra. And then his mouth was there, nuzzling and nipping. Then again on bare skin as he pushed the bra aside.

Rachel traced the hard contours of his chest. Drank in the heat and taste and smell of his bare skin. She loosened his belt and jeans. Then he was standing with her in his strong arms. Linking his mouth to hers as he set her down. Toying with her breasts as she moaned with pleasure.

They left a trail of clothes and shoes and inhibitions behind as they made their way to the bedroom.

When they were naked, Josh lay down on the bed beside her. He stroked his hand across her belly and kissed her neck, stringing her taut with frantic desire, and easing her lingering fears.

"Will the baby be okay?"

She covered his hand with hers, touched by his concern. "We can't put direct pressure on her. And you'll have to wear, uh… Oh, no. I didn't even think of that."

Josh kissed her soundly on the mouth and came up grinning. In his right hand he waved a small foil packet. "I've got you covered, Doc. So to speak."

She stroked her fingers across his strong, handsome mouth and gazed into eyes that were fiery with passion, yet gentled by some sweet inner light that spoke to the heart of her woman's soul. "I haven't done this for so long. I wish—"

"Shh." He kissed her fingertips, then kissed her. "I've *never* done it like this. So fast. So perfect. I'm dying to be inside you right now, Rachel." When he pulled back, the expression on his face was uncharacteristically serious. "Is this what you want?"

She *did* want to feel this way again. She wanted to feel like a woman. His woman.

"This is crazy," she whispered, wanting to believe in the approval and desire in his eyes. "I've never done *crazy* before."

"You haven't been with me before." His matter-of-fact statement bespoke confidence, not ego. It spoke promise, not doubt.

"Josh. What if I can't—?"

"You can." He stopped her protest with a deep, drugging kiss. The hand on her abdomen slipped lower, until he cupped her most tender center. Her thighs clenched around him, her body heating like a steaming kettle at each stroke of his fingers. His mouth dropped to tease her tight, sensitive breasts. With his hand and mouth he brought her to the brink of paradise.

And when she thought she would burst with the pleasure her body had been too long denied, he rolled her onto her side and entered her from behind. With one hand hugging her breast, the other cradling the precious miracle she carried, he pressed his lips to her neck and plunged inside.

He took her far beyond her cautious dreams, far beyond her fears. And when he thrust inside her one final time and ignited her explosive release, Rachel cried out with the sheer bliss of being a woman. Josh's woman. His only woman.

JOSH AWOKE to the touch of a tiny shove against his stomach and the weight of a beautiful sleeping beauty draped against his side.

He ignored the first long enough to visually appreciate the lush contours of Rachel's ultrafeminine body.

This was how it should be between them. No holds barred. No rules. No reservations.

In Rachel's heart, she had to know the same thing. That a man and a woman this in tune with each other's wants and needs belonged together.

There was no psychology to explain the connection they shared. It just was.

It was the kind of connection that should withstand outside threats and demanding jobs and an age difference.

The baby punched again, telling Josh in no uncertain terms that he needed to move out of her way. He grinned. There was another Livesay female he'd have to open up to another way of thinking.

He pressed a kiss to the crown of Rachel's hair. He kissed his fingers and touched them to her belly. Then, moving slowly so as not to wake her, Josh slipped out of bed and went in search of their scattered clothes.

As he stepped into the living room, the phone rang. After Rachel's stressful night—and physically demanding morning—the woman needed her sleep. Josh ran back into the bedroom and picked up the phone on the second ring.

"Livesay residence."

Rachel awoke to the energetic greeting in Josh's low voice. Before even opening her eyes, she sighed in deep contentment. He was taking care of her again.

"Who is this?" he asked, apparently repeating the caller's question.

Her eyes snapped open. Caller? Question? Her contentment vanished as if turned off by a light switch.

She reached for her covers. Oh God. They were tangled at her feet. She was lying in her bed, completely naked! Her lumbering pregnant body exposed for all the world to see.

"Could I take a message, Dr. Jeffers?"

"No." Rachel sat up. *Dean Jeffers?* Josh smiled down at her, listening to whatever message the dean was giving him. She tried to scoot to the edge of the bed, but the baby wouldn't cooperate. Why hadn't he let the answering machine pick up? It was ten in the morning, for goodness sake. How could she explain having a man in her condo? She wasn't equipped to deal with this right now.

A lot of years had passed since her disastrous marriage. A lot of years had passed since she'd made love. That was a lot of years to be overcome by a single morning of blissful passion.

Finally, she got up the only way she could, by rolling onto her hands and knees and crawling to the edge of the bed. Any memory of her restful sleep was erased by the panicked feeling of being caught where she shouldn't be. She snatched the phone from Josh's hand.

"Give me that."

With a reeling lack of grace, she stumbled to her feet and put the phone to her ear. "This is Dr. Livesay." She tugged at the corner of the sheet, but the damn thing was caught under the corner of the mattress and wouldn't budge.

Frantically, she looked around for her robe. It must still be hanging behind the bathroom door.

"Rachel?" William Jeffers' voice rasped with a timbre

somewhere between confusion and concern. "I want to see you in my office. As soon as possible."

She spotted the chambray shirt in Josh's hand and grabbed it. She clutched it to her chest, letting the length of his shirttails cover her breasts and baby in a tardy show of modesty. "What's this about?"

She could hear the dean tutting. "I don't want to do this over the phone," he said. "Please."

"I'll be there in about thirty minutes."

"Good."

As soon as she hung up, Rachel slipped her arms into the sleeves of Josh's shirt and hooked a couple of strategic buttons. She rolled the extra inches of sleeve length above her wrist. Seeing her panties lying in the doorway, she grabbed them and tugged them on. Then she found her leggings, her bra, her sweater.

She had everything but her boots on in record time. And it wasn't until she'd zipped the boots that she realized Josh had been watching her the whole time. Standing in the doorway to her bedroom. Outrageously sexy. Gloriously naked. A young buck in the prime of his life.

"I guess the rules are back in place, huh?"

"Josh, please. The dean still thinks you're one of my students. We have to act as if you still are, right? I'm sorry." She gestured toward the bedroom behind him. "That should never have happened. It was wonderful. But I shouldn't have let it happen. Someone could find out." She glanced at the phone on the end table. "I think someone just did."

"You mean someone could find out that a healthy, beautiful woman is sleeping with a man who's falling in love with her?"

"No." Rachel felt herself go still with shock. Completely still, except for the foolishly active baby in her belly whose rolls and punches seemed to be cheering the announcement. "Don't say that. You're too young to know what you're talking about."

"I'm a man, Doc. Not a kid."

"I'm sorry. Something's up with the dean. I can't deal with this right now. I'm sorry."

Neither arguing nor accepting her apology, he moved. In two long strides he stood in front of her. Before she could guess his intent, he reached out with one hand and palmed the back of her head. He lifted her up to his mouth and kissed her. Soundly.

He released her just as quickly. She rocked back on her heels. He grabbed his T-shirt from the sofa and started to dress.

"Think about this, Doc." His eyes, looking tired and strangely ancient beyond his years, never left her. "Are you sure you regret this morning because you've been caught in flagrante delicto with a so-called student? Or are you worried that the truth will take away your best excuse for pushing me out of your life?"

"WHY DID YOU GO to the dean?" Rachel demanded, blocking Curt Norwood's path as he came out of his lecture class.

"Good afternoon to you, too."

"Forget the pleasantries, Curt." Several stragglers filed out of the lecture hall, forcing Rachel to step aside. But she wouldn't let him go without an explanation. "I've just been 'strongly cautioned' by Dean Jeffers to watch my moral and ethical behavior. Why on earth would you tell him I might be risking my personal life and professional career?"

"Because you wouldn't listen to me." Curt folded his

coat over the crook of his arm and headed down the hall toward his office.

Rachel fell into step beside him. "Your accusations are slanderous."

"I have it on good authority that your young friend, Mr. Tanner, is running with a pretty dangerous crowd."

"What are you talking about?"

Curt pushed open the door to his secretary's office and invited Rachel to precede him in. He hung his coat on the rack next to the door and offered to take Rachel's. She impatiently went through the motions of letting him take her hat and coat, simply because he refused to say anything more until they'd gone through the standard niceties shared by old friends. He set his bag on the secretary's desk and checked a stack of messages before continuing.

"Last night he was seen at a club downtown, accepting a large sum of money."

"Maybe he works there."

"Only if he sells drugs. Or takes them. It's that kind of place."

Rachel's eyes widened in shock. Hearing Josh say he was a cop and hearing details of the sort of undercover work he was doing were two different things.

Last night at the hospital it had frightened her to think about how easily Josh stepped into dangerous situations. Taking three men on in a fight. Subduing a crazed drug addict without harming the youth. Would he step in front of a bullet to protect someone? Take on an entire army of drug dealers?

And she'd never seen Josh armed. The only weapon she'd noted was the gun locked in his truck. The one she had foolishly thought he'd hurt her with.

She'd tracked down Curt on his way out of class intending to defend herself against the dean's suggestion that she was spending an inappropriate amount of time with one certain student. That, because of *concerns reported by Professor Norwood,* he felt compelled to reprimand her about spending any more private time with said student.

Instead, she found herself defending Josh against Curt's allegations. "Josh Ta— Tanner isn't a drug addict. He's too bright, his eyes too clear. He's too health-conscious to be involved with that kind of thing."

"Maybe." Curt pursed his lips as if trying to hold back an unpleasant comment. He guided Rachel to the chair behind the secretary's desk. "I heard about Kevin Washburn's episode yesterday. He's one of my advisees."

The one you refused to listen to when he tried to ask for help.

"Someone had to have sold him that meth. Guess who his newest friend is on campus." He didn't wait for her to answer. "Josh Tanner."

"Josh doesn't sell drugs."

"How do you know?"

"He's a good man—" she lowered her voice and corrected herself "—a good kid. He helped me with a flat tire the other night."

"In the middle of the night? What was he doing on campus then?"

"He had been at a party."

Curt nodded his head as if that revelation proved his point.

Rachel crossed her arms. What was she supposed to do now? Did Curt's deduction mean that Josh was doing his job well? Or did it mean that he was in danger? Oh God. She didn't want to care about this. She didn't want to care about Josh.

But she did.

He might walk out of her life and break her heart tomorrow, but that didn't stop her from caring today. Josh was right. She was too paranoid to let the relationship between them happen. Too frightened to take a chance on happiness because of the hurt that was sure to follow.

Curt softened his expression with an indulgent smile. Misinterpreting the cause of her extended silence, though recognizing the sadness and confusion she must be projecting, he took her hands in his and sat down on the edge of the desk. "Rache. If you're in some kind of trouble because of this Tanner kid…"

"Trouble?" How could her life be any more troubled? The dean considered her a scarlet woman. Her baby's father was spying on her. Rachel's breath caught in a silent gasp as her rational mind took over the confusion in her heart. Spying. She raised her gaze to Curt. "How do you know Josh accepted a payment at a club downtown?" She eased the accusation with a bit of humor. "Were you out cattin' around last night?"

Did she imagine the tension that momentarily stiffened his shoulders? In an unexpected show of tenderness, Curt raised her hands to his mouth and kissed them. "I don't cat around, Rache."

Then he tugged a little harder and urged her to her feet. She willingly stood, expecting to fall into one of their friendly hugs.

"Sorry," she said. "I didn't mean to impugn your character."

Instead of a hug, he settled his hands at either side of her distended waist. He veed his legs apart and pulled her between them. "There's only one woman I keep my eye on."

When she realized his lips were zeroing in on hers, she

flattened her hands against his shoulders and pushed him back. "Don't do this, Curt. Don't spoil our friendship."

He shook his head and gave a laugh filled with regret. "You should have married me all those years ago, Rache. I'd have treated you better than Simon."

Touched by his understanding and never-failing support, Rachel slid her arms around his neck and gave him one of those friendly hugs. "Anybody would have treated me better than Simon."

They laughed together and separated. "So, you never answered my question." Rachel sat back down. "How did you find out about Josh's questionable activities?"

"I'm just looking out for you, Rache, you know that."

"I know."

Curt dug inside the canvas attaché he'd set on the desk and pulled out a folder. He found the one he wanted and passed it to her. "One of my students saw Tanner and reported it to me this morning. This one."

She opened the folder and wearily sank back into the chair. The familiar brown eyes and smug grin seemed to be laughing at her, even from the still photograph. "David Brown."

"I know you have reason to discount his word. But—"

She cut off his quick apology. "I've reconsidered my opinion of Mr. Brown. I'm dropping the plagiarism charge against him."

"You are?"

Rachel rubbed her hand around her belly, feeling a bit queasy. Anne-Marie was fine. *She* wasn't. She couldn't look Curt in the eye. How did Josh do this? How did he sell his principles in the name of doing his job? A plagiarist or a drug dealer? KCPD needed her cooperation. Today the plagiarist would win.

"I still intend to put a reprimand in his file, but he can come back to class." She closed the cover on the hated picture and returned the file to Curt. "You owe me one."

"Let me take you to dinner sometime?" He raised his hand as if making an oath. "Just as friends."

"Dr. Norwood? Dr.—" The hallway door swung open, and a short woman—red-faced and out of breath, came in. "There you are. I tried to catch you after class."

"We must have passed each other in the hallway. What's up, Sandy?"

Rachel stood, preparing to turn over her seat to Curt's secretary. The shorter woman smiled and waved her aside. "No, thanks. Dr. Norwood, you said to let you know as soon as the armored-car delivery team arrived."

Curt's face lit up like that of a kid at Christmas. "It's here?"

"What is it?"

"A Bat Masterson revolver. I plunked down a chunk of money to curate it here for the next nine months." He jogged to the coatrack and slipped into his coat.

Sandy finished the explanation. "They're delivering it straight to the museum. I thought you might want to see it."

"Rachel?" Curt was trying to be polite, but he was already halfway out the door.

"Go. Go." She laughed as she waved him away. Men and their toys.

Sandy grabbed her coat and hurried after him. Rachel walked more slowly to the coatrack to gather her things.

"Is he gone?"

"Josh!" The familiar blond giant filled the doorway for only a moment before stepping inside and closing the door behind him. "What are you doing here?"

"Signing up for a research project."

She followed him across the room to the door of Curt's office. "You just missed Dr. Norwood."

"That's the idea." He quickly opened the door and went inside.

"Is this legal?"

"Shh." He went straight to Curt's file cabinet.

She dropped her voice to a whisper. "Josh, is it safe for you to be in here?"

He opened drawers and thumbed through files. Closed them and moved on. "You worried about me, Doc?"

Maybe. Yes. A shiver rippled down her spine. His grin didn't reach his eyes. This *was* dangerous. "Don't you need to have a search warrant to do this?"

"I'm a student, remember?"

Green eyes met blue across the top of Curt's desk. That was clearly no joke, but a reminder of the distinction she'd made this morning. She was wrong. He was in charge here. He was the one mature enough to admit where their relationship was going.

"Josh, I..."

But this wasn't the time for discussions or explanations. He stopped his search and angled his head to a point beyond her shoulder. "Watch the door for me, will you?"

"You haven't answered any of my questions." She turned and faced the outer office, wondering just what good it would do Josh if she spotted someone coming. Short of breaking one of the sealed windows, she was standing in the only entrance to or from the room. "What are you looking for?"

"This—"

She turned to see the folder he held in his hand, but he twirled his finger in the air, telling her to turn back around and keep watch. She obeyed, and settled for listening to the sound of papers being rifled through behind her.

But she had to talk this out. "Curt says you're trouble."

"I will be if he puts his hands on you like that again."

At the matter-of-fact tone of his voice, she glanced over her shoulder. Though the words had a possessive stamp to them, he never looked up from his perusal of the file in his hand. Should she be thrilled by the claim he'd just made or laugh it off as an example of Josh's teasing humor?

She did neither. She stuck to a safer line of questioning. "Do you watch me all the time?"

"Pretty much. When I can't, I've got a couple of friends who're keeping an eye on you."

"There are other cops watching me?"

He looked up at her then. "I said I'd keep you safe."

Locked in the promise of his gaze, she forgot that she was supposed to be keeping watch. But Josh never forgot the danger at hand. He made a copy of the papers in his hand, replaced the folder and then grabbed Rachel's coat—and Rachel—and guided her out of the office.

Several minutes later they were out in the crisp winter sunshine of the late-February afternoon. Despite the dean's warning, she found it easy enough to walk side-by-side with Josh across campus, though she kept her hands jammed in her pockets and her head turned down against the cold. It kept her from linking her arm through his and snuggling into the warmth and strength that radiated from him.

"You've led several student-based research projects in your career, right, Doc?"

Interesting question. Unexpected, but interesting. "Dozens. The university pays the kids a small stipend to serve as guinea pigs for thesis and doctoral studies. As long as the student meets the profile for the study being done, it's a good opportunity to build their resume and earn some money. Why?''

''Did you ever conduct a project on nineteenth-century forensic medicine?''

''Why would I? That's not my field of study.''

''Then, why would a professor of criminal studies be overseeing a genetic research program?''

''What?''

He pulled the rolled-up copies from his jacket and handed them to her. She quickly scanned the contents of the first page. Shocked by what she was reading, she flipped through the other pages. ''Sperm donations? That's Curt's research program?''

He brushed his fingers against her back to turn her toward the parking lot and his pickup. ''You know something?''

''I saw Joey King yesterday. He thanked Curt for the job tip that helped him pay rent this month.''

They stopped at the bright-red Dodge Ram. Josh pulled out his keys. ''Joey, too?''

''Joey, too, what?''

He opened the door and helped her climb in. ''According to David Brown, these so-called projects are a cover for the campus's small-time dealers. They get their name on the list, make a donation, and then use the payment to explain their sudden influx of wealth.''

''You think Curt's involved with the drugs?''

''I don't know if he's the brains behind it, or just an unwitting dupe that someone else is using.''

He shut the door and walked around the truck. She couldn't picture Curt Norwood as any kind of dupe. She couldn't imagine him spearheading a group of drug runners, either. There had to be another explanation.

As Josh started the engine, she flipped through the

pages again, looking past the names and reading the details of the research itself. "All of these donors participated in the study at the Washburn Clinic." She reeled as an ice-cold shock of discovery swept through her. She dropped the papers and clutched her arms around her baby.

"Oh God. Oh my God."

"Easy, Doc. Are you having contractions again?" Josh's warm hand squeezed her thigh. There was resolute strength in that hand but panic in his eyes. "What's wrong?"

She latched on to his hand and squeezed, feeding him a bit of her own strength with a reassurance. "The baby's fine."

But she wasn't.

"One of those students—one of *my* students—could be her father."

Chapter Twelve

"Why can't we go to the Washburn Clinic and find out if one of those names on the list is 93579?" Josh watched Rachel's hands gesture emphatically through the air. "You broke into Curt's office to find that list of names in the first place."

She sat at the far end of the sofa, propped against a pile of pillows with her legs up in his lap. Josh shook his head and continued to rub the long, delicate arches of her feet. "Doc, c'mon. Your blood pressure, remember?"

"My blood pressure is going to go through the roof if you don't answer some questions for me."

He let his massaging stroke slide up to her knee. She had such pretty legs. And a stubborn streak that refused to surrender. He needed to tell her something to get her to calm down—for the baby's sake and for his own conscience. "David Brown gave me the idea for looking up research projects with the guinea pigs for hire. Since he's my best lead, I tracked down the ones he was a part of. The research center directed me to Norwood's office."

"And the next logical step is to go to the Washburn Clinic, right?"

He stilled his hands and demanded her full attention. "We can't, Doc. I've got a friend running the list of names right now—cross-checking to see if any of those students have arrests or rehab time on their records. If we go to the clinic now, we might tip somebody off and they could cover their tracks. I'm too close to risk that right now.''

"But I could find out who *Daddy* is."

Her plea touched his heart. But it couldn't change his mind. "I know." He reached up and smoothed the hair away from her temple. "But we will find out, I promise you."

She covered his hand with hers and pressed it against her cheek, giving him hope that maybe she was learning to trust him a bit. "Your mother raised a good man."

She turned her head and kissed his palm. The sensation of her soft warmth tickled his skin and skittered along his skin straight to his heart.

"I'll wait—"

But she wasn't all softness. Josh laughed as he saw this one coming.

"—but I won't wait long."

"I didn't expect you would. Patience isn't your best virtue." As her eyes widened in reaction to his effrontery, Josh leaned in and kissed her full on the mouth, silencing any argument. "You're a woman of action."

"And you're a frustrating pain in the butt."

"Yeah, but it's such a cute butt."

Her cheeks flamed with color at his flirting. She swatted his shoulder. "You're going to be seeing that butt when I walk out of here and call your mother to tell her what mean things you're saying to me."

"Lady, you look good coming or going."

"Josh!"

He leaned in for another kiss. He loved sharing this teasing banter with her. Loved them interacting as a couple. Loved the reward of her answering kiss. Loved the feel of her long fingers in his hair, stroking and grabbing and—

His coat chirped from the hook by the front door. "Damn." Josh tore his mouth from Rachel's and rested his forehead against hers. Just when she was beginning to let down her guard. Just when things were getting…interesting.

She still had his face framed in her hands. "Your coat's ringing."

"Yeah." He pressed a quick kiss to her lips and moved from beneath her. "Hold that thought."

He hurried to the door, pulled his cell phone from his coat and punched the connect button. "This is Josh."

A.J.'s softly accented voice was laced with laughter. "Busy?"

"In the best way." Josh glanced across the room at Rachel, a look of rare contentment relaxing her expression as she leaned back against the pillows and picked up a book for expecting mothers she'd been reading. He wanted to see her like that every day of his life, secure and happy.

But he had to take care of business first. He had to do his job as a cop before he could do his job as a man and make her see that they belonged together.

"What do you have for me?" he prompted, feeling suddenly eager to get business taken care of.

"Almost every name on that list has some kind of record. Not a lot of convictions, but the names keep popping up on the computer—possession, possession with intent to distribute, you name it."

Josh turned the phone away from Rachel. "What about Norwood? Is he clean?"

"Spotless. If he knows what these kids are doing, there's nothing to prove it here."

Damn. Maybe it was just jealousy that had him thinking Norwood was up to no good. Rachel kept talking about their being old friends. Norwood was Rachel's age. And he was interested in her. Even if the feeling wasn't mutual.

"What's our next step, then? A search order for the clinic? They easily could have converted one of their laboratories into a meth lab. No one would question the chemicals being shipped in—fertilizer for the grounds, formaldehyde as a preservative..."

He could hear A.J. up and moving already.

"I'll write up the order. Too many suspects are ending up with a connection to the clinic. I'm sure the judge will go for it."

Josh felt a familiar anticipation. Like that old TV show where someone lit a fuse in the opening credits. The beat of the music crescendoed as the team of agents in the show closed in on their man. Then, *boom!* The show was over, the bad guys were caught and the good guys drove off into the sunset.

He wanted the *boom*.

They were closing in on the source of the campus meth ring. And though it was only one drug ring and one group of kids he'd be saving, he was finally making a difference. It was payback time for the tragic loss of Billy Matthews and so many other victims of the drug trade.

"You want to tell Cutler, or should I?"

A.J. laughed. "You're his golden boy, Josh. I'll let you have the glory."

"Your time will come, Rodriguez, and Cutler will be breathing down your neck, too."

"In the meantime I can watch you suffer."

"Right." He looked over at Rachel, hating that he had to leave her again so soon. He'd better make this quick so he could get back to her. He had a whole lot of things he needed to say, a whole lot of future he needed her to believe in. "I'll meet with Cutler, then, and set up the raid. You get the judge's order."

"Done. Watch your back."

Josh smiled, appreciating the routine of his newfound friendship. "Always."

He disconnected the call and reached into his coat for another item. He flipped open the badge, taking a moment to reflect on the star and the number and everything it meant to him. Then he stuffed it into the front pocket of his jeans and pulled out his gun.

As always, he checked the safety, checked the magazine and secured the gun in the holster. Then he slipped his arms into the holster and pulled the black leather strap across his shoulders.

"Where are you going that you need to strap on a gun?"

He turned at the sound of Rachel's husky voice and crossed the room. After making sure the gun rested comfortably in reach of his shooting hand, he took the book from Rachel's lap and set it on the coffee table. "When I'm not undercover, I wear it to work every day."

"Sounds like a grown-up job."

"Doc." He took her hands and pulled her up beside him. "There are a lot of things—" She wrapped her arms around his neck and hugged him close. Surprised, though heartened, by Rachel's initiation of more intimate contact, he gladly settled his arms around her and held her. "It's okay, Doc. This is what I do. It's what I'm trained for. It's what I've lived and breathed for as long as I can remember—wanting to be a cop, like my cousin and my older brothers. I'll be okay.''

"This is hard for me." Her sweet lips brushed against his neck in an unintended caress. "I know you're a grown man and not some kid. But it's hard for me to..."

He tightened his hold on her, offering her his support to continue.

"It's hard to let myself think of you as my equal. Because that means a real relationship could happen here."

He kissed her hair, his concern turning to hope. "I wouldn't mind."

She brought her hands down to his chest and began fiddling with the buttons of his shirt. "It also means investing my heart in something that might not last."

Josh wrapped his hands around hers and stilled the nervous fluttering of her fingers. "Because of my job?"

"No. I mean, I worry because of the danger, but—"

Josh's heavy sigh filled the room. He didn't want to hear this. So he said it himself. "But because I'm nine years younger than you?"

She was strong enough to raise her gaze to his, stubborn enough to want him to see her point. "Twenty years down the road, when I'm pushing sixty, you'll still be a man in your prime. You're gorgeous, Josh. And you're funny and brave. Women are going to want you."

"But you won't?"

"Josh—"

"I'm *not* your ex-husband. I'm not Simon Livesay. You can't judge me by his standard."

"It's the only standard I know." She pulled away, hugging her belly, protecting herself and her little girl from the hurt she expected to find one day.

"You work at a university, Doc." His own brand of hurt—that rejection, that not measuring up to someone's standard—turned into sarcasm in his voice. "Maybe it's time for you to learn something new."

But the clock was ticking. The Washburn Clinic and the answers to this case were waiting for him. He reached for Rachel's hand, and despite her reluctant protest led her to the window.

"I have to go. But this conversation isn't finished, not by a long shot."

"Josh, I have to be honest about the way I feel."

"So do I." He pulled the curtain aside and moved behind her. He hugged her waist, with one arm laying a possessive claim to the life in her womb. He nudged open the blinds. "See that green pickup truck down there?" She looked out the window and nodded. "That's one of Lieutenant Cutler's men, my superior in the drug division. He'll keep an eye on you while I'm gone. You're to stay put and rest and think about how much I love you."

"Josh—"

"I'm going to prove myself to you, Rachel. If it's the last thing I do." He put his other arm across her chest above the swell of her breasts, laying a possessive claim to the woman herself. He slipped his fingers up to her neck and turned her head to bury a kiss in the soft hair at her temple. "I want to marry you. I want your little girl to be my little girl."

He hugged her as tightly as he dared without crushing the baby. Then he turned her and kissed her swiftly on the mouth. "You stay put and stay safe."

He left her at the window and strode across to the front door. He pulled on his leather coat and zipped it closed to mask his gun. "I'm coming back to you, Doc. I will always come back to you."

He closed the door behind him and prayed she wanted him to return.

I WANT TO MARRY YOU.

Josh Taylor—young stud of the world, Sir Galahad with a wicked grin and ancient eyes—wanted to marry her.

Rachel rubbed her stomach as she waited for the herbal tea to steep in its pot. "What are we going to do, little one?"

Could she let go of the past and believe in the future? A long-term, forever kind of future with Josh?

I'm going to prove myself to you, Rachel. If it's the last thing I do.

What more could a man do? He'd risked his life for her. He'd made beautiful love to her. He treated her child with tender care. He'd opened up his heart and spoken the truth that was inside.

She was the one with something to prove.

Rachel sank into one of the kitchen chairs, stunned and ashamed to realize that the only thing keeping her from happiness was her own fear. *She* was the one with the immature attitude about a relationship with Josh Taylor. *She* was the one who refused to see the wisdom of following her heart instead of her head.

Anne-Marie thumped her right below the rib cage. "Ow." Rachel massaged the tender area and smiled. "I know, sweetie. Mommy's slow. But she can be taught."

She sat and enjoyed a moment with her daughter before her need to do something kicked in. She was a woman of action, after all, according to Josh. "So, what do *we* do to prove ourselves to Josh?"

She hadn't really expected an answer. But when the phone rang, she jumped, as if a higher power had suddenly responded. Smiling at the foolish notion and pressing a hand over her rapidly beating heart, she went into the living room and picked up the phone. "Dr. Livesay."

Her hopeful dreams were shattered in an instant.

"Shame, shame, shame, Doctor." The hoarse, muffled

voice tightened its evil grip around her baby and her heart. "Didn't you understand my message? I was with you at the hospital when you almost lost my baby."

"Who is this?" Anger at the unjust threat gave her strength. "Why are you doing this to me!"

"You think you can keep playing with that boy toy of yours. With *my* baby between you. Well, that's not going to happen anymore."

"Stop this!"

"I know he's a cop—"

Rachel froze at the stark threat in his tone. The anger that had whipped through her became a fear that chilled her to the bone.

"That's right. I know."

"How?"

"I was there when he told you. Remember?"

With her at the hospital. *Daddy* had been with her at the hospital. Rachel squeezed her eyes shut and tried to replay every face she'd seen that day. But she'd been in so much pain. She'd been so afraid. She just couldn't think. The details escaped her.

"What do you want?"

"Just what I've always wanted." He gave a croaky laugh. "I want what's mine."

Click.

The silence at the end of the line pounded like drumbeats inside her head.

She had to think. She had to do something.

What was Josh's number? She ran over to her bag and rummaged through the contents. Then she threw the whole mess down on the table. She didn't have Josh's number. She'd never needed it. He'd always been with her when she needed him.

She opened the end-table drawer and pulled out the white Kansas City phone book. "Taylor, Taylor, Taylor." She thumbed to the *T* section and her heart sank. There were hundreds of Taylors in the phone book. At least twenty *Joshua*'s or *J*'s.

"This is ridiculous," she chided herself. *Just call the police.*

And not just any cop.

She picked up Mac Taylor's card and dialed the number. He picked up on the first ring. "Taylor here."

"Mac Taylor?" she asked, though she recognized his voice right away.

"Speaking."

"This is Rachel Livesay. I just got another call from *Daddy.* I'm not sure what to do. But I think Josh is in trouble."

JOSH WAS RIGHT. Patience and waiting were not Rachel's strong points. She'd put Anne-Marie to sleep with all her pacing.

Mac Taylor's visit had been brief. And despite all his reassurances that Josh had been given the information and that he was well-protected, she didn't feel very reassured.

She needed to *do* something.

Maybe she should call Simon about her classes and discuss her counseling caseload. Dean Jeffers was sure to meet Simon's price and hire him. Apparently he'd be taking over her position sooner than any of them had planned.

The doctor wanted her to stay at home, but she hadn't specifically said Rachel couldn't work. She might not be able to help Josh as he and a group of fellow cops searched the Washburn Clinic, but she could help some-one else. And maybe, in a way, ease some of Josh's con-cerns about the world he fought so hard to make right.

She got out her day-planner and her cell phone and sat on the couch to check on some of her clients. They needed her more than Simon ever had. She'd rather talk to them, anyway.

"Hey, Lucy. How are you feeling today?"

"A little better. I have an appointment with an obste-trician tomorrow to make sure I'm pregnant. I probably shouldn't have told Kev until I knew for sure." There was a heaviness in the girl's voice that reflected the bur-den of guilt she carried. "I didn't mean to set him off like that."

"It was the drugs that set him off, Lucy. You wait and tell him again once he gets out of rehab. And then I want you both to come work with me. Together."

"I'd like that."

They chatted a while longer before hanging up. Kevin Washburn wasn't allowed to receive phone calls during his first week at the center, so she looked up the number for Kevin's father.

She was almost ready to hang up, when the phone picked up. Silence greeted her.

"Dr. Washburn? Is this the Washburn residence?"

"This is Andrew Washburn." His once-booming voice sounded weak and tired.

"Rachel Livesay," she said. "I was calling to see how you're holding up today."

"You tried to save my boy, didn't you."

"I tried. I wish I could have done something more."

Andrew's pause lasted an eternity. "So do I. I mean, I wish that *I* had done something more."

''Would you like to talk about it?'' She had nothing but the time and heart to listen.

''Yes.'' The energy in his voice lifted from depressed to almost hopeful. ''Yes, I'd like that very much. But not over the phone. Would you be able to come to the house?''

''Right now?''

Dusk was falling, transforming the glittering sparkle of a sunny winter's day into the gloomy gray shadows of a moonless winter twilight.

''Yes, if you can. The house is unlocked. Just knock and come in. I'll be in my study.''

What about the cop outside her condo?

What about Josh's *stay put and stay safe?*

''Rachel? Please.'' His voice took on the apologetic tone of a confession. ''There's something I'd like to discuss with you.''

''About Kevin?''

''About your baby.''

''THIS BURNS MY ULCER to say this, but—'' Lieutenant Cutler paused to show just how much it pained him ''—good work, Taylor.'' He almost smiled as he surveyed the orderly chaos of crime-scene technicians, uniformed police and plainclothes detectives bustling around them, taking pictures, cataloging and carting away everything from the Washburn Clinic's main office that might be used as a scrap of evidence. ''Imagine, a trashy little meth-lab hidden away inside a ritzy country club clinic where babies are made.''

The lieutenant's praise had been a long time coming, but Josh didn't feel he deserved it. Yet. ''Ethan Cross is rounding up warrants for all the students on the donor list.

They may not all be runners in the meth ring, but he'll bring them in, just in case.''

A tall, lanky man wearing the distinctive navy blue uniform of the Kansas City Fire Department—and sporting the brown-eyed, dark-haired version of the Taylor features that made Josh a handsome man—walked up and slapped Josh on the shoulder. "The Haz-Mat unit has everything loaded up. It's safe for your men to go back into the lab now."

"Thanks, Gid."

Lieutenant Cutler took the announcement and ran with it, barking orders and herding his men into the lab to work the scene in there.

"They're lucky the place didn't blow up in their faces." Gideon Taylor normally worked as an arson investigator. But when Mac had called to tell Josh his cover had been compromised by the so-called *Daddy,* his third eldest big brother had suddenly shown up to serve as the fire department's liaison. Josh could well imagine that the rest of the Taylor clan had been mobilized in a similar fashion.

Josh grinned down at his older brother, taking full advantage of the one inch of height he had over Gideon. He might be the youngest Taylor, but he was by no means the smallest. "You know, you don't have to baby-sit me."

"I know."

His steady brown eyes looked so much like their father's that Josh had often seen his relationship with Gideon in the same way. Eight years older than Josh, Gideon had always seemed grounded. Mature. In recent months, he'd also seemed a little sad. But Gideon wasn't one for talking about stuff. Not until he was ready and wanted to.

"Mostly I'm just checking in. We haven't heard from

you in a while. Ma didn't believe for one minute that you were at a training session in Jeff City."

"Well, you can tell Ma this—I'm fine. I have been fine. I'm going to continue to be fine."

Gideon shook his head. "Anything more specific?"

He hoped... "Tell her—" Maybe he was jinxing this by even thinking about it. "Tell her I met somebody. Tell her I want her to meet a pregnant friend of mine. You think she'd be cool with that?"

"Did you have anything to do with the pregnant part?" Now that was the parental tone of voice he expected to hear from Gideon.

"I wish. But no."

Gideon grinned. "Ma's baby-radar is probably going off right now. She'd got a sixth sense about these things."

"It's not a done deal yet."

His big brother smiled and gave him a playful punch on the shoulder. "I won't say a word. You take care of what you need to. You know we'll support you, no matter what."

"Thanks."

The brothers shook hands.

Then Gideon thumbed over his shoulder. "I'll be around. But I'm going to go double-check that everything's cool on the truck before they take off."

Bursting with the possibilities for his future, Josh pulled out his cell phone and punched in Rachel's number.

They still had to bring in the bigwig of the campus meth ring. Maybe it was Andrew Washburn himself. Maybe that's why he felt so guilty about his son's addiction.

The phone continued to ring.

Of course, Cutler's big plan was to push every kid they arrested for information. A team of specially trained cops would work the interrogation rooms, trying to get one or more of the kids to turn on their boss. To give the cops a name in exchange for a lighter charge or dismissal.

That was the plan.

He, too, was going to be one of those cops on the interrogation team. This had been his case from the get-go, and he had the most at stake in bringing in the leader.

But he wanted to talk to Rachel first.

Josh frowned. The imminent success of his first undercover mission, and expected promotion because of it, suddenly didn't seem very important.

Rachel's phone rang and rang until the answering machine picked up.

Why the hell didn't she answer?

Chapter Thirteen

"Dr. Washburn?"

Rachel pushed the door open and knocked one more time.

"Dr. Washburn? It's Rachel Livesay."

The entryway was black without its chandelier, but enough light streamed in from the porch light for her to see that the mess of broken glass and metal was still lying in its twisted heap in the middle of the foyer. Had Andrew Washburn been alone with all the filth and ruin left over from Kevin's destructive frenzy yesterday? No wonder the poor man needed to talk. He needed to move beyond yesterday and start thinking about tomorrow.

Steeling herself, she waved back at the officer who had driven her here and moved on inside. "Dr. Washburn? Andrew?"

Using the outside light to guide her, she crept along the outer wall of the foyer and down the main hallway, trying not to cringe at the crunch of broken glass, and screech of metal against marble, beneath her feet. The house was too quiet, too creepy, too horrible a place for a grieving man to be alone.

As she moved past the staircase, a second, brighter light caught her eye. Rachel smiled in relief. The study.

Leaving the wall, she walked straight toward the light streaming through the open doorway. She paused in the ornate walnut doorjamb to blink and let her eyes adjust to the light.

She saw the shock of snowy-white hair that readily identified Andrew Washburn, and smiled. "There you are. I was worried when you didn't answer." Rachel froze halfway to the desk. "Oh God."

And then she ran to the desk. Ran around to the man in the chair to make sure her eyes hadn't played tricks on her.

Her eyes filled with bitter tears, obscuring the scene before her: Andrew Washburn, leaning back in his chair, looking for all the world like he'd dozed off. But the bright-red blood draining from his mouth and staining the chair at the back of his head told her he was dead.

She blinked away the tears and tried to make sense of what she saw. A sixty-year-old man, grief-stricken and guilt-ridden over his son's addiction to drugs. Wealthy and accomplished and yet absolutely helpless when it came to helping his own flesh and blood.

The hand that lay in his lap held a revolver. And as she sniffed back tears, a burning scent stung her nose. Gunpowder? Had he just now shot himself?

Rachel pressed two trembling fingers against his neck and then jerked them away as if she'd been singed. "You're still warm."

She wiped her fingers on her coat, unable to dispel the sensation of death from them.

Automatically, she looked about for the phone. Maybe she should be looking for a suicide note. Maybe she should just go notify the police officer parked in his truck outside waiting for her.

Liking the idea of escaping from the grisly, sad scene

better than any of her choices, she took a deep breath and started to leave. But she kicked something with her foot. Something that had fallen from Andrew Washburn's other hand.

A file from the Washburn Clinic.

Knowing she shouldn't touch anything before the police entered, she couldn't help herself—she balanced herself against the desk and squatted down to get a better look.

Shocked by what she read on the cover she lost her grip and balance, and fell back on her bottom. Not caring how gangly and awkward she looked as she crawled onto her hands and knees to right herself, she turned her focus back to the number she'd read on the folder.

93579

This was what Andrew wanted to talk to her about. He was going to reveal her baby's father.

Was the secret so hideous, so awful, that revealing the truth was worth taking his own life? Or had depression made that choice inevitable—and giving this information to her was his final good deed?

Knowing she could debate his reasons *ad infinitum,* Rachel chose instead to thank him. Then she opened the folder.

"No."

She glanced up at the dead man, wishing he could answer her questions. This didn't make sense.

Rachel picked up the folder and pushed herself to her feet. She laid it on the desk and looked at the picture inside—in the clear light—to make sure she wasn't mistaken. 93579. *Daddy.* The father of her baby was...

"Curt Norwood."

Her head snapped up at the man's voice from the doorway. "Curt!" Her gaze dropped just as quickly to the gun he held in his hand. "What are you doing?"

He smiled. The face that had once been handsome now leered at her with a sick hatred that Rachel had never seen before. Had never wanted to see.

"I'm taking what's mine."

"WHERE ARE YOU TAKING ME?"

Aside from the nonchalant way he'd pulled the unconscious officer from his truck, or the way he kept his black steel pistol trained on her stomach as they drove through the night, Curt Norwood was every inch the charming intellectual she'd always known.

"We're going to school, of course. There's a problem with a student I need to take care of."

"You mean Josh?"

"He's too young for you, Rache. He's all wrong for you." He lifted the gun and caressed her chin as if the weapon were the extension of a caring hand instead of the symbol of deadly control. "He'll hurt you. Just as Simon did." He flashed her a smile. "I don't want to see you hurt again."

Rachel breathed in through her nose and out through her mouth, willing herself to stay calm against the threat of such irrational violence. *Keep him talking.* Hadn't she used that strategy before on stressed-out patients? *Keep him talking. Keep him calm.*

"Josh hasn't hurt me."

"He will," Curt asserted. "He will."

"Why do *you* want to hurt me?"

"I don't." He looked away long enough to steer the truck onto Volker Boulevard. "I'm trying to take care of you. I've always wanted to take care of you, Rache. But you wouldn't let me."

"How is scaring me to death with those sick messages 'taking care' of me?" Another question popped into her head. "How is bringing Simon back into my life, and encouraging him to take my place at school, 'taking care' of me?"

"I knew it would be difficult for you to see Simon again. To work with him. And I knew protecting your 'miracle' baby would make you desperate. I just wanted you to turn to me. I've loved you for so long, Rache." He turned his tired eyes on her. "I just wanted you to need me."

"You've been my friend forever, Curt. I've always needed you."

His soft tone snapped and a vein pounded near his receding hairline. "But you never loved me! You fell in love with Simon instead. You should have loved me!"

Maybe talking wasn't the best way to go.

Rachel shrank back into her seat, tightly hugging her belly. She kept her eyes glued to the gun. "Could you point that somewhere else? This is your baby, too. You don't want to hurt her."

He actually obliged by putting both hands on the steering wheel, though the gun stayed wrapped in his fingers. "You never would have guessed that, would you? That I was the baby's father. You wanted a baby so badly. I would have given one to you. I would have married you and laid you and given you that baby."

Not the most romantic proposition, even from a sane man.

"How did you make sure I got your sperm and not someone else's?"

"Blackmailed Washburn."

"How?"

Curt laughed and turned the truck toward campus.

"You're full of questions tonight. Sort of like that boy-friend of yours."

I know he's a cop.

So he'd said on the phone during his last threatening calls.

"What are you going to do to Josh?"

He laughed again. "You'll see. That boy toy thinks he's got it all, where the babes are concerned."

The gun waved toward her again and Rachel flinched. Curt saw the movement and laughed. He stroked the gun along her chin again, down her arm, toward Anne-Marie.

Rachel swatted his hand away, risking Curt's wrath to protect her baby.

"*I* was supposed to rescue you that night. *I* was supposed to get your gratitude. But no, lover-boy showed up and beat the crap out of my kids."

"You set up David Brown, and Lance and Shelton, to attack me?"

"Not to attack you. To threaten you. Your boy toy is the one who turned things violent."

"He was protecting me. He's always protected me from you."

Curt's mouth thinned into an ugly, unforgiving line. "I'm counting on that."

"What do you mean?" Oh God. He was using her as bait.

Curt seemed to read the understanding in her eyes. "He'll piece together the trail soon enough. The cop I knocked out at Washburn's. Washburn himself. It was amazingly easy to convince him to put his gun in his mouth. Taylor will see the blood and my file. He'll know you were there."

How could she fix this? How could she warn Josh?

Because she had no doubt that he would come charging

to her rescue. Only, this time his strength and charm and determination to do the right thing wouldn't be enough to save her. They wouldn't be enough to save him. This time, the consequences could be deadly.

Curt pulled the truck into the faculty parking lot and shut off the lights and engine. "When Washburn called me and said he had a guilty conscience about the deal we made and was going to tell you the truth, I got the idea for the perfect way to get your annoying little boy toy out of my way."

"If you think I'm going to somehow fall in love with you after this—"

"You're the mother of my child!" he barked, leaning across the seat, pinning her against the door.

Trapped with his hand on her hip, his gun at her breast and his hot, wet breath in her ear, Rachel fought the urge to gag.

Now his voice was just a whisper. "If we can't be together, then you can't be together with her. I'll take her. She's mine. And since I told Dean Jeffers about your illicit relationship, I know I'll get the promotion. I'll have everything and you'll have nothing. Nothing but that shallow boy toy who ruined your life."

Rachel's breath came in shallow gasps. Her heart thumped in her chest. She could feel her blood racing, charging ahead of the fear that nearly consumed her.

"I'll do whatever you want, Curt. Just don't hurt my baby."

"Our baby," he corrected her. But the promise appeased him. For now. He opened the door behind her and pushed her out of the truck. His rough grip on her arm kept her from falling.

Then he shoved her along beside him, toward her classroom. To set the bait in the trap that would lead Josh to her.

The trap that would get him killed.

"CAN'T YOU DRIVE any faster?"

Under any other circumstances, Josh would have marveled at A. J. Rodriguez's skill and precision behind the wheel. The man was one cool customer, taking the streets of downtown Kansas City at eighty-plus miles per hour.

But not these circumstances.

"Rachel needs me."

"Backup's five minutes behind us, *amigo*. We don't want to get there too soon."

"We have to get there before he hurts her."

If he hadn't already.

Josh had always felt like a grown man around Rachel. But he'd never felt old.

Tonight, in the Fourth Precinct's interrogation room, when David Brown told him that he was Curt Norwood's right-hand man, Josh had felt world-weary.

The pieces suddenly fell into place. A criminal studies professor who knew the in's and out's of police procedure. Who had access to hundreds of students who needed money. Who wanted drugs. He'd set up a covert empire built on the blood and death of innocents like Billy Matthews and Kevin Washburn.

Norwood wanted David to hire Josh. Hire the cop. Bring him into the game so he could keep an eye on him.

His brother Mac had been the first on the scene at the Washburn place. He didn't think it looked like cut-and-dried suicide, judging from the position of the gun. Mac had told him about the folder.

About 93579.

About *Daddy*.

Curt Norwood was using Rachel to get to him.

He would purposely hurt Rachel—or her baby—just to hurt him.

"We're almost there, man." A.J. checked the twin sidearms strapped at either side of his waist.

Josh checked his. He'd added an extra ammo clip in his pocket. Put a knife in his boot. Strapped on a flak vest. He cracked his knuckles beneath his taut leather gloves.

One way or another, Curt Norwood was going down.

A.J. spared a glance at Josh as he turned off the flashing lights and slowed to turn into a parking space on the street. "Are you sure he'd bring her here?"

"Positive. He's king here. He owns these kids. He's in line to get a promotion from the dean." Josh smiled. A smile of knowledge. A grim-eyed smile that held no humor. "He wants me to come to him as a student. Someone inferior in age and status."

A.J. shut down the car. "Does he know you want to tear his heart out?"

"If he hurts Rachel, he'll be tearing out mine."

"CURT, DON'T DO THIS. Please don't do this."

Rachel twisted her wrists against the rope that tied her to the desk in the second row, but the bonds held fast.

The lecture hall was completely dark. Curt was here. Somewhere. She could hear him breathing. But he didn't speak.

He was positioned so that he had a clear shot at any door, he'd said. Positioned so that he had a clear shot at her.

True to form, when Rachel needed her to be quiet, Anne-Marie tossed and turned up a storm. The baby was sitting square on Rachel's bladder. She didn't think she could be more uncomfortable.

But she barely noticed the pain and pressure.

Josh was coming for her.

And Curt was waiting.

JOSH SILENTLY COUNTED to twenty, giving A.J. the time he needed to get into position at the main entrance to the lecture hall. *He* was going in the back way. By now his eyes had adjusted to the darkness. He figured he'd have about half a second once they broke in, to spot Rachel and Norwood.

Then he'd pray that he chose the right one to shoot at. The right one to protect.

Seventeen… Eighteen.

Josh took a deep, steadying breath and prayed.

Twenty.

A.J.'s shout came first. "Give it up, Norwood!"

"Rachel!" Josh pushed the latch and shoved the door open with his shoulder. He dove for the floor of the lecture stage and rolled as all hell broke loose.

A flash of gunfire from the far side of the seats. A.J. returned fire from his position up top. Shouts. Curses. More gunfire.

"Josh! No! Get out of here!"

"Rachel!"

He climbed to his feet and threw himself toward her husky cry. He fired to the right, knowing his shots would go wide of their target. But he could pin Norwood down. Shut him down. Keep him from hitting Rachel with any stray bullets.

"Dammit, Josh! He wants to kill you." She was sobbing now.

He reached her and swore. She was trussed up like some damn sacrifice. Forced to sit upright. Centered in the room in the line of fire from almost any direction.

"Shut up, Doc." He ripped the knife from his boot and slashed at her bonds while A.J. laid down a line of fire that kept Norwood busy. He cut her free from the chair and wrapped his arms around her. "By the way," he whispered. "I love you."

"Get away from her!"

Crack. His shoulder burned. "Damn."

"Josh!"

"Now, Taylor!"

He rolled to the floor, taking Rachel with him.

The doors burst open from every corner and light flooded the room. Lieutenant Cutler and Ethan Cross and every other cop in Kansas City, it seemed, charged into the room.

In a matter of seconds, it was over.

Josh never moved, never eased his grip on Rachel. He shielded her with his body, past the last gunshot, past the command to surrender, past the announcement that the suspect was dead.

He lay there holding Rachel and her baby until A. J. Rodriguez tapped him on the shoulder.

"Do you know you're bleeding, man?"

"Josh?" Rachel's hands were still tied, but she moved those magic hands together, touching his face, his neck, his chest, his arm.

"Ow!"

"Josh, you've been sho—"

He silenced the ragged concern in her voice by claiming her mouth with his kiss. He stamped his mark on her. Laid claim to her heart. Offered her his.

When he came up for air, she was smiling. A beautiful, kiss-me-like-that-again smile. But her words stopped him short.

"I love you, Josh."

He grinned. "I'm glad you finally realized that."

"And Josh?"

"Yeah, Doc?"

"My water broke."

SWEAT RAN INTO HER TEMPLES and pooled between her breasts.

"You're doing fine, Rachel," the shift nurse praised her. "Now relax and breathe."

Rachel dropped her head back against the pillow and looked around the sterile birthing room. She saw the nurse, the cart with the blood-pressure monitor. The long tube that was anchored to Anne-Marie's scalp, monitoring her baby's heart rate.

It was too soon. Her baby was coming too soon.

The doctor had checked her once, announced she'd dilated to seven centimeters, and promised that everything was progressing normally, even if Anne-Marie was three-and-a-half weeks premature.

But now she was alone. Except for the kind nurse whose name she couldn't remember. And the soft balloon sculpture on the wall. And the intense pain that invaded her abdomen and forced her to sit upright.

"Ow-w!" She breathed out, rapidly. *Hoo-hoo*'s and *hee-hee*'s.

When the contraction passed, the nurse scurried out and Rachel leaned back. She was so thirsty. So tired. So alone.

She and Josh had been taken away from the campus in separate ambulances and she hadn't seen him since.

He'd been bleeding. His blood had soaked his sleeve and the back of her tunic where he'd held her tight—putting himself between her and Curt Norwood's bullet.

Oh God. If she had any energy to spare, she'd cry out at the unjust irony of the past few hours. This was Curt's baby she was bringing into the world. Obsessed, murderous, evil Curt Norwood was the father of her baby.

How could she ever explain to her little miracle that her father had tried to kill her?

"Oh God." Her despair was barely a whisper as she gathered strength for the next contraction.

"Josh?" She squeezed her eyes shut and prayed. She desperately wanted, needed, his strength right now. She needed to apologize. She needed to know he was all right.

She needed him, period.

"Hey, Rachel." Another nurse had replaced the first. Mac's wife. Her kind eyes and gentle smile were a welcome sight.

"Hi, Julia." A tall blond man came up behind her. Rachel tried to hide her disappointment. "Hi, Mac."

"How are you feeling?" he asked in that distinct raspy voice of his.

"Like I'm having a baby." Did they have something to report? "How's Josh?"

Julia smiled as she wet a washcloth and pressed it between Rachel's parched lips. "The doctor just got done stitching him up. The wound was clean and superficial. They'll put him on antibiotics just in case."

Rachel sucked on the washcloth before Julia removed it, nodding her thanks for both the good news and the drink. "Thank God. I saw the blood on him and—*Ow-w!*" Another contraction seized her.

When she was breathing normally again, she noticed that Mac had made a discreet exit.

Rachel felt the next contraction coming and looked away, concentrating on her breathing and ignoring the impossible-to-ignore pain.

"Where's Josh?" Rachel panted.

"I'll go see," Julia said.

As she left, Dr. Conway hurried into the room, followed by the shift nurse who'd been with Rachel since she was admitted to the hospital.

The nurse propped Rachel's feet onto a set of stirrups while the doctor set up shop between her legs. "Ten centimeters."

Rachel burned inside. But she was so tired. So alone. So afraid that Anne-Marie was coming too soon.

"Are you ready to push, Rachel?" The doctor sounded like that was a good thing.

Rachel could only nod.

"You're not having this baby without me, are you, Doc?" The tall, bronzed giant with the wicked grin and deep, sexy voice stood in the doorway smiling at her.

"Josh!"

She reached out to him and he came to her. He bent down and kissed her full on the mouth. She dug her fingers into his hair and kissed him back, drinking in his strength and love.

She only came up for air as the next contraction hit her.

With one arm bandaged in a sling, Josh sat behind her and propped her up on the bed as she pushed. He fed her chipped ice and wiped her damp forehead and whispered words of love and encouragement into her ear.

And together they brought her bright, bellowing baby girl into the world.

"Josh?" Rachel could barely breathe. She could barely see through her tears. "Oh, Josh, how is she?"

She blinked and saw the tears shining in Josh's eyes. He kissed her soundly, stealing her breath and healing her heart. "She's gorgeous, Doc. Absolutely gorgeous."

"Would you like to cut the cord, Mr. Taylor?"

Cocky, confident Josh Taylor's mouth dropped open in stunned surprise. He looked down at Rachel, doubt clouding the azure depths of his eyes. Rachel reached up and brushed a tear from his cheek and smiled. She'd trusted her life to this man. She'd trust her baby to him as well. "Go ahead."

Minutes later, the nurse laid the baby on Rachel's stomach and Josh Taylor kissed both his girls.

His charming persona, tempered by the love shining in his eyes, was back in irresistible force. "You and Anne-Marie are my family. She's the daughter of my heart just as you're the woman of my dreams. Will you two marry me?"

Secure in the love of this strong man, Rachel no longer saw the differences in their ages. She saw his strength. His humor. His fiercely protective nature.

She knew this was the champion she wanted her child to learn from and love. Another man might have provided the DNA, but Joshua Taylor provided the heart that would make him a real daddy to her little girl.

She knew that Josh was a better man than her ex. True and faithful, with eyes and a lusty libido meant only for her. She knew that Josh loved her.

And that she loved him.

"Yes," she answered, letting the love she felt shine straight from her heart. "We'll marry you."

* * * * *

Look for the next installment
of Julie Miller's
TAYLOR CLAN series
in July 2003:
KANSAS CITY'S BRAVEST.
Available only from Harlequin Intrigue.

HARLEQUIN®
INTRIGUE®

No cover charge.
No I.D. required.
Secrecy guaranteed.

CLUB UNDERCOVER

Where the innocent go when there's nowhere else to turn....

Discover the underbelly of Chicago's sultry nightlife with the hot new romantic suspense miniseries from

PATRICIA ROSEMOOR

🔫 **FAKE I.D. WIFE**
March 2003

🔫 **VIP PROTECTOR**
April 2003

Look for them wherever Harlequin books are sold!

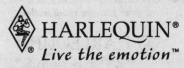

HARLEQUIN®
Live the emotion™

Visit us at www.eHarlequin.com

HICUFI

Two women in jeopardy...
Two shattering secrets...
Two dramatic stories...

VEILS OF DECEIT

USA TODAY bestselling author

JASMINE CRESSWELL

B.J. DANIELS

A riveting volume of scandalous secrets, political intrigue and
unforgettable passion that you will not want to miss!

*Look for VEILS OF DECEIT in April 2003
at your favorite retail outlet.*

HARLEQUIN®
Makes any time special®

Visit us at www.eHarlequin.com

PHVOD

HARLEQUIN®
INTRIGUE®

Elevates breathtaking romantic suspense to a whole new level!

When all else fails, the most highly trained, covert agents are called in to "recover" the mission. This elite group is known as

THE SPECIALISTS

Nothing is too dangerous for them…
except falling in love.

DEBRA WEBB

does it again with an explosive new trilogy for Harlequin Intrigue. You'll recognize some of the names from her popular COLBY AGENCY series, but hang on to your hats this time out. Because THE SPECIALISTS are more dangerous, more daring…and more deadly than any agents you've ever seen!

UNDERCOVER WIFE
January

HER HIDDEN TRUTH
February

GUARDIAN OF THE NIGHT
March

Look for them wherever Harlequin books are sold!

HARLEQUIN®
Makes any time special ®

For more on Harlequin Intrigue® books, visit www.tryintrigue.com   HISPEC

If you enjoyed what you just read,
then we've got an offer you can't resist!

Take 2 bestselling love stories FREE!

Plus get a FREE surprise gift!

Clip this page and mail it to Harlequin Reader Service®

IN U.S.A.
3010 Walden Ave.
P.O. Box 1867
Buffalo, N.Y. 14240-1867

IN CANADA
P.O. Box 609
Fort Erie, Ontario
L2A 5X3

YES! Please send me 2 free Harlequin Intrigue® novels and my free surprise gift. After receiving them, if I don't wish to receive anymore, I can return the shipping statement marked cancel. If I don't cancel, I will receive 4 brand-new novels each month, before they're available in stores! In the U.S.A., bill me at the bargain price of $3.99 plus 25¢ shipping and handling per book and applicable sales tax, if any*. In Canada, bill me at the bargain price of $4.74 plus 25¢ shipping and handling per book and applicable taxes**. That's the complete price and a savings of at least 10% off the cover prices—what a great deal! I understand that accepting the 2 free books and gift places me under no obligation ever to buy any books. I can always return a shipment and cancel at any time. Even if I never buy another book from Harlequin, the 2 free books and gift are mine to keep forever.

181 HDN DNUA
381 HDN DNUC

Name	(PLEASE PRINT)	
Address	Apt.#	
City	State/Prov.	Zip/Postal Code

* Terms and prices subject to change without notice. Sales tax applicable in N.Y.
** Canadian residents will be charged applicable provincial taxes and GST.
   All orders subject to approval. Offer limited to one per household and not valid to
   current Harlequin Intrigue® subscribers.
   ® are registered trademarks of Harlequin Enterprises Limited.

INT02

eHARLEQUIN.com

For great romance books at great prices,
shop www.eHarlequin.com today!

GREAT BOOKS:
- **Extensive selection** of today's hottest
  books, including **current** releases,
  backlist titles and new **upcoming** books.
- **Favorite authors:** Nora Roberts,
  Debbie Macomber and more!

GREAT DEALS:
- **Save every day:** enjoy great savings
  and special online promotions.
- *Exclusive* online offers: FREE books,
  bargain outlet savings, special deals.

EASY SHOPPING:
- Easy, secure, **24-hour shopping** from the
  comfort of your own home.
- **Excerpts, reader recommendations**
  and our **Romance Legend** will help
  you choose!
- **Convenient shipping and
  payment methods.**

**Shop online
at www.eHarlequin.com today!**

INTBB2

HARLEQUIN®
INTRIGUE®

They are tough…they are determined…
they are *damn* sexy….

They are:

**Military men trained for
combat—but tamed by love.**

Watch for this exciting duo of books featuring men in
uniform, who are both officers and gentlemen.

MARCHING ORDERS BY DELORES FOSSEN
March 2003

TOUGH AS NAILS BY JACKIE MANNING
April 2003

Available at your favorite retail outlet.

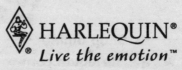

HARLEQUIN®
Live the emotion™

Visit us at www.eHarlequin.com

HIMOM.